Godfall and Other Stories

Sandra M. Odell

Hydra  House

978-0-9979510-0-4 (trade paperback)

Library of Congress Cataloging-in-Publication Data
Names: Odell, Sandra M., author.
Title: Godfall and other stories / by Sandra M. Odell.
Other titles: Godfall
Description: Seattle, WA : Hydra House, 2018. | A collection of 23 stories previously published in various journals and new stories not published elsewhere. | "A collection of speculative fiction short stories" -- Hydra House website. | Description based on print version record and CIP data provided by publisher; resource not viewed.
Identifiers: LCCN 2018002812 (print) | LCCN 2018010229 (ebook) | ISBN 9780997951004 (ebook) | ISBN 9780997951004 (trade : alk. paper)
Subjects: LCSH: Speculative fiction, American. | Fantasy fiction, American. | Horror tales, American.
Classification: LCC PS3615.D455 (ebook) | LCC PS3615.D455 A6 2018 (print) | DDC 813/.6--dc23
LC record available at https://lccn.loc.gov/2018002812

Hydra House
2850 SW Yancy St. #106
Seattle, WA 98126
http://www.hydrahousebooks.com/

Cover art: Dave Whitlam (davidwhitlam.com)
Cover design: Tod McCoy (todmccoy.com)

"Blue" appeared in the *Drabblecast* podcast, #260, October 19, 2012 • "The Business of Rats" appeared in *Stupefying Stories*, March 2017 • "Curtain Call" appeared in *Galaxy's Edge* #12, January 2015 • "Exchanges, No Refunds" appeared in *Daily Science Fiction*, October 2, 2014 • "Godfall" first appeared at *GigaNotoSaurus*, January 2016 • "Going to the Chapel" appeared in the *Drabblecast* podcast, #156, May 25, 2010 • "How Toby told Time" appeared in *Bards & Sages Quarterly*, January 2011 • "The Hydra Wife" appeared in *Jamais Vu*, December 2013 • "Ink" appeared in the *Podcastle* podcast, #376, August 11, 2015 • "Just Be" appeared in *Ideomancer* Vol. 10 Iss., 1 March 1, 2011 • "Life Line" appeared in *Crossed Genres* #31, June 30, 2011 • "Listening to It Rain" appeared in *Fireside Fiction*, September 2013 • "Lost in Translation" appeared in *Futristica* Vol. 2, ed. by Chester W. Hoster, Katy Stauber, published by Meta Sagas Press, 2017 • "Parting is Such Sweet Sorrow" appeared in *Kasma Science Fiction*, July 15, 2012 • "The Poison Eater" first appeared in *Deep Cuts*, ed. by Angel Leigh McCoy, E.S. Magill, Chris Marrs, published by Evil Jester Press, 2013 • "Samaritan" appeared in *Lost Trails 2*, ed. by Cynthia Ward, published by Wolf Singer Press, 2016 • "Telling Stories" originally appeared in the *Podcastle* podcast, #433, September 13, 2016 • "A Troll's Trade" appeared in the *Cast of Wonders* podcast, #182, December 1, 2015 • "Truth Is A Stranger To Fiction" appeared in *Breath & Shadow* Vol. 12 Iss. 2, Spring 2015 • "The Vessel Never Asks for More Wine" appeared in *Jim Baen's Universe* Vol. 4 #5, February 2010 • Original to the collection: "Black Widow," "Good Boy," "Home for Broken," and "Scarecrone."

Table of Contents

Introduction

In 2013, as a wet-behind-the-ears editor who had just taken over from Barry J. Northern and Graeme Dunlop at *Cast of Wonders*, I read my first Sandra M. Odell story. "A Dictionary's Apprentice" is a brutal, beautiful tale of a post-literate society, where life and limb are risked to keep the printed word alive in silent, unyielding protest again oppression.

Reading Sandra's work can be daunting. Fearless on the page, her work refuses to retreat behind opaque allegory as it drags injustice and prejudice before the reader's eyes. I think that's why her work translates so well into audio: even when we might want to close our eyes and gloss over the unpleasant realities, the strength of her literary voice demands attention. Stories like this volume's "Good Boy" and "Black Widow", along with the recent "Meat" showcased at *Pseudopod*, refuse to yield, confronting the reader head-on with realities sharp and horrible.

But as a survivor herself, Sandra takes exquisite care that her brutal worlds are never nihilistic spectacle. There is hope and laughter, along with the hard choices and painful realizations. Hope for everyone, including trolls and rat-catchers and past their prime robotic divas. Lesser-skilled authors would cavort through the grimdark muck of their own creating, leaving readers to wallow in her wake.

Instead, there is a rich, strong thread of inclusive justice to most of Sandra's stories. Scalding condemnations of gaslighting, child abuse, and addiction. Explorations of imprisonment—cultural and environmental, as well as psychological and physical. Of the way the disabled are vilified, misunderstood, or discarded not only by society but their own families.

Engaging with Sandra's work can be an act of trust, one that is always rewarded, even as Sandra herself acknowledges the switchbacks and bumps along the road. Her notes regarding "Black Widow" and her Clarion West experience are some of the bravest process-writing I've ever seen. It's hard to admit you're wrong, and harder still to be willing to go back into the mess you made determined to clean it up for yourself and the others you may have impacted along the way. I hope her classmates realize what an act of courage it must have been to not only complete the workshop, but to publish the final piece.

This collection is a fantastic introduction to the staggering range of

Sandra's short fiction. From robot noir to tattoo parlors, Sandra brings us with her through candid explorations of genre and identity, liberally signposted with unflinching self-awareness. I'm honored to have published four of her stories at *Cast of Wonders* to date—eleven across the Escape Artists podcasts in total—and I'm even more honored to call her a friend.

The heroes of these pages do not have farmboy journeys—this is darker, stranger fare. No easy answers await you, and you'll want both flashlight and tissues to hand. Be brave, be trusting, accept that reality is messier and sadder and more wonderful than the surface reveals as you harvest meaning from fallen gods.

Marguerite Kenner
Editor and host, *Cast of Wonders*

For Doug, my light and my faith.

*For Harlan, for teaching me it was okay to be angry
and to ring the black bell.*

Godfall

Tully brought the skiff in from the south. The blue mountains of Maya's feet rose against the sky, each toe adorned with a massive gold ring inlaid with cobras crowned with lotus blossoms. By the looks of the gold and white flags, the feet had already been claimed by the Vatican. It must have galled Pope Innocent XVI to accept the UN award for the feet of a Hindu god.

Maya's legs rested to one side, knees slightly bent, thick thighs leading to the fleshy invitation of her belly. Tully couldn't see the upper arms, but the lower right arm lay across the midriff, while the lower left arm lay flung to the side, a cosmic afterthought. Immense gold bracelets at the wrists framed the wealth of rings on both hands. Beyond her breasts would be the treasures of her shoulders and head. This looked to be a good haul. Plenty of gold and industrial grade diamonds in the rings, while uranium and other heavy metals could be extracted from the bones.

A rush of wind brought the mingled smells of iron, copper, patchouli, and a special scent that was distinctly ... Maya. Tully couldn't think of any other way to label it. The think-boy who figured out a way to bottle that scent would make millions.

Marco nodded in the direction of the UN flyers patrolling the boundaries of the fall zone. "The dogs are out in force."

Tully allowed himself a moment to admire the view of the younger man against the fore rail. Dark skin, dark hair, nice ass. Too bad Marco had signed on as a helper. Tully made it a point to never mix business with pleasure.

"They're just doing their jobs," he said.

Marco looked up. "How long did you say we have?"

Tully squinted at the flyers circling the distortion in the air high above Maya's midriff. The tangle of colors, the improbable angles that echoed in his joints, made them want to bend in sympathetic symmetry. He returned his attention to the controls. Gates always made him a little queasy. "It's still small yet. The UN says three days, maybe four."

He eased the skiff around Maya's toes to the tops of her feet, dark with henna. Workers on the maze of scaffolding in the ankle creases

watched them pass overhead. A message ping warned them that the skiff
had violated Canadian airspace and should depart immediately. With a
slurp of coffee and an acknowledging ping, Tully turned the skiff over
the ankles to Maya's calves. The Canadians had ground-to-air missiles.

Maya had settled into the ground five, maybe ten feet. In the
muggy heat, it wouldn't take long for the god's skin to pale from bright
blue to a meaty gray. Then she would start to swell. And stink. It would
be bad. With any luck and a returned call from Ali Bob, they'd be long
gone by then.

A mob maybe five-hundred strong milled around the Red Cross
tent city set well back from Maya's out-flung left hand. They screamed
at the flyers, at Her Most Revered Corpse, at the scrapper teams
plundering Maya's remains, at the aid workers searching for survivors in
the surrounding rubble of stone, steel, and shattered lives. Radio chatter
claimed at least three million dead, possibly as high as five and a half
million.

Marco settled on the front deck. "You think the mummers are
already here?"

Tully took another sip of coffee. After the bumpy 18-hour non-
stop to the sub-continent and the four hour flight inland, the inside of
his eyelids felt like 40-grit sandpaper. "I've never been to a fall where the
mummers didn't get there first."

Marco put his back to the railing, dada locks flapping around him.
"I used to think about them all the time as a kid, you know? I still have
every issue of the Mummers' Parade."

Great, a fall fanatic. Tully hadn't scoped that out when he took
Marco on. It was going to be a long scrap.

Dagda fell first, his ornate leather armor filled with the sun and his hair a
golden tide in the Irish Sea. Millions dead, two thirds of Dublin destroyed.
Numb with grief and the scope of the devastation, those searching for
survivors continued until the sky split wide and the worms tumbled down
for the feast.

Massive, eyeless, segmented horrors, they swarmed over the body,
tied themselves in knots to gouge out massive chunks of flesh and bone.

They devoured every bit of skin or drop of blood, no matter where it fell—concrete, wood, stone, metal, or human flesh.

Twelve hours later, the sated worms rose from the devastation and returned through the hole in the sky to the unknown, leaving cold, sinking confusion in their wake.

Tully set down at a clear point half way between Maya's ankles and the backs of her knees. Ten minutes later, the UN approved his acreage request, and together he and Marco secured the skiff, pitched their tents, and set the claim lines. This close, the overwhelming smell of patchouli coated the inside of Tully's mouth and clung to his clothes and hair.

A dozen or so other independent scrappers had set up similar camps. A few had already set their hooks and started torching lines into the blue skin to mark for later harvest. So long as they stayed clear of the choice bits, most corps and countries didn't have a problem with smaller licensed operations picking at the scraps.

While Marco made fresh coffee and heated dinner pouches, Tully went around to other camps for introductions and scuttlebutt. Two crew chiefs greeted him with suspicion, newer claimants judging by their high-strung nerves and clean skiffs, but the seasoned scrappers welcomed him with cautious camaraderie.

Farther down the calves, he was pleased to find Lovie Tepaka leading her own team. They'd worked together at Maniisoq when Sedna fell and he'd pulled her out of the wreckage in Athens back in '21, when a stretch of scaffolding collapsed under the weight of Athena's skin.

Lovie offered him a flask and a comfortable crate for a quick sit. "You hear about Richmond and his crew?"

Tully took a sip, passed the flask back. "Yeah. Did any make it out?"

"Not a one. The UN said they lost maybe a thousand men and a couple of million in hardware to the worms."

Tully let out a low whistle. "Were their estimates off for the gate?"

She shrugged. "No idea. I'm just glad I got held up with repairs. You?"

"Just came off of Apollo and couldn't close on the payout in time. I did okay, though." He did even better if he didn't count how Edgars and Victor had walked after hearing the news, or how he'd had to scramble to find a new hand willing to sit on call until the next godfall. Tully couldn't blame them, though. There were old scrappers and bold scrappers, but ...

Lovie nodded and took a drink. She offered the flask a second time, slipped it back in her shirt pocket when he refused. "It's rough work, you know? Just because you make it in doesn't mean you'll ..."

Her words gave way to uncertainty, a touch of darkness and fear. Not at all like the Lovie he knew.

Tully slid his foot to the side until his knee bumped hers. "Hey."

Lovie blinked, shook her head. She gave him a lopsided smile. "Sorry. Scrapper brain. You know how it is."

"All the time."

The touch of fear returned, then settled out in her shrug. "It's like it's on the tip of my tongue."

Tully understood that, too, fear and all. Scrappers made their livings off of death. Forgetting things was the best way to stay sane.

Lovie looked past him and made a small, irritated sound. "Shit. Mummers."

"Hmmm?" Tully turned around in time to see a troupe of twenty or more masked figures in brightly colored robes, playing drums and bells, go by in two skiffs. "Yeah. Marco was asking about them."

"One of your new boys?"

"The only one."

Lovie looked at him sidelong. "He cute?"

"Of course. Knows his shit, too." Tully watched the troupe skirt the outside of the claims barriers. "He's hot on the mummers."

Lovie spat in disgust. "You kidding me? When Ukko fell in '23, they came skulking around our camp in the middle of the night saying they only wanted to touch our torch sites so they could celebrate him. We got so tight for time driving them off that we almost didn't make it out before the alarm sounded. Nearly lost our entire haul."

The mummers stopped on the far side of Maya's knees to make camp, well away from the Red Russians' extensive claim to the thighs. The whisper of their bells was lost in the whine and sizzle of torches as nearby crews methodically butchered the dead god.

Tully hitched his shoulders. "It takes all kinds."

She shook her head. "I never thought I'd see the day when you went soft."

He stood, putting his hands to his lower back. "It's nothing about soft. I just don't see a reason to pull a gun when the other guy's got nothing but a butter knife."

Lovie laughed long and hard and got to her feet. "That's the Tully I know. Hey, what about Maui? I thought you'd be busy fishing by now."

Tully grinned. "I get a big enough payout this time and I will be."

She slapped him on the shoulder. "Keep the dream alive, man."

Best advice he'd gotten all year.

Odin, Guan Yin, Raven fell in the space of a year. Tnee Kong and Jok two years later.

Hardline Christians claimed the end times were upon the world, and all should repent. Buddhists saw the end of the Wheel and settled down to wait. Environmental activists blamed European conservatives, Israel the Hebrew States, Egypt the West African Collective, Canada the United States, Space Proponents the Grounders. Worldwide suicide rates spiked. Thousands of godfall survivors went mad. Troupes of godfall fantatics took to traveling from site to site to honor the corpses of the dead gods.

Where had the gods come from? What had happened to them? And what were the worms?

The top two inches of Maya's skin curled over itself and dropped slowly to the deck of the skiff secured halfway up her lower calf. Properly cured, the epidermis could be fashioned into fireproof leather, or body armor that could stop a .50 caliber round. The trick was getting it off the body without passing out from the stench of burning meat. Tully extinguished the torch, set it on the plank, then climbed down the scaffolding to the skiff three meters below.

Marco stacked the folds of blue skin into large, non-reactive plastic bins. Buckets under the corner box spigots captured anything expressed under the weight of the folds. He wore a godskin jumpsuit and industrial grade nitrile gloves identical to Tully's. "This shit gets worse all the time."

The complaint sounded low and fuzzy through the comm in Tully's breather.

Tully stripped off the breather, gagging with that first breath. Someone had filled his mouth with dead rats and cotton, and added lead weights to his eyelids. He and Marco had set to work immediately after dinner the night before. Since then they hadn't slept more than a dozen winks apiece.

He pulled off his welder's goggles. "Still pays well, that's all we got to ... where the hell are the spare filters?"

"Don't ask me. They were there when I changed mine out."

"Well, they're not there now. I can't work up there without ... here they are. You got to put things back where they belong. We don't have time to go looking for every little thing."

Marco stared at Tully for a tense moment, then turned back to stacking. "Whatever, man."

Fuck. Tully ran a hand through his hair. "I'm going to make some coffee."

Marco shrugged.

Tully went forward and set water to boil in the thermos. All around the skiff, scrapper crews worked double time stripping everything of value from the dead god, an efficiency of gore. Far above, a swarm of flyers surrounded the gate as it throbbed and thrummed, intent on mapping its every nuance.

He was getting too old for this shit. His father had been a scrapper before he'd settled down to raise a family. Exercise, fresh air, good money, his father said. The good old days. He never mentioned the broken bones, the stench, having to leave a payout behind or risk not making it out in time.

Tully dropped two coffee bags into boiling water and waited. He would make it big with this haul and catch the first flight out to Maui. No more scrapping for him.

When the thermos timer flashed, he filled two mugs and carried them aft. He nudged Marco with an elbow. "Hey."

The younger man looked over his shoulder, squinted through his blood-splattered goggles.

Tully held out a mug. "Take five."

Marco pulled off his breather and accepted Tully's apology.

They sat together in caffeinated silence until Marco spoke up. "What's it like for them, you think?"

"For who?"

"The Indians. They had another god fall. This is, what, the third? Fourth?"

Tully rubbed his eyes. "India is a country, Hindu is a religion."

Marco rolled his eyes. "You know what I mean."

The coffee was defective. Tully didn't feel any more awake. "Yeah, but that doesn't mean you have to get it wrong. Does India care? Sure they do. They just lost millions of people and a major city. Do the Hindus care? Of course. Ganga, Shiva, and now Maya. Three gods in eight years line a lot of wallets, but can't be easy on the faith."

Marco grunted. "You think they still believe?"

"The Christians are still hanging on after Jehovah fell, so why not the Hindus? Seems to me they'd have the better claim. They still got hundreds of gods to go."

The silence stretched another few sips. Marco crumpled his cup. "I saw the mummers last night while you were setting up the bucket feeds down below. They were singing and dancing up a storm, skiffs all lit up like they were having a party or something."

Tully stifled a yawn. "Mmmm."

"You ever think about them? Why they do all that shit?"

"Not really."

Marco sucked on the ends of his mustache. "Why not?"

Tully considered their progress since the first cut. They should be able to make it to the top of Maya's right calf by early afternoon. If they busted ass, they could make it a third of the way up her left calf before midnight. "No harm, no foul so long as they keep away from my operation."

"Yeah, but what's in it for them?" Marco persisted. "It's not like the gods can hear them, so why the big party every time one of 'em comes floating down from the sky? You never hear about them getting excited about the scavengers."

Tully chuckled. "Dead gods don't eat you if you get in the way."

The younger man fiddled with the cuffs of his jumpsuit. "Yeah. Listen, if it's okay with you I was thinking about heading that way tonight. Check them out, see what's going on."

Tully shook his head. "No can do. I need you here."

"What's to need? It'd only be for a couple of hours, and the radio says we've got two days at least."

Tully yawned with his whole body. Maybe he needed a coffee IV. "A couple of hours is another five yards of skin. You signed on to work, not get a leg up with a tambourine band."

Marco snorted. "Work, shit. I can go when we bed down."

"If we can spare the hours, you're going to need to sleep so we can keep going."

Marco laughed. The sound died when he noticed Tully didn't join in. "That's bullshit. You know that, right?"

Tully pointed to the gate writhing far overhead. The unraveling knot of reality had taken on a blue iridescence the color of Maya's skin. "I know what I see, and that says you stay."

Marco threw his cup into the garbage. "Fuck that, man. You can't make me work all the time. I got rights."

Not enough coffee, never enough sleep, and Marco mouthing off. Not what Tully needed. "Sure I can. You work or I slash your percentage."

Marco got to his feet. "The hell you will. It's a piss ass fifteen percent but it's mine. We got a contract."

Marco glared down at him with such pure loathing Tully had to laugh. He stood, topping the younger man by a good three inches. "You got to live long enough to collect, kid. Get on up there with the torch and I'll spell you here. I want at least another eight yards before we break for lunch."

By the time Pele fell on Kilauea, humanity had learned to identify the look of the gate that set the tocks ticking for the worms' arrival.

The dead gods promised resources to a starving world: gold, uranium, calcium, iron, sulfur, phosphates, diamonds, and more. Soon every country had a plan to get scrapper teams to a godfall site and safely away before the worm gate opened.

The faithful revolted against this final insult. The bombing of Mecca when Jehovah fell on Jerusalem and nations divided the remains. A dirty nuclear strike that wiped out Rio de Janeiro after Ci's harvest. Odinists gutted the Icelandic president and eight members of his cabinet when they approved the butchering of beautiful Baldur.

You will not take our gods from us, part them out like so many fish or bits of wood, they said. *We shall remember. We shall overcome.*

The world answered with grim practicality. *Look to the dead for your memories. We do what we must to survive.*

Ali Bob's arrival an hour after lunch saved Tully from listening to more of Marco's whining.

The broker peered into the skiff's hold with his flashlight. "Not much to show for your work, eh?"

Tully snorted and leaned against the aft rail. Ali Bob claimed to have his father's sex appeal and his mother's love of fine clothes. Tully could have added bad breath, body odor, and a few less complimentary qualities to the list, but the man usually paid the best prices so he kept quiet. "Give me a break. We hit the clock last night and haven't so much as stopped to take a piss."

Ali Bob dropped the flashlight in his linen suit coat pocket. "Ah Tully. Always so poetic."

Fifty meters overhead, Marco secured the last of the scaffolding to the topmost edge of the lower calf. "Good to go!"

Tully moved to the skiff controls. "Hang on a minute."

He roused the engines, released the hooks, and guided the skiff up until it hovered below the top scaffolding planks. While Ali Bob wiped his hands clean, Tully helped Marco secure the mooring hooks. He passed Marco the torch. "Get on it."

Near-by crews crawled their way up Maya's fleshy calves, ants conquering a tree brought down in a storm. Three acres away towards the ankles, Lovie's team peeled away massive strips of epidermis and sectioned off the first layers of the dermis from the lower calves. Above the knees, the Red Russians stripped muscle and fat from both thighs. Only that morning they'd shot down two skiffs that had nosed too close to their claim.

The largest crews had teams on the ground to suction run-off blood and viscera into 55-gallon drums. Radio chatter had it the Japanese working the left shoulders had figured out a way to automate the entire ground clean up. Big surprise.

Ali Bob mopped his brow and gestured over the side of the skiff. "Those buckets are filled with blood?"

Tully nodded. "Yeah, most of it from box run off, but three from burn weepage. We should have twelve, maybe fourteen, by the time we pack it in. Get me a couple more men and another skiff and I can double that, maybe triple."

The broker folded his handkerchief and returned it to his breast pocket. "My crews are already spoken for. You are aware—"

The high whine of Marco's torch split the conversation in two. Ali-Bob's penciled eyebrows expressed his opinion of the interruption. He leaned in towards Tully and continued. "You have heard that the gate is growing faster than expected?"

"What? Really?" Bad news. Very bad. Tully looked at the sky. The gate still thrummed blue, but didn't seem any larger. Not really? Maybe? He didn't have the sensors and gadgets to tell for certain. "Nothing's come over the radio. Are you sure?"

"Am I ever not sure when I share information?"

True. Ali Bob always gave good intelligence. "Any idea why?"

The broker spread his hands, palms up. "The humidity? The equinox? The phase of the moon? The average rainfall on the Serengeti? My sources did not say. Sometimes the gates open faster than others. You know that."

"Did you bother to tell anyone else?"

Ali Bob arched a brow and sniffed. "Of course."

That was a load off. How long until word came across the radio? "How long do we have?"

"Until midday tomorrow at the least. I would, however, make certain to stow your harvest in case of the unexpected."

Easy for him to say. "Crap."

"Have you seen the French water drill? Cuts through dermal and sub dermal like that—" Ali Bob snapped his fingers. "—and straight to the muscle. Such clean lines, too. Three months ago at Hongor I watched a team excise whole tendons from Ay Dede, three meters long at least. You harvest muscle tissue and tendon and I can offer you double the going rate for your poundage. Doctors in Istanbul are screaming for all the muscle tissue they can get to study limb regeneration."

Tully rubbed his face. He needed sleep, not borderline panic. "I'll keep that in mind."

He pinged Marco's comm. Marco grunted in acknowledgement.

"Change of plans. Clear a space. I'll be right up with a torch."

A three note signal sounded over the radio. "Gate update on all channels. All channels, gate update in three, two, one ..."

Tiamat. Ameratsu. Dionysus. Osiris. Marduk. Hera. Monkey. Ah Muzencab. Xi He.

Research hinted that more worms left a godfall site than arrived. Other research suggested the worms devoured one another in the frenzy, driving the numbers down. No hard numbers could be obtained to support either claim.

Godstuff expanded new horizons of scientific discovery, lifted third-world countries out of suffering, and challenged the underpinnings of philosophies and religions worldwide.

Tully jerked his head up, blinking against the glare of a passing searchlight from a UN flyer overhead. Uncomfortable warmth spread over his left thigh and knee. He looked down, swore, and turned off his torch. How long had he been asleep? Couldn't have been too long. "Marco?"

The younger man was nowhere to be seen. Not in the skiff, not on the ground as far as he could tell. Louder: "Marco?"

The comm line remained clear.

Searchlights from UN skiffs swept back and forth over the beleaguered corpse, catching glistening stretches of bare muscle and fat. Spotlights from the ground made taffy of the workers' shadows, stretching them to impossible lengths. Local crews pushed themselves to eke out the last few feet of harvest before they had to abandon Maya to the scavengers. From farther up the body came the muted pop of ribs pulled free. Or maybe vertebrae. He was too tired to tell.

Tully scrambled down to the skiff, hitting the deck two steps before he expected. He clutched the scaffolding until the world stopped shaking. "Marco?"

In the musty, sour space below deck, he found Marco's bloodstained jumpsuit and breather in a heap on the younger man's bunk. "Shit."

The faint buzz of an echo came from Marco's breather.

Tully ripped off his own breather, swallowing past the upswell of bile. Suit and breather left behind, same with the rifle in the rack. He hurried back to the deck and looked thighward. No sign of Marco, and the mummer camp was lost in the glare of the work lights. "I don't need this right now. I. Don't. Fucking. Need. This."

What to do? What to do? Drag Marco back to the job? Had to find him first.

Tully focused on the bloody expanse of his harvest claim stretching to an equally bloody gate far overhead. Red? How did it get red? What happened to blue? Never mind.

Coffee. More coffee. Tully made himself a quick thermos, burned his tongue on the first swallow. "Fah."

He'd left the torch perched on the corner of the scaffolding. Should he pack it up? Another swallow, and a third. He'd have to finish the packing, secure the barrels of blood and plasma down below. Load the skiff himself. It would go faster if Marco had hung around.

Fucking Marco. Fucking mummers. Fucking fuck fuck!

The radio was filled with the usual prep chatter for clear out. Crews called in commands, supply requests. A few wanted load out clearance. No news about the gate. If he held off until dawn to load out, he could get at the subdermal layers, maybe even the fat or some of Ali Bob's muscle. A bigger pay out meant fishing and no more scrapping. Ever.

Screw Marco. Let him live it up with the tambourine brigade. He'd drop the kid off at the nearest bus stop on the way out.

Tully carried the thermos, a spare breather, and the rifle back up the scaffolding. He was stupid tired, not tired stupid. You never worked a scrap alone without a gun in easy reach just in case.

He sparked the torch to life and set to work. 40 grueling minutes later, the strip of epidermis came away and dropped to the skiff. He set to work on the dermis, not particularly concerned with size or shape, only finished work. No payout if he didn't get the scrap out. He eased the first chunk down the first two rungs and let it drop. One down, who knew how many to go. He exhaled and kept working.

Cut, twist, pull, drop. The cut lines blurred; his hands began to shake. Blood and bits of detritus splattered his goggles. Three pieces, four. Patchouli curled insidious and thick through the filter. Five, six.

Had he finished the coffee already? Tully shook his head and kept working.

The world ran like watercolors in the rain, spilling over his hands. Maya smiled down at him, wide blue lips opening to devour his name in the wild abandon of her hunger. The torch traced a path across the sky, a bright white star carving his name on the back of her tongue. Maya would swallow him whole and let him fish out the rest of his days. Yeah, Marco could rot in the belly of a scavenger. It would serve him right, running off like that. Dumb kid. Dumb ...

The torch dropped from Tully's hand. He jerked backwards, staggered, and went down on his right knee. It popped, and a grinding fire exploded up his leg. His stomach clenched and he barely got the breather off before the coffee came rushing out and over the railing.

Bone ground against bone, screaming under the skin. Tully dropped to his side, praying someone would knock him out, cut his leg off, fucking kill him it hurt so bad. He lay there until the haze of pain receded, staring up at the dull black sky. No stars, nothing but the occasional UN flyer and the red gate twisting in on itself.

Tully began to cry. He couldn't do it. No way he could pack it all in now. Make it down to the skiff and the radio? Hell, he couldn't even reach the gun to fire a couple of shots to attract attention.

You got to live long enough to collect, kid.

Tully closed his eyes, only for a moment, and fell into Maya's waiting mouth.

Isis. Buffalo Woman. Inanna. Amadioha. Ngalyad. Pan.

The godfall treasures inspired greed that shattered treaties, destroyed governments, left millions dead, and millions more homeless. The havenots became the haves, the haves became the want mores. Riding on the coattails of that greed came the realization that the worms could open their massive mouths and someday take it all away.

One by one the gods fell, and humanity adapted.

Maya spit Tully out and he slammed into the railing. He put weight on his right leg to stand and fell back with a scream, a spike of fire rammed through his knee.

The scaffolding lurched again. Tully gripped the railing and pulled himself upright, biting through his lip with the focus of a pain he could control. Voices and the clamor of sirens filled the night. Metal screamed against metal. The scaffolding bucked under him. Maya jerked, rumbled, twitched on the Richter Scale. No, something inside her moved.

Above spun the gate, an angry throbbing red. White threads curled around the edges and dropped from the hole, swelling, stretching, black mouths gaping. They fell on Maya's belly like calving glaciers, ripples causing the body to convulse. Worms. The gate was open and the scavengers had come for him. "No."

He was going to die in the belly of a worm.

Fear trumped pain. Tully tumbled to the skiff and dragged himself to the controls. Over the staccato radio chatter and the howl of lifter engines came hollow chanting from below, a tinny jangle of tambourines. He pulled himself along the rail until he reached the front of the skiff.

Far below, in the strobe and shadows of the U.N. search lights, figures moved at the base of his claim. He caught the flash of gold, the swirl of scarlet. How many? Five? Seven? More? The figures gathered around the blood buckets and there came the pop of a breaking seal.

Tully clutched the rail. "Hey! The gate's open! Get out of there!"

He swung the skiff spotlight around and down. A dozen mummers stood around the buckets, hands raised. One looked up at the light with a fixed, filigree smile on its gold mask, then turned its attention to a figure on its knees in front of one bucket.

"Are you crazy? I said the gate is open!"

Maya's body jerked again, trembling under the assault of hunger. The skiff bounced against the god's bloody flesh with a meaty, metallic squelch that trembled through the deck.

The mummers didn't move. The kneeling figure turned its face to the light and Tully's reality slid sideways. Marco stared up at him with filmy, white eyes, lids swelling and stretching to seal them away from the light. His bloodied mouth stretched beyond the limits of flesh, a lipless black pit ringed with jagged teeth.

"I am become. I am become," the younger man sang above it all. "I am hunger, and I am become."

Other voices joined his. Tully swung the light around and

something twisted and maggot white bored through his mind. Worms as far as the eye could see. One scooped up a mouthful of people and debris. Another plunged headfirst into Maya's bloody flesh, twisting itself to tear away chunks of muscle and fat.

The mummers raised their hands and sang as the scavengers rolled and thrashed back and forth, shattering matchstick scaffolding, sending men and women screaming to their deaths. Worms everywhere, sliding over one another to reach Maya's body. Fires burned unchecked, equally hungry and destructive. Black smoke poured from punctured fuel tanks, blotting out the stars.

Reality jammed a railroad spike through Tully's left eye, the god-eye sacrificed for knowledge. He focused the spotlight on his hired hand far below. No one left behind. No. One. "Marco! We have to get out of here! We—"

Marco dipped both hands into the bucket and bent his head for another drink. The mummer's chant rose to an ululation clashing with the strident voices coming over the skiff radio: "All remaining crews are to evacuate the site immediately. Repeat, all remaining—" "Get your skiffs out of here! Leave the carts, dammit!" "immediately. UN forces—"

And Lovie's voice: "Tully, are you still there? Jesus Christ, get your ass out!"

Marco lifted his face to the light. His eyes bulged like blind fruits above the black maw, bone-white hairs burrowing into his cheeks. In the pool of light, Marco stretched like old-fashioned newspaper putty, distorted along the X&Y to an infinity shown in his beatific, bloody smile.

Tully's mind filled with a throbbing sonic scream, the gut wrenching sound to herald the end of all things. Death, rebirth, and death again. People, civilizations, gods. Changed, made new. Renewed. People made new. The death of faith, the birth of reason, someday to cycle round again.

Marco expanded, became a bloated, corpse white, writhing creature of endless hunger for sweet god flesh and all reality beyond. As the newborn worm plunged into Maya's bloody flesh, the mummers raised their arms and sang its praises.

The spotlight popped and sprayed Tully with shards of hot glass. The world went dark for whole seconds before the gate aurora and the strobing lights of fleeing ships brought it back to life. Far below, the mummers, the thing Marco had become, were gone.

Tully stood at the rail, unable to move, until a yellow spotlight from above pinned him to the deck. A voice, harsh and commanding: "Get your ass up here now!"

He turned his face to the light, stepped away from the rail, and collapsed.

A cargo skiff. Rough hands. Lovie's voice from somewhere near: "Get us clear!"

Up, up, up they went and headed north at full speed. Away from the god, away from the worms. Away from something else Tully couldn't remember.

Two men carried him down below to Lovie's bunk space, stripped him out of his jumpsuit, splinted his knee. Lovie clambered down the stairs soon after, shaking with anger and something more. Fear. She was afraid.

"What the hell were you thinking, huh? Were you trying to get yourself killed? Jesus, Tully, I can't believe you."

Someone shot him up with something. Tully's bicep burned and then a languid warmth poured through him. "Sorry. I had to—"

"Had to what? There's nothing so important that you needed to hang around back there. You heard the claxons. You could have been killed."

"I wanted to get to the buckets." Tully blinked the world back into focus. "Yeah."

Lovie dismissed the men, grabbed a towel, and began to clean his face and hair. "Next time leave 'em. What about your new man?"

Something white and barbed slithered through Tully's memories and out again. He looked at the bulkhead.

Lovie swore and kept working. She fed him sips of whiskey until the world took on a golden hue. "I should have left you, you know that, right?"

Tully nodded, drifting in the shallows of her words.

"I should have, too. Those things were, were ..."

Her hands stilled on his cheeks. She looked over his head, her gaze distant, fixed on something he could almost see and was terrified he might.

"There were things, weren't there? I thought ..."

Tully licked his lips. "Thought what?"

Lovie shook her head and chuckled under her breath, an uneasy, brittle sound. "Never mind. It's not like I could never leave my man

Tully behind."

She stood. "Anyway, I'm heading topside. You rest here, and I'll check on you later."

He grabbed her hand. "Don't leave me."

She leaned down and kissed him on the lips. "I got to check on my boys. I'll be right back."

Tully couldn't breathe. He smelled patchouli and blood, heard the distant ringing of tambourines. He held on tight to the only proof he had that he hadn't been left behind while the scavengers devoured his world. "But you're coming back, right?"

He couldn't make sense of the words, but they felt important so he said them.

"I said I would, didn't I?"

He nodded—"Yeah, yeah you did."—and let her go, his hand cold without someone to hold onto.

Another kiss, and Lovie walked out, closing the door behind her.

Tully settled back on the pillow, thoughts circling themselves like sharks. He'd ask Lovie for another shot of whatever it was when she came back. She was coming back, right? She wouldn't leave him alone with ... something.

Tully shivered in spite of himself and burrowed under the thin blanket. He stared at the bulkhead until visions of scavengers gave way to fishing boats off the coast of Maui, and he closed his eyes.

Author notes

"Where do you get your ideas?"

There is a phenomenon called "whale fall" where the carcass of a whale sinks to the deep ocean floor and becomes its own eco-system, attracting scavengers for years and miles. Many whale falls are deliberate for the sake of studying marine ecology, some are natural and equally spectacular. While watching a documentary about the deep ocean, I saw my first whale fall, the sharks, the crabs and small fish, and most of all the worms. This started the wheels turning and soon whale fall became god fall. How would humanity react to a wealth of gods falling to Earth? And how would they survive when the scavengers arrived?

The Home for Broken

A knock at the front door.

You set down your toast, wipe your mouth with your napkin, and hurry to answer. Who would call so early? You weren't expecting anyone at this hour, and the post isn't delivered until well after noon.

The answer is a short, freckled woman with a tumble of brown curls held back by a blue plastic clip. Broad shoulders, wide hips, a smile of uneven teeth. She holds out her right hand. "I'm Becky Ward from the Home for Broken."

You accept the hand out of habit; she has a strong, confident grip. "Yes?"

She presents you with a piece of paper. You take the crisp, white sheet, note the letterhead embossed in gold, scan the text, something about care, perfection, termination of parental rights. The world drops out from under you. "Oh! From the Home. We weren't expecting you so, so soon."

"That's perfectly all right. May I come in?"

Like that, she is beside you in the entryway, in your home, an uncomfortable reality. She nods in approval at the end tables, the family portraits beside the coat rack. "Is she here?"

"Who? Melody? I mean - wait!"

Miss Ward is at the stairs before she looks back at you. "Yes?"

You can't do this on your own. You clench your hands together, crumpling the paper. "I need to call my wife. Carol isn't here right now. I mean, she's at work, and we thought we'd have more time." Even to your ears, that sounds overly clinical. "More time with our daughter."

She smiles again, a disarming quirk of the lips. "I understand, but a space just came open and Melody will be a perfect fit."

She continues up the stairs. There is an odd hitch to her step, an unevenness on her left side that pulls her knee out of alignment. An off-tempo metronome. You feel like a gawker backstage at a gaudy show. Is she broken, too?

You hurry to the phone stand and ring Carol's office, fingers trembling as you spin the dial. Five rings, no answer. Why doesn't she bloody answer? Right, right. She's at her morning team meeting. You glance up in time to see Miss Ward reach the top of the stairs. The handset tumbles to the floor. "Please. You can't ... I mean ..."

This is your house, your space, yet you race up the stairs to find this stranger opening doors. Ethan's room. Angie's room. Linen closet. Bathroom. Your room. Fear pushes words out of your mouth willy-nilly. "Miss Ward - Ward, is it? - I don't understand. Carol and I agreed to placement, but that was months ago. We've changed our minds. Melody's perfectly happy here with us now."

"I didn't see her in any of the family pictures downstairs."

You flush. "She doesn't photograph well. And she's easily excited."

"Of course."

Miss Ward reaches the door at the end of the hall, plain wood with no identity beyond the closed hasp with the open padlock hanging from the staple. "Would you mind opening the door, please?"

A question so courteous it burns.

"She doesn't sleep much. I mean, she wanders and we have to keep her door closed."

"So she's inside."

Is there something different about her posture? Shoulders back? Standing a bit taller?

"Well, yes. We keep the door closed, otherwise, not all the time, mind you, – "

While you fumble with the words, your hands fumble at the lock. Melody does wander at night, and you need your sleep, so does Carol, and the kids complain that Melody gets into their stuff.

Miss Ward opens the door. "Hello, Melody."

The closed air is redolent with machine oil and diapers changed as an afterthought. Dim light filtered through the heavy curtains captures the slow motion ballet of dust. Melody sits perfectly still in the center of the room, hands on knees, head tilted to one side as if in contemplation of the blocks arranged in front of her. She has your coarse black hair, Carol's high cheekbones, your mother's button nose. Not unattractive, you tell yourself. Not really. More plain than ugly.

There is little else of Melody in the room. A bed, a low four-drawer dresser, a toy chest filled with hand-me-downs from her brother and sister, none of them as interesting as her blocks or her favorite cardboard shoe box.

Miss Ward walks straight to your daughter, lowers herself to the floor, favoring her left leg. "My name is Miss Ward. How are you today?"

Everything is happening so quickly. You should try to reach Carol again. No. You need to get control of the situation. "Melody is non-verbal. She's been evaluated twice now. The doctors have never seen a child like her. She was born this way. I mean, she's not like normal flesh and blood people, and the therapists feel she doesn't have the capacity for speech."

"That doesn't mean she doesn't have the capacity to listen. Ah, here we go." Miss Ward feels around the lump between Melody's shoulder blades, reaches under the back of your daughter's shirt and turns her hand once, twice, three times, with the fast ratchet of gears.

Melody blinks, straightens her shoulders, and begins to stack the blocks largest to smallest, one, two, three, all the while mouthing "ca, ca, ca" which never made sense to you.

"There." Miss Ward pulls Melody's shirt down, sits back. "She just needed to be wound."

"You knew about her key?"

"Of course. More common than you might think, really. We have a comprehensive therapy and self-maintenance program at the Home. She'll fit right in."

You can't watch the key turn under your daughter's shirt with undulating intent. "We usually keep her wound, but sometimes when the other kids are off at school we let her wind down, I mean she prefers it, really." Why do your best intentions sound like excuses? "We're good parents."

"Ah." Miss Ward only has eyes for Melody. "Hello, Melody, my name is Miss Ward. You're building a nice tower. Crash! And they all come down."

You wince at the way Melody's head bobs back and forth when she rebuilds. Miss Ward helps, then offers praise when Melody knocks it down again. You could never find the time to play with Melody this way; besides, she should have outgrown blocks years ago. Angie is interested in boys, likes to read *Glamour* and *Cosmopolitan*. Melody tears the pages of her sister's magazines into strips and would eat them if you let her. After a long day at the office, you sometimes tell yourself a little paper can't hurt just so you don't have to chase her around the house.

This is ridiculous. You have nothing to be embarrassed about. Even though she's different, you love your daughter, right? Right?

"Miss Ward, I must insist we wait for my wife to come home."

She still doesn't look at you. "There's no need. You already signed away your parental rights."

"That's preposterous." You take a step back, bump against the doorjamb. "We didn't know what we were signing."

"Of course you did."

You did. You even remarked to Carol how nice it would be to have a normal family like everyone else. The truth burns like dry ice in the pit of your stomach.

"I'll ring my solicitor. The police."

"Go right ahead, but the courts have already approved your termination request." Miss Ward gives you a quaint, sad smile. "There's no reason to worry. We have a program already in place for Melody. Daily therapies, vocational training. We'll request her records from the school district."

You look at your shoes.

"Melody is enrolled in school, yes?"

That damnable courtesy again. "The district felt she wasn't benefiting from her class time so we removed her from school. Not that she noticed. I mean ..." You gesture at your daughter's diligent, incessant stacking and knocking over. Ethan has a 4.0 Grade Point Average. Angie earned a place at the district's summer science camp. "You can see she's much happier at home."

So is the rest of the family. The kids no longer get teased about their "weird" sister. Carol no longer risks being late to work if Melody's special bus doesn't show up on time. You no longer have to explain to your supervisor why you sometimes need to take machine oil to Melody's class.

Miss Ward touches Melody's shoulder. Looking at the woman's left hand, the way the fingers knot against the palm, makes your soul itch, much like when you wind your daughter.

"I'm sure you know what it's like, being broken I mean," you continue. "Not that being broken is a bad thing, but none of our friends have a child that requires winding. It's hard for them to relate to a child so ... different."

"Of course." Miss Ward stands. "Let's get you packed, Melody. Do you have a suitcase we can use?"

You step into the room. "Miss Ward, I can't let you take her."

That weak protest is all you can muster.

There's that smile again. "You already have. You don't have a suitcase? Here, Melody. Put your arms out like so. You can help me carry the clothes down to the car. Thank you."

You rush downstairs to the phone and try Carol's number again. No answer. You swear, and dial the front office. The line is busy. Why doesn't anyone answer? Don't they realize your world is changing too fast for you to catch up?

Miss Ward calls from upstairs, "I found a suitcase at the back of the closet. Might I have a hand?"

You hurry up the stairs, intent on stopping this foolishness, and before you know it you're bringing Melody's toiletries from the bathroom. Miss Ward is too matter of fact and genial. Why isn't she the ogre your guilt needs her to be? Why are you carrying the suitcase to the front door while Miss Ward helps Melody down the stairs one step at a time?

You aren't about to let a broken woman show you up when it comes to caring for your own daughter. You set the suitcase in the entryway and hurry back to the stairs. Melody is on the third step. You take her free hand from Miss Ward— "Come along, Melody. Don't dawdle." —and tug her forward.

It happens in slow motion like a heart-wrenching moment on the telly. Melody's foot catches on the next step, slips, her hand pulls free of the rail, she tumbles towards you. You could break the fall, but her key is turn, turn, turning like a great ugly thing. You let go of her hand. You mean to step forward but step to the side instead, and your daughter falls to the floor on her hands and knees. She makes no sound, not the slightest whimper. Turn, turn, turn goes the key.

Miss Ward is down the stairs and reaching for Melody before you gather yourself enough to do the same. "Oh, my," Miss Ward says. "Up you go. Are you all right? Let me see your knees."

You break out of slow motion and help ease Melody onto the bottom step. "Is she all right?"

Melody is a right pain at the doctor's office, and you have things to do today. Not that you mean to be cruel ...

"She's fine. A bit bruised up is all," Miss Ward says as if reciting the day's weather. "We have aspirin powder at the Home."

"I didn't think I'd pulled that hard. I tried to catch her."

"Accidents happen."

Are the words strained? Polite to the point of anger? "I didn't want to break her key."

Miss Ward lifts the back of Melody's shirt. You should look, but can't.

"It's fine." Miss Ward takes Melody's hand. "Let's get you in the car, Melody. It's time to go."

As they move to the door, you stand by the stairs, flotsam in the wake of their passing. Ring your wife. Ring the authorities. Ring somebody! Yet you think of all the things you could get done with Melody gone. Guilt clenches tight around the shallow thought. Maybe you're not fit to be a parent after all.

You take a step, then the next until you join them at the door. "Do you . . need help with the suitcase?"

"No need to put yourself out. We'll be fine." Miss Ward opens the door. With Melody in one hand and the suitcase in the other, Miss Ward turns to you and smiles. "We'll ring for the rest of her things later in the week. You're free to visit any time you like. We love having family over for dinners and outings."

You look at Melody rocking back and forth, moving to music you can't hear over the turn, turn, turning of her key. She has your hair, Carol's cheekbones, your mother's nose, and looks rather pretty in the bright light coming through the cut glass window. "Certainly."

The word is meek and ashy in your mouth.

"Let's give your father a hug and we'll be off."

Melody makes no move, so you go to her and hesitantly put your arms around your child. Her hair smells like strawberry shampoo. You step back. "Good-bye, Melody. I, um, I love you. I'll see you soon, all right?"

Melody's free hand flutters to her stomach, her throat. She looks at you, through you.

Miss Ward directs Melody to the door. "We'll keep in touch. Come on, Melody, let's get you home. Everyone is so looking forward to meeting you. Do you like dogs?"

Together, the uneven metronome and the wind-up girl make their way down the front path and out the gate to a small blue sedan parked along the curb. You should try to ring Carol again. She needs to know that Melody is gone. To the Home for Broken.

As you watch the car ease into traffic, something swells inside your chest. The car turns left at the light. How had you never noticed that your daughter's hair smells like strawberry shampoo?

The swelling pops and runs down your cheeks, but this is what you want, right? Right?

Author's Note

At 21, my youngest son is non-verbal, not toilet trained, and has global developmental delays in addition to other facets of his multiple diagnoses. He is also loving, vexing, annoying, sly, funny, heart-wrenching, and a joy to have in my life.

I could go on for days about how people react to disabled people, the "cripples", the "broken". They're contagious, a punishment, a blessing, a burden, a hassle, an angel, a victim, a lodestone, a puzzle no one has time to solve. To those beliefs I say no, no, no, and most of all no. Disabled people are not items or curiosities for your wonder. They are not broken. They are people.

I knew when I wrote this story that it would never find a market home. That's okay. I wrote it for me, and have no regrets.

The Poison Eater

Doby eats half a pack of cigarettes without so much as flinching. Camels. Breaks them in half, eats them filters and all. Same with a Marlboro Menthol Spence pulls out of a pack he unwraps himself. Takes three bites, chews, and washes it down with a swig of Mountain Dew.

A swallow of dish soap, then an air freshener stick, then cigarettes. The rest of us stare.

Doby burps and wipes his mouth with the back of his hand. "Pay up."

We do, even Spence, though he doesn't look happy, which is messed up because this was his idea in the first place.

Doby stuffs the wad of ones into the front right pocket of his jeans.

Spence frowns. "So that's it?"

Marty's Mart closed at one so we have the back lot to ourselves, us and a couple of cats sniffing around the dumpsters. The night smells like garbage, scotch broom, and diesel exhaust from the semis passing by on the 422 overpass on their way to Akron. That's all the world does any more is pass Youngstown by.

And my folks wonder why I want out so bad.

"That the best you can do?" Spence says.

Doby sort of looks pissed but I can't really tell in the shadows. All we got is the moon and the streetlights on the corner for light. "Like what?"

Spence can be a real jerk sometimes, and the mosquitoes are getting to me. I say, "Stop being an ass. He did it, didn't he?"

"Big deal, he ate soap and a couple of cigarettes. I got a kid cousin who can do that. Then he shits himself for a week and it's all good."

Eddie nods like he agrees. Doby grits his teeth.

Spence reaches into his backpack. "You want a real pay up, I got something for you."

He pulls out a fat white plastic bottle with a blue cap and sets it in front of Doby. "You think you're the man and shit, let's see you down some of this."

I catch the edge of the label in the light. Bleach? That's too much for me. "C'mon, man. That shit's poison."

Doby cuts a look from Spence to the bleach and back.

Spence taps the lid and smiles like a shark. "He's the one who said he can eat anything, made a big deal of it, so let's see him do it."

He's playing Doby is all. Before I can tell Spence what he can do with his bottle and offer my grandma's hot water bottle for the job, Doby reaches into his jacket and pulls out a thin yellow and blue can. "All right. You want it so bad, let's make it interesting." He tosses the can into Eddie's lap. "But you gotta make it worth my time."

Eddie picks the can up like it's a snake. "Cigarette lighter fluid?"

This time Doby taps the cap. His smile is cold and crazy. "Squirt it in, as much as you want. Ten bucks a swallow."

Suddenly the night's real quiet. No trucks, no mosquito buzz, no nothing. Spence isn't smiling so much now.

I stand up. "All right. That's it. You guys are crazy if you think—"

"Siddown," Spence says to me without looking away from Doby.

"He's not going to do it, and you're a 'tard for thinking he will. I got better things—"

"You pussying out, Connor? Sit your ass down."

I want to kick Spence in the teeth, want to pour the bleach down his throat and watch his stomach eat its way out his ass. Spence is a 'tard, but Jenna says she loves him. Mom wants me to hang with him so the baby has a father when it's born. Like anything I do will keep Spence around.

Eddie looks like he wants out, too, but Spence leads the pack. Maybe I'm the 'tard. I sit down.

Doby nods and smiles like a razor.

"Show me the money," he says.

We dig in pockets and wallets and come up with a wad of bills Spence passes to me. Bastard. I count it out. "Sixty-five bucks."

"Seven swallows," Spence says.

Doby nods, shrugs. "Whatever."

Spence looks even whiter, if that's possible. He's got to know Doby won't do it, but it's his turn to put up or pussy out. Doby's playing him now.

Eddie stares wide-eyed from Doby to the lighter fluid until Spence punches him in the arm. "Do it."

Eddie squirms and says, "Listen, I got to get goin'—"

Spence twists off the cap like he's wringing Doby's neck. The smell of bleach cuts through the dumpster stink. "Do it," he snarls at Eddie, and Eddie does. His hands shake so bad he squirts lighter fluid down the side of the bottle before he gets the red nozzle inside. The smell of the two together has me rethinking if I should leave.

Doby grabs the bottle, swirls it around. "Seven swallows."

Spence kind of nods.

Doby brings the bottle to his mouth. He's not going to do it; he can't do it. I'm reaching for the bottle. Eddie tells him to stop.

Doby tips the bleach back, and we're groaning and swearing and gagging as he chugs it down. The smell fills my head, coats the back of my throat; my stomach twists and burns. Somehow my cell phone is in my hand and I'm calling 9-1-1, but I can't look away. Four, five, six—

"Nine-one-one. What is the nature of your emergency?"

Seven.

Doby lowers the bottle and smacks his lips, looking straight at me. "Pay up."

"Nine-one-one. What is the nature of your emergency? Caller, are you there?"

I wait for Doby to scream or hurl or burst his stomach or something. He lifts his eyebrows and holds out a hand.

"Hello? Caller, are you there?"

I close my phone, and pass the cash to Doby.

Spence stares, mouth wide open, and then gets all pissed because he got owned. "You crazy or something?"

"I'm sixty-five bucks richer than you, that's what I am," Doby says.

Spence grabs the backpack and stands. "Well, you call or do whatever you want. I'm not stickin' around for the ambulance when you explode. I didn't do nothing."

He takes off without looking back, Eddie too, then it's me, and Doby.

As Doby arranges his money into one roll, my cell goes off. I check the number: 911. I hit silent and stuff the phone in my pocket.

We stand up. Doby kicks the bottle of bleach over, and it suddenly smells like a laundromat on a Saturday. The mix pools dark rainbows on the asphalt.

Doby zips his hoody. He lights a cigarette, a Camel, with a match from a wrinkled matchbook. "What are you waiting for?"

I have no idea. Spence put him up to it; I didn't do nothing but hold the money. It wasn't my fault, yet I can't just leave him. "Maybe you should stick a finger down your throat or something. I got a pencil if you want."

Doby takes a drag, the ember making wicked shadows across his wide nose and cheeks.

"You really need to get to a doctor." It sounds lame, but I can't exactly knock him down and drag him to the emergency room when that might mess him up more. What's the number for Poison Control? How long do I have before he starts screaming? Maybe there was more water than bleach, and the lighter fluid was really vegetable oil.

Doby French inhales another drag. "I'm fine."

Lit end first, he eats the cigarette in two bites and walks away.

I catch hell when I get home because 911 called my house when I wouldn't answer my phone, and Mom was late for work because she waited for me when I should have been home. She takes my phone and tells me Dad is going to "set you straight" when he gets home from his back shift. Later, Dad rolls his eyes and tells me not to worry Mom so much.

I don't expect to see Doby at school the next day, but he shows up for homeroom like nothing's wrong. He looks straight at me on his way to the back row in math like he's daring me to say something.

Eddie lets on how Spence rags on Doby in American history, but won't go near him. "Not like Spence gave a shit first off, but I feel where he's coming from," he says around a mouthful of fries at lunch.

I finish my cheeseburger, and roll the tomato up in the lettuce for a salad burrito. "That's bogus, man."

"I'm serious. What he did, that was messed up. I mean it."

"You scared of Doby?"

Carlos downs his milk. "What? Oh, hell no."

"You totally are, aren't you?"

"Gimme a break."

"I'm serious. You're just like Spence."

Eddie stuffs his napkin in the milk carton, doesn't look at me. "What you think?" he says, almost too soft to hear over the cafeteria noise.

We talk about something else.

Five minutes before the end of lunch, I walk by Doby on my way to drop off my tray. He's alone at the table, earbuds leading to a hoody pocket, tearing apart a slice of pepperoni pizza and eating it a greasy piece at a time.

He doesn't look pale or sick or anything. "Hey, Dob."

Doby stops eating just long enough to make me think he hears me, but doesn't look up.

As far as I know, Doby's an okay guy. He's odd man out; even dweebs think he's not cool enough to make up for being smart, but I don't have a hard spot for him or nothing. Really never gave him much thought until he mouthed off to Spence. Sort of. I mean, he's not bad looking. "You got, um, a partner yet for the environmental presentation?"

He pulls out an earbud and stares up at me with that same look from homeroom. He's the kind of thin my dad calls no chin pencil neck. My dad's a dork sometimes. "No. Why?"

"Just asking. I mean, I looked at the packet and started taking notes, but I don't have a partner yet. You interested?"

Doby finishes his pizza, and wipes his hands on his jeans. "Sure, I guess."

Why'd I ask? The warning bell sounds. Benches and tables scrape across the floor as everybody hurries towards the garbage cans. Eddie cuts us a look from across the room, but doesn't stop.

"Yeah, um, okay." I hitch up my backpack, take a step towards the garbage cans. "See you in class and we can set something up?"

Doby shrugs. "Whatever."

I don't stick around.

Two days later, I'm out the door with the escape bell and on my way to the bus when I see shit going down by the planters out front. Eddie and a couple others have Doby cornered, knuckling him in the arm, getting up in his face. Some nearby keep an eye out for school security. The rest pretend not to watch.

Doby is pissed, *gut you and leave you to bleed* pissed, his face flushed and shoulders hunched tight. He wants to hurt them bad; I feel it in my stomach, the way he wants to grind their faces into the cement. Eddie and the rest keep pushing him to make the first move, but Doby doesn't do shit back, never does, which only makes it worse.

I'm moving before I realize it. Next thing I know, Doby is at my back and I'm leaning into Eddie, talking low. "Wassup, man? C'mon, you don't wanna do this, huh?"

Everyone's watching us.

"What the fuck, man?" Eddie says in my ear, breath hot and sour against my cheek. "This got nothing to do with you."

I don't want to do this for a whole bunch of reasons. I've known Eddie since the third grade, he's a bud, but treating Doby like the meat of the week is all because of Spence's dare and that's not cool. I don't play that. "I know, I know, right? So, why you doing this?"

"I heard he's talkin' shit about me."

I step closer so Eddie can feel me, letting him know I'm not going anywhere. I keep my hands flat against my legs so I don't make fists. I keep it on the low. "Doby doesn't talk shit, man, you know it. He didn't do nothing to you, right? What's really going on?"

I see the memory of the weirdness in his eyes, his frown. "He went and said— "

"You hear him say anything, huh?"

That's when Eddie looks over my shoulder and I don't have to turn around to bet money he's not looking at Doby but at Spence. I tell him, "I got it, you know. Leave off, huh?"

I slide my left foot back.

Eddie finally looks away, jerks his head to the side. "Yeah, man, be right there," he says to the distance.

I didn't hear anyone call him. I back up half a step. He does, too.

We bump fists and it's over. Eddie and the others head to the buses and cars. I think I see Spence watching from beside his car at the end of the bus line, but I can't be certain.

I'm twitchy; my shoulders ache from coming down. I turn around. "Listen, I—"

Doby puts a chunk of blue and white in his mouth. He chews it like a thick wad of gum, drops his skateboard, and rolls off without a word, eyes wide and hating.

Had to be gum. Had to be. It couldn't be one of those dishwasher gel packs. I breathe through my mouth so I don't smell detergent.

Doby sucks as a partner. He doesn't do much except tell me when I'm wrong, like he knows all about mercury levels in fish. At the library, he sits with his feet on the table and listens to music, doesn't crack a book or log on to the net, and corrects everything I do. Thing is, he's right every time, which pisses me off even more.

Jenna flips me shit. "I don't think you can get any more 'tarded than asking Doby Chuckman to be your partner."

Like she has room to talk. She's going to end up working part time at Taco Bell and taking night classes at the community college for her GED while the rest of her friends walk come June. I tell her where to get off. Mom gets on my case; it's bad for the baby.

It's all about the baby anymore. What about me? I may not be the smartest in my class, but the recruiters liked my test scores back in February and took down my name. Mom freaked, and Dad told me he could get me a job at the recycling plant. Screw that. No way I'm sticking around.

Doby doesn't show up for homeroom for two days. Eddie says he hasn't seen him all week. I'm sweating. The presentation draft is due tomorrow and I was stupid enough to give him my thumb drive when he said he'd check the references. For five bucks Anna gets me Doby's address from the office during third period and I catch the express transit after school.

As soon as I step off the bus, it starts to rain. Great. By the time I get to his house, I'm soaked and set to finish everything myself. Fuck Doby and his freak stomach, fuck the rusted cars and sacks of garbage in his yard. Then the front door opens and I swallow everything I was going to say.

A small guy with a face like a hemorrhoid squints up at me through the screen door. "What?"

I can see the resemblance. His dad? "Yeah, uh, is Doby home?"

"Doh-ber-min! You got someone at the door!"

Doby's named after a kind of dog? That's messed up.

The man turns away. "Come on in. He's in his room, end of the hall. Mind the cat."

The cat is sad, with bald patches and bug-eyes. It hides under the coffee table piled with newspapers and garbage and hisses at me on my way down the hall.

The far door has posters of Tony Hawk and 50 Cent. I knock. Doby opens it, a paler shadow in a house of shadows. I'm still angry, but this place looks like it has enough anger. I kind of wish I could make Doby smile.

"Hey, man."

Doby looks me up and down. No smile. He steps to the side and motions for me to come in. "Hey."

The room smells like sweat, cat pee, and pot. A bed, a dresser, a couple of broken down chairs. Piles of clothes and junk make it hard to walk. Can hardly see anything with the light off and the blinds closed. "Where you been? Haven't seen you in school."

He pushes magazines and clothes off a chair, then drops onto the bed. "Not feeling good."

I sit, put my backpack at my feet. "That sucks."

He shrugs.

Does he have a stomachache? I want to ask, maybe as a joke. I'm not really sure.

"Doh-ber-min! I told you to take out the garbage, dammit!"

Doby gets that look again, the *hurt you, hate you, make you bleed* look he had at school. An ugly look. It busts through the wall beside me, grabs Doby's dad, and snaps his pretzel neck.

Doby is up off the bed, gets his hoody, stuffs a bottle in the pocket. "C'mon."

He scoops up the garbage on our way out. I say good-bye to his dad because I don't want to be rude. His dad smokes and watches wrestling, doesn't answer. He does yell something after Doby slams the door behind us. I don't catch what. Doby doesn't turn around.

We walk. Doby looks straight ahead, working his jaw the same as my dad when he grits his teeth. I can't get any more soaked. I didn't come to hang out, but I don't want to up and split. Doberman. A dog gets kicked all the time, you want to do the right thing and help. "You okay, man?"

Doby pulls out the bottle and has it open and two swigs gone before I smell pine and see enough of the label to realize it's not iced tea. "Yeah."

The question tumbles out of my mouth: "Dude, what's wrong with you?"

I expect him to tell me to mind my own business. Instead he snorts and takes another drink.

Do I stop him? Knock him over and call 911 this time like I should have done at Marty's Mart? "Are you trying to kill yourself?"

Another drink, half the bottle gone now. "What's it to you?"

That catches me by surprise. I'm not his friend, not really, I don't think.

"I dunno. It'd be a waste is all. You're smart; you could be someone." I look around at the rundown shoebox houses with pastel siding, the 7-11 next to a boarded-up liquor store. A dead end street in a dead end town. Dad could have made it out, but he quit college and came back to Youngstown when his dad died. Mom wanted to be a nurse; instead, she got married and works at fucking Wal-Mart. "I mean, Youngstown ain't worth dying for."

We cross against the light, cars laying on the horns as they swerve around us.

"It's all I got," Doby says. "All I'll ever have."

I shake my head. Water drips into my eyes. "Not me. I walk with my paper next year, and I'm gone, no looking back."

"Really?"

"Yeah."

We don't say anything for a couple of blocks.

"You ever get angry, Connor?" he says.

I nod. "Yeah."

He looks at me full on, not from the side, not with a snarl. "I mean pissed, hate someone mean."

That's harder to answer. Those feelings are like a genie. I got this fear that if I admit to it, I'll never be able to stuff it back in the bottle. Kind of like other feelings.

"Once or twice, I guess."

Half a block more. Where are we? No idea.

"I do," he says. "I hate all of them, the fucks, the dorks, the douche bags." He finishes the bottle and throws it into the bushes. "This is food, right, for when I want to kill them. All of them. I might still someday."

"Dude."

"Give it all back."

That last part is as dark as his look. What does he want me to say? I think of the kicked dog, how it can turn on you without warning, and don't say anything at all.

Doby pulls out the cigarette lighter fluid, squirts a stream into his mouth. I try not to watch, but it's like a wreck on the overpass and can't look away. He pulls my thumb drive out of a back pocket. "Here."

I take it. "Thanks."

He brings out a plastic packet of green pellets, the label a cartoon dead mouse holding a lily. "Whatever."

I turn in the presentation rough and get to work on the finished project. Doby corrects me and eats bleach tablets.

Jenna starts having contractions. Mom says they're Braxton-Hicks or something. Spence gives me the eye if I'm around when he picks Jenna up for birthing classes at the hospital.

He only talks to me once, when Jenna's upstairs getting ready and Mom's in the kitchen. I'm on the couch with a Dr. Pepper and chips, he stands in the doorway watching me play HALO 2.

"Hey, Connor."

I don't look up. "Hey."

"You still a pussy for the freak?"

I give a Brute Spence's face and press down hard on the fire button, blowing his ass away. "Bite me."

"Pussy," he says. I hear Jenna coming down the stairs and suddenly he's all smiles. Mom tells them good-bye from the kitchen, and they're gone. Then she nags me to get off the game and clean the cat box.

Doby and I don't hang out so much as go for walks at night after the library closes. He drinks lighter fluid and listens to his music. Sometimes he acts like he might want me to do more, but I don't. Sometimes in bed at night, I wish I did. Him and me, we're not from the same neighborhood but not that far from the same life. We don't talk much.

This is how Spence finds us, on a walk. Maybe he didn't set out looking for us, I don't know, but we're cutting through the back lot at Marty's Mart and I hear him over the traffic: "Hey, freak!"

It's late, not as dark as it was the last time we were here. I see his sneer as he walks over to us, the glitchy eyes. The bastard's tweaking. I wasn't home when he picked Jenna up. Was he tweaking with her in the car?

"Wassup, freak and pussy. Freakin' pussy." He jangles his car keys in time with his steps like some sort of Clint Eastwood wannabe.

"Whatever." I nudge Doby with my elbow. "C'mon."

Doby doesn't move. He puts the can of lighter fluid back in his hoody pocket.

"What you got there, freak?" Spence says. "What is it this time, huh? Gasoline?"

"Fuck you," Doby says, his voice low and hard.

Spence rattles his keys. "Ooh, big man."

"Fuck. You." Lower, harder, ugly.

Spence is close enough I smell the beer on him. Pictures of Jenna wrapped around a tree, in a body bag, the baby in a little casket, are lightning behind my eyes. The anger and what I want to do to him comes hot and fast, and scares me enough to speak up. "Get lost, Spence." To Doby: "Let's go, man."

That Goddamn sneer. "You suck him off yet, Connor? His dick taste like bleach?"

Doby explodes. He knocks Spence to the dark rainbow asphalt, drives a knee into his chest and grabs handfuls of Spenser's hair.

I can't move, I can only watch as Doby slams Spence's head against the pavement. Spence bucks, punches Doby in the side of the face, the ribs, again, and again, but Doby doesn't care. He's all hate, and scariest of all, Spence is swearing but Doby doesn't make a sound.

Doby pulls his left sleeve up with his teeth and begins to gnaw on his wrist, his own freaking wrist, like a, oh God, like a dog. He puts a knee in Spence's face, digs around his pants pocket, brings out a Swiss Army knife. He flips out a blade and saws at his wrist until it glistens, flows. He drops the knife and jams his wrist into Spence's mouth. "Drink, motherfucker."

I couldn't be half as frightened if he'd screamed it.

Spence gags, jerks his head to the side.

Doby wrenches it back and clamps a hand over Spence's nose. "I said drink, you cocksucker. Swallow it." I can't see Spence's mouth, only Doby's hand and wrist with a black line oozing around it. "Swallow."

Doby puts all his weight on Spence's face. There's a terrible sucking, puking sound that goes on forever, then Doby takes his wrist away.

Spence coughs, and I swear he tries to scream but all that comes out is foam. Black and blacker, it shoots out like he's puking up his soul. His eyes roll back, and in the bare light I see the veins of his face crawl like worms trying to escape acid rain. Doby's hate and anger and ugly eat Spence alive. He spasms and shakes. His insides pool around his head, ooze foamy and stinking in my direction. He stops moving.

"What?" The word hangs up in my throat. "What did you ... ?"

Doby slides off, licks his wrist, looks at me sidelong.

Looks at me like he wants to kiss me the way he does in my dreams. Looks at me like a dog kicked one time too many, ready to turn.

He holds out the lighter fluid. I can move again, almost reach for the blue and yellow can, take a step back.

Doby smirks and looks sad at the same time. He goes through Spence's pockets, takes his wallet and keys, grabs the knife. Then he's sucking on the blue and yellow can on his way to Spence's car. I hear the squeal of tires and see the flash of metallic blue less than a minute later.

Spence's dark and foamy spreads towards my feet. Got to get home. Home. Veins like worms. Mom and Dad. Home.

Jenna is sorting through baby clothes and chatting on the computer when I stumble through the door. She looks up from something with strawberries and ruffles.

I sag against the wall, try not to puke. Shaking like I'm going to fall to pieces on the outside the way my life has on the inside.

She frowns. "You okay?"

Mom calls from upstairs: "Everything okay down there?"

Jenna says, "Yeah, just Connor." To me: "Gawd, what happened with you? You look like crap."

I stagger towards the couch. Does she see what happened? What I let Doby do?

Mom calls down again: "Any word from Spence?"

Jenna fiddles with her phone. "Not yet. He said he'd text when he got home. Probably stopped to get cigarettes."

I gag, make a sound, not a word, and Jenna looks my way again. "What?"

"I-I ..."

Veins like worms, and the baby, oh God, the baby.

It's over, my life is over. I am so hungry.

Turn and run, no idea where. Try to outrun the taste of lighter fluid and bleach as Youngstown closes in.

Author's Note

Why do we hate? I don't know. The question of why we hate, that base, bare question is one of the hardest to answer, second only to "Why do we love?"

Many of my stories begin with a particular image or scene. This one is no exception. A circle of boys behind a convenience store, and one boy who accepts the dare to do something dumb. Only it's not dumb, not to him, and that may well be the most horrific part of the story.

Listening to It Rain

Alan found me at Cook Creek, near where it fed into the summer sludge of the North Raccoon River. He dropped down beside me, on the log where we used to tell our folks we went fishing. Sometimes we brought home a blue gill or channel cat, but mostly we touched and tasted, lazing in the sunshine, laughing when it rained.

"Hey, Ben. What's up?"

I hitched my shoulders, and kept my eyes on the water.

We skipped rocks and didn't say much for a while. The creek talked to itself on the way downstream and somewhere a jay let everyone know it was angry. Without a wind, leaves hung limp as dishrags from the branches and the place smelled ripe with green and rot, witness to another muggy Iowa summer.

Finally Alan said, "You should be heading back to the cemetery."

"Don't want to."

I dared a quick look at him. New lines crinkled sad at the corner of his mouth.

"You got to, Ben. You're dead."

At least he had the good grace not to mention my face or back. Stitches could put a body back together, but never make it whole.

I skipped another rock. "Not my fault."

How'd he get so old in six months? Black crew-cut growing out, a few hairs playing pretend as a beard, something sad and lonesome I wished I could soothe away.

He took a deep breath and, real easy, he said, "Yeah, I know, but you still got to go back. It's Sunday, and your folks might come around after church."

"Not my problem." I wished I could put feelings behind the words, but I didn't have none no more.

Alan leaned back on his elbows and I risked another look. The sunlight through his shirt hinted at his chest underneath. I kept my hands to myself.

He must have seen me looking, cause he turned and smiled full on. Once upon a time I would have gone all warm at the sight, but I didn't have no heartbeat no more, either. I didn't have nothing but the cold,

cold grave, and worms for company.

"You get the classes you wanted?" I said before he could open his mouth.

His smile went away, and he looked back at the creek.

"All but the college placement biology," he said. The words were thick and slow in coming. He cleared his throat. "I got Mister Jayger for language arts."

I nodded, though not so much as to tear out the stitches under my hair. "He still got that ugly station wagon?"

"The Meat Beater? Yeah."

"He should get himself some decent wheels."

Alan laughed. "You should have seen him at the game against, um ..."

He looked away and cleared his throat again.

We settled into silence. I wanted to say lots of things – "I miss you.", "You have any idea what it's like to need something so bad and not know what it is?", "I'm scared." Maybe even wanted to cry, but my tears went out of me with my heartbeat, splattered on my bike and the hood of a beat-up fifty-nine Chevy Impala.

I looked at my hands, long waxy fingers, dirt and bits of wood and grass under the nails. I wondered what Alan would do if I put a hand on his arm, leaned my head on his shoulder. Would he wrap his arm around me like he used to? Pull away? Run screaming cause I'm so cold anymore? In all the times I'd wandered from the cemetery and all the times he found me, I never even so much as let my hand brush against his. I so wanted to touch him, but the wanting came from far away, tucked in a place I couldn't reach no more.

My grandpa had no use for Alan's family, said Alan's dad had yellow fever and his mom spent years in one of those camps for the Japanese. Ma always said Grandpa was still bitter about the war, and that I shouldn't listen to him. Herself, she boasted how she talked to Alan's mom at the bakery if no other customers came around.

Alan and me never cared about what we couldn't and shouldn't do. We just did because it felt right together.

Used to feel right.

I picked up a rock. "You applied for any colleges yet?"

He nodded, still looking at the water.

"I don't know why I can't stay in the grave, Alan. I just can't, you know? I got ... I should still ..."

He nodded again. I thought maybe I saw tears in his eyes.

"You're righteous smart." I tossed the rock in the creek. "Maybe I'll come visit you in college."

Alan smiled. He reached out and touched my elbow just for a second. I almost felt it.

The shadows had shrunk and started to grow long again when he stood. "Come on, Ben."

I looked at the ground, then at him. "Why?"

He held out a trembling hand. "Because it's time."

He flinched when I put my palm in his, but didn't pull away.

Hand in hand, we walked back across Shilling's Bridge to the cemetery. I knew my row and place; so did Alan. His backpack and camp shovel sat behind the mound of dirt and splinters, just out of sight of any passers-by. He let go of my hand and picked up the shovel.

There were tears in his eyes when he said, "You need to rest, Ben."

I eased myself back into my coffin. Hand on what was left of the lid, I finally got my courage up. "Don't forget me."

I hoped it was true when he said, "Never."

I eased the lid closed, my feet already lonesome for the trail. Alone in the dark, I listened as the dirt rained down on me again.

Author's Note

Ben told me his story while I walked the nature trail behind my partner's game store. My steps crushed bright orange leaves slick with rain, I listened closely to the whispering creek as I crossed the wooden bridges, and I wondered what would make a body so lonesome for the trail, and a heart ache for something it couldn't understand.

The Business of Rats

Early evening rain trickled inside the collar of Ratty Tomlin's tattered long coat. He touched his cap to the night watchman sitting on a one-legged stool.

"Evening, sir. Is this the Beckett and Brownman stores?"

"So it says up there," the watchman said, tipping his head back to indicate the whitewashed lettering above the doors. The rain stained the wood dark as it collected in thick drops that fell from the cross frame. "Help you with something now?"

"Ratty Tomlin at your service, finest rat catcher of the south Thames." He straightened his shoulders. "Mister Beckett's man sent me along to catch some rats. Said I would be expected."

A lantern beside the stool gave off meager light in the pungent fog coiling up from the Thames. The watchman set his hands on his knees and gave Ratty Tomlin an eye from beneath his bowler's brim. "And who would his man be?"

"That would be Mister Harris, sir."

The watchman's scowl lifted to a smile. He stood, setting the stool off to the side. He extended a hand. "Right you are, then. I was expecting you earlier."

Ratty Tomlin tucked his cudgel under his left arm and accepted the offer. His hand engulfed the larger man's. "A fellow keeps busy, and gots to break bread when he can." He didn't see a need to mention that pretty Maggie Boyle at Tugger's Fish House had served the bread, as fine a reason a man could find to make oneself tardy.

"True enough." The watchman nodded toward the grip. "They's quite some mitts you have there, eh?"

"Lucky that way, I suppose." Hands three sizes too big for a man so small, massive and knobbed with scars and gristle, they showed Ratty Tomlin's work, missing two knuckles worth of the ring finger on the left, and all but the barest stub of the thumb on the right. Rats had sharp teeth, and didn't fancy being caught.

"And who have we here?"

Ratty Tomlin glanced down at the brown and white terrier looking up at him. He reached down and rubbed the dog's ears. "Why, none other than Prince Albert, the finest ratter in all London."

"Ah." The watchman chuckled, rumbling deep in his chest. He tipped his hat in exaggerated courtesy. "Good evening to you, Your Royal Highness."

Prince Albert obliged the introduction with a sniff of the man's boots, back end wagging for all his worth.

The watchman fished a ring with two stout keys out of his vest pocket. One key opened the broad lock that secured the chain around the door handles; the other unlocked the iron brace that held the wooden cross beam in place. The watchman looked up and down the street before he lifted the bar and secured it upright with a wooden pin. "Here you go, then. Not that I envy you none."

Ratty Tomlin did his best not to shiver with the weight of childhood memories. "Ratting isn't so bad as all that. Sure a sight better than the workhouses."

The watchman pulled open the right-hand door wide enough to let a body through, then picked up his lantern. The wisp of flame caught full of itself with a twist of the knob. "Can't argue that none. Just seems to be getting rattier around here of late. Likely's why they called for you. Mind your feet."

What first took Ratty Tomlin's notice when the door opened was the smell. Musty burlap, wood and tar, stale sweat and beer from the work day, and threading through the lot of it, the sharp musk of rats. He stepped in after the watchman. "How so rattier?"

The big man shuddered. "This place is fairly crawling, it is, but never so much as the past ten, maybe twelve, nights. Up and down the storehouses, in fact. I hear them, the rats, skittering about. I come in here once a night, and only once, to have a look around, but never see nothing."

"I would wager there's a fair number of them if I can make the smell," Ratty Tomlin said, and knew it for right. He'd never been schooled in numbers, but he figured on earning a good many thruppence a live rat from Mackleby's rat pit before the night's end. Wouldn't that be a sweet bit for his purse on top of Mister Harris's quid?

The watchman harrumphed. "Can't imagine the fellows working here with them rats about."

The lantern revealed stacks of boxes to the right and rolls of what had the look of rugs to the left. Above seemed a loft. Shadows caught the edges of the light and stretched themselves into the darkness beyond.

"They might see one now and then, but rats is as likely to stay out of sight during the day."

The watchman stepped to the side. "That's for you to say, then. His Highness coming along?"

"Hmm?" Ratty Tomlin looked down and then over his shoulder. Prince Albert still stood outside the door, ears back, tail tucked between his legs. "Come along, boy. Rats, Albert. Rats."

The terrier whined pitiably and hunkered down.

Ratty Tomlin set down his goods and stepped outside to collect the little dog. Prince Albert leapt into his hands and jammed his nose into the crook of his arm.

"Here now," Ratty Tomlin said softly, rubbing the terrier's ears. "What's this?"

Something more than the cold and rain had set him to trembling. Ratty Tomlin kept his back to the watchman as he coaxed his little friend's head up with kindly whispers and a few scraps of dried beef.

"Finest ratter in London, hmmm?" came from behind.

Ratty Tomlin scowled. "He's hungry is all." He gave over another bit of beef. Prince Albert scoffed it down and licked his master's knobby fingers. "That's a good boy, Albert. Let's do it now, shall we?"

Ratty Tomlin gathered his tools, stepped back inside, and set Prince Albert on the floor beside him. The terrier made no complaint, but kept his tail between his legs.

The watchman guffawed and scratched the whiskers under his chin. "Well, I can't say I blames him for being hungry, is it? I wouldn't fancy being hungry in here myself."

Ratty Tomlin had had enough from the larger man. "There's rats to be had, and Mister Harris ain't paying me to stand around nattering."

The watchman shrugged. "Right."

They took a bit of the watchman's light for Ratty Tomlin's lantern, then the watchman stepped outside. "The doors need to be locked tight, so give a bang and holler when you're ready to come out."

Ratty Tomlin turned up his lantern. "You're on all night, then?"

"Until Mister Harris comes round in the morning." With that, the watchman pushed the door closed.

A lonely, shivering sound, the rattle and clank of being locked inside. The dark settled in close around the lantern light. Ratty Tomlin emptied his satchel into his coat pockets—bags, a lancing kit with two needles, a tipper of strong whiskey, and a wad of packing. He rubbed sweet-scented oil into his calloused hands, working it in until the slick was gone. Then with lantern held high, he listened. The patter of rain on the roof, the muted clatter of horse and carriage somewhere outside, and, yes, the pick of tiny claws. Ratty Tomlin smiled and set to work.

Rats liked the dark places out of sight, the crawls behind crates, nesting in bales of hay or rolls of cloth. He took his time and listened close; patience and a keen ear made fine friends for a rat catcher. In no time he heard the telltale scritch most folk would shun in a bad dream. Not Ratty Tomlin, though. Sounded sweet as money in his ears.

He followed the pick and squeak around, about, set down the lantern, eased a hand into a furrow of a cotton bale. Wait for it, wait for it, and there!, the brush of whiskers on his knuckles. Ratty Tomlin brought his hand around and grabbed the squeaker by the head, easing it out with a thruppence of satisfaction.

He shifted his grip to the loose skin on the rat's back, and brought the lantern close for a better look.

The smudge black of the London night sky, and as long as his hand from twitching nose to the tip of its wormy tail, the rat made for a fine first catch. The beastie's whiskers quivered and its front paws twitched and clutched like tiny four-fingered hands. "You're a handsome fellow. Here go."

Into the bag it went, and on to the next rat went Ratty Tomlin.

His special blend of oils did the trick every time. Rats lean and quick or wobbly fat sniffed out a hopeful treat and were grabbed up and stuffed in a sack. Prince Albert stayed close at first, but it wasn't long until the sight of a rat dashing away and his master's eager "Go on, boy!" had him darting this way and that. He was allowed the first catch for himself; after that, the rats were given over to his master alive, if a touch bloody.

With two squirming burlap bundles by the time his belly rumbled, it had the makings of a good night. Ratty Tomlin found the pot in the water closet to relieve himself, then settled down for a wedge of cheese and a pint by the front doors. "What, maybe fifteen rats so far? Mick'll be stump smiling when he sees what we have for him." He fed Prince Albert a crumb. "Couldn't have done it without you, Albert. You're my boy. Not so fine a sight as Maggie Boyle, but you'll do."

Ratty Tomlin wiped the shallow nicks on Prince Albert's muzzle with whiskey before searing them shut with a needle heated in the lantern's flame. The little dog whined and ducked his head each time the glowing needle came near. "You don't want to fester, Albert. Hold ... still."

A curl of smoke, the sharp smell of burnt fur, and it was done. "There."

Ratty Tomlin made certain there were no holes or tears in the burlap before he made for the back of the storehouse. What with the crates and bales and piles, there was certain to be at least another five rats in the mix, perhaps as many as ten, and every one of them pretty pennies for his wallet. Ratting wasn't a gentleman's job, but it kept Ratty Tomlin in most comforts and out of the workhouses.

Rat stink and mold soured the air toward the rear of the building. Ratty Tomlin stepped careful through the stacks, lantern held high, pausing now and again to sniff, listen. The dark pushed back against the light, refusing to give way. He found the occasional tuft of hair caught in a loose board, or a scattering of tiny black turds where a trunk was cocked off row, but no rats.

Ratty Tomlin got down to hands and knees to peer behind a row of barrels marked as salted pork, but found nothing there but darkness and the sound of his own heartbeat. He sat back on his heels.

"Where do you suppose they made off to, Albert? Upstairs?"

That's when he heard a scratching, faint for all it sounded above and near.

Prince Albert backed away, all ruff and teeth and barking.

Ratty Tomlin gripped his cudgel. A mad dog? A vagrant? "What is—?"

Something dark dropped on him, driving the breath out of him in a crush. It kicked the lantern away, snatched the cudgel, and was sudden on the stacks and gone round around the corner with Prince Albert chasing it in a fury.

The lantern snuffed out, and the stench of oil caught Ratty Tomlin's stomach unawares. He gagged as he rolled to his side and brought his knees under him. Coughing, he swallowed something foul and sucked in a painful gasp of air, and then the next. Something wet his upper lip, and there was a taste of blood in his mouth. Where was his cudgel? Right, the bloody mug-hunter what jumped him made off with it.

Ratty Tomlin pulled himself to his feet against the stacks. No time to fuss with the lantern, and the light would only give him away. No matter, he'd wager he knew this place like the knobs of his hands. Ratty Tomlin slipped the shiv from under his coat and staggered off after

Prince Albert's fierce complaint. Rat catchers knew how to take care of
street rats, too.

Dim moonlight from windows high above took the edge off
the dark, but Ratty Tomlin kept his hand out in front as he stumbled
through the heavy shadows. Prince Albert's barks sounded just around
the corner close when there came a sharp yelp of pain and then silence.
His stomach clenched tighter than his chest. He bit his tongue to keep
from giving himself away by calling for his friend.

Chiv held tight, he rounded the corner quiet as he could.

"What have we here?" came from above. The thick, growly voice
held an odd squeak at the end of the words.

Ratty Tomlin glared up at the shadows with nothing to see.
Whatever fellow was up there must have had a mouthful of rotted
wooden teeth to talk so strange. "Come down here and I'll show you
what I have for you."

A small bundle dropped to the floor at his feet. Ratty Tomlin gave
a start and cursed soft and foul. Seeing nothing above, he cautiously
nudged the thing with the toe of his boot, and made it out to be one of
his burlap sacks empty as could be.

"I doubt it." A piece of darkness on the crates above shifted, settled.
"I doubt it."

Ratty Tomlin stood. The sharp stink of rats was thick enough to
chew. "What? You a coward hiding up there? Let me get a look at you."

"You wants a look, little ratster?" Scraping, a spark, and the dim
stirring of a flame before it caught full and well. A wicked clawed hand
jammed a torch of plank wood and oil rags into the top of the crate as
the light parted the shadows. "Satisfied?"

A chill caught Ratty Tomlin's spine. He took a step back.

It was a man wearing the skin of a rat, a rat wearing the body of
a man. Mangy brown fur, dull yellow teeth surrounded by a droop of
whiskers on a rat's long face that weren't no mask. Crouched atop the
stack of crates, clawed toes gripping the edge of the wooden box, the
creature leaned forward and peered down with greedy black eyes. Gold
and silver hoops pierced the edges of the round ears set high on its head.
The wet pink nose twitched, and black lips pulled back in a beastie smile.

"Wassa matter, little ratster? Scared?"

Knocking knees said to run for the doors and scream for the
watchman, but what if that thing got him on the way? Worse, what if it
had Prince Albert? Ratty Tomlin squared his shoulders with courage he

didn't rightly feel. "Should I be?"

A slender pink tongue dragged itself along the black lips, corner to corner. "Fits t'piss y'self, I say."

Ratty Tomlin tightened his lower belly to keep from doing just that. "Just what sort of ugly pug-arse are you?"

"I'm a rat, is what I am. You knows rats, don't you?"

"Oh, I know rats."

"Yesss, you does." The rat thing held up a squirming burlap bundle and tore it open with a swift swipe of its claws. A knot of rats tumbled out the bag, squeaking and scurrying over the beast. One scampered up the side of the thing's face and stuck its head in the round shell of the thing's ear. Was it licking? Whispering? Ratty Tomlin couldn't tell. The rat hopped to the creature's shoulder, down to the crate, and disappeared after the others.

Ratty Tomlin grit his teeth. Not only had this rat thing done him over and probably uncorked one on Prince Albert, it had undone all of the night's work, adding insult to injury of the highest order.

The rat thing must have seen the frustration on his face. "Poor little ratster," it said with a vicious snigger. "You gots nothings now."

Knobby fingers tightened around the comfort and strength of the chiv grip. "Not quite. Them ears'll fetch me a fist of quid when I sell them for dinner plates."

The beastie smile came back somehow twice as sharp and wide. "Ain'ts you full of y'self."

Ratty Tomlin shifted his weight, slid his right foot forward. "Come get yourself a taste, you muck-eyed, shit-bottomed beastie."

"What's the rush, little ratster? You ain't goin's nowhere." The rat thing reached behind it and brought Prince Albert into the light, claws dug into the terrier's bloodied scruff. It shook the little dog and laughed at the bare, wet whimper.

Ratty Tomlin's gut clenched with anger and fear for his friend. "I'm going to string you high is where I'm going."

"That so, eh?" The rat thing lifted Prince Albert to its mouth, took the left rear paw between its yellow teeth, and bit down with a sickening crunch and a high dog squeal. The rat thing spit the paw at Ratty Tomlin's feet. "Get rids of the knifes now, ratster."

Ratty Tomlin dropped the shiv.

"Betters than that, ratster." It licked at Prince Albert's remaining back paw.

Ratty Tomlin kicked the shiv into a corner. "Let him go."

The rat thing took up the torch— "No." —and put the fiery head in its mouth. Dark swallowed the storehouse as the black lips swallowed the flame.

The dark was all the more blinding for being sudden. Ratty Tomlin squeezed his eyes shut and crouched low, listening, ready, but not fast enough for the silence. Hands took him by the shoulders and threw him up and back into bundles of shakes that scattered under his weight. He came up slashing the dark with a broken slat, but heard nothing but Prince Albert whimpering and his own heart pounding as loud as the Queen's cannons. "Bastard!"

"Not so sporting when the rat's big as yous, eh?" Laughter lean and low shadowed the words. "Pissant ratsters, thinks yous so fine."

Ratty Tomlin spun left then right, thin planks splitting beneath his boots. The shadows moved, not enough to be rightly dark now that his eyes were settled, but not to his liking at all. A tail slithering one way? Two shadowed ears twitching another? He ached, and quivered, and sweat, cornered and small with nowhere to hide.

Prince Albert whined. Then came the sound of paws dragging close by, bigger than a rat's, not so big as the rat thing. Ratty Tomlin grabbed the sound and held on for both their lives. Noise meant Prince Albert was alive, good enough for him. Weren't no bully of a rat going to run them off, not Ratty Tomlin and his trusty Prince Albert, no sir.

He staggered off the shakes, no more steady on flat footing. He took a breath. "Sporting? I put money down on rats bigger than you at Mack—"

A rustle and snap from his right. A weight caught Ratty Tomlin low and quick in the legs.

He jammed the stake into the rat thing's back, put his shoulder into it and twisted, thick splinters wedging deep into his palms.

The rat thing squealed and bucked up. It came up with a snarl, caught Ratty Tomlin by the left hand, and hellfire exploded up his arm as the rat thing's teeth went through his palm like a hammered awl through leather.

Ratty Tomlin howled and lunged at the mass of shadowed fur and muscle. He tore his hand free and drove the rat thing into a stack of crates that came down on them in a rain of sharp corners.

Somehow he lost the stake, but he didn't care. He still had his right hand and the fiery club of his left, and he beat the rat thing down with the claws and teeth and rat stink of his pain.

The rat thing tumbled him off to get away, but Ratty Tomlin came right back. With his knees hard in the rat thing's chest, he grabbed one ratty weak hand in his good strong hand, and bent all four fingers back with a kindling snap. The rat thing screamed, music to Ratty Tomlin's ears.

The grate and rumble of sliding wood came from the front of the storehouse, and with it a sliver of dull gold light.

"What's with the Devil's own ruckus in here?" the watchman said at the top of his lungs.

The rat thing made to grab Ratty Tomlin by the face. Ratty Tomlin knocked its hand aside and grabbed it around the throat, his thick hands clenched like a miser's on a penny. Gristle and bone slid under the rat thing's skin as he bore down. He leaned in close. The rat thing's breath reeked of mash and rotten meat. "Better money ... at the pit."

A hard jerk to the left. The rat thing's neck snapped like a wet stick.

Ratty Tomlin had his hand wrapped tight in his shirt, and Prince Albert bundled in his coat and on his lap, by the time the watchman blustered to the back of the storehouse. The tipper of whiskey was empty beside him.

"Look at this. You've gone off your bob, then?" the big man said, thrusting his lantern at Ratty Tomlin. "You any idea what Mister Harris is going to—Mother's Mercy!" His gaze dropped to the gruesome mess in Ratty Tomlin's lap.

Ratty Tomlin stared at him for two slow blinks before he held up a blood-soaked rag strip. "Lend a hand, would you?"

The watchman blanched. He motioned with the lantern, the shadows jerking about. "Jesus wept. How did ... ?"

"A rat. Come on, now."

Together they tied off Prince Albert's stump and bound Ratty Tomlin's hand. Even the watchman's flask was called to service, though the watchman turned away as Ratty Tomlin poured the last of the whiskey over his mangled hand before they wrapped it tight in strips of muslin from a nearby bundle.

"That needs to see a doctor," the watchman said, wiping sweat from his brow.

Ratty Tomlin sat perfectly still, surprised it didn't hurt more, surprised he had a hand left to hurt at all. Even with his eyes closed he saw the hole clean through the center of his hand, the way his ring finger stump and little finger twitched like merry madmen. "Mmmm."

The watchman looked even more grieved when Ratty Tomlin directed his attention to the rat thing. How he'd missed it coming back, Ratty Tomlin couldn't say.

"I thought that was ..." He leaned in close, drew off. "No, that's not a ... Is it?"

"It is." Ratty Tomlin wedged Prince Albert into the crook of his left arm, held out his right hand.

"Bloody hell," said the watchman.

"That, too."

The watchman helped Ratty Tomlin to his feet. "What you going to do with it?"

"I was hoping you could help me stash it around back, maybe under some scrap."

The watchman blinked and looked him full in the face like as if he'd suggested taking an axe to the Queen. "Me?"

Ratty Tomlin twitched his left hand. "Can't really do it myself."

"Why keep it at all?"

"For a better look in the light, and so's Mister Harris understands what happened."

And to cut off the ears, but that didn't seem worth saying. "I'll make it worth your time."

With a promise of ten bob upon Ratty Tomlin's return, the watchman shouldered the burden through the front doors and around back where they hid it under a tumble of tarps and brick. With nothing else for it, they headed around the building once more.

Low slung clouds hid the first hints of sun, leaving the lamplighters to greet the morning by snuffing out their work of the night before. Ratty Tomlin swayed on his feet as he watched the fellows mark the start of day along the damp cobbles of Orney Way.

The watchman frowned. "You goin' to make it home safe?"

Ratty Tomlin nodded, wishing for more whiskey and a good salt bath. It would hurt something fierce, but better a salt bath for his hand than a sear.

The watchman reached out to the little dog wrapped in his master's coat. "His Majesty going to be all right?"

Ratty Tomlin shied the terrier away. "He will be," he said, and made another silent promise to the same. "Two of his legs is broken, and his paw, well, you'll see. You can't keep a good ratter down." He stroked the top of his friend's head. Prince Albert whined and closed his eyes.

"What about, um, what about ... ?" The watchman jerked his head toward the storehouse.

"Tell Mister Harris I'm right sorry about the mess, and that I'll be back in a night or so to finish up." Ratty Tomlin would set Prince Albert up with Maggie Boyle, then tend to hisself. "Tell him I won't pay for any damages, but he don't owe me one penny until I clear out all the rats, every last mother's son of them great and small."

Ratty Tomlin was good for it. After all, he was the finest rat catcher in the south Thames, and he knew his business.

Author's Note

Confession time. I am a child of documentaries: nature, history, science, math, theater, literature, politics. You name it, I'll watch it. I don't recall much of my childhood, but I do remember curling up beside my mom on the couch to watch Nova or the latest episode of Elizabeth R on the local PBS channel. She said the trick to watching documentaries was to pay as much attention to what's not said as to what is, and note the source material for the production. Are the sources verifiable?

One such documentary series detailed some of the worst jobs in history, and rat catcher was one of them. I loved it! I went from the documentary to researching rat catchers in Victorian-era England, the neighborhoods along the Thames river, rats, Jack Russel terriers, and Queen Victoria's ratter, Jack Black. Luckily I was able to pull myself out of the research rabbit hole long enough to write the story.

Now, if you'll excuse me, there's a new series about religious icons ...

Telling Stories

Sam knew there would be trouble the night the saguaro came to call. "Evening," she said, and stepped aside for her unexpected guest.

The cactus scrunched down as far as it could and skittered through the door on its roots, bringing with it the breath of rocks, sagebrush, and the cold Sonoran desert night. It stopped in the middle of the cabin's sparsely furnished main room and straightened until its spines brushed the roof. "I hope I didn't come at a bad time."

"Not at all. I don't get many saguaros stopping by."

She didn't have many anybodies stopping by anymore, but saying so would have been rude. She settled into the rocker by a bookcase crammed with dog-eared issues of *Popular Mechanics* and *National Geographic*. "What can I do for you?"

The cactus tried to straighten to its full height, but the roof got in the way. "I wish to marry a Gila monster."

Sam stopped rocking. She stuck a finger in her ear to clean out a bit of wax. "Um ... Come again?"

"I wish to marry a Gila monster."

Sam took a moment to gather her thoughts and clean her glasses with the tail of her shirt. "You don't say."

"She hunts in the early morning, and I am rooted near her burrow. We started talking, and now we spend most of our mornings together. She is lovely, all black and pink and yellow skin, and has a very dry sense of humor."

The cactus quivered with what Sam supposed was laughter.

"I see." She let her glasses drop to the end of their beaded chain. "And?"

The saguaro twitched. "We don't know what to do. We both love the sand, but I stand far above it, and she burrows beneath. I drink in the glory of the sun; she feasts on mice, and eggs, and such." Its arms slumped. "I gave her one of my fruits, but she could not eat it."

"Of course not." Sam looked at her hands, short, wide fingers with nails worn ragged from working in the garden. Growing up on the Taos Pueblo, PopPop Donner used to say her hands were "beautiful with hard work." "Why come to me?"

"You are very wise. Your family has been here for always."

Sam snorted. "I wouldn't say always. I moved to Arizona in '73."

"But your people know the desert ways."

Sam shook her head. "Not so much. Ma was a nurse at the Taos clinic, and Pa worked as a handyman any time he climbed out of the bottle." She scratched the back of her head. "My grandfather kept to some of the old ways, and I used to, but that was a long time ago."

"For the always, yes," said the cactus.

Sam set her glasses back on her nose. "I spent thirty years fixing cars, and working the liquor store counter in Yuma. I'm too damn old and set in my ways for magic anymore."

"The Gila monster and I do not need your medicine."

Well, that was a relief, but it didn't tell her what she wanted to know. "Then why come asking me for help?"

"Your family has the always." The saguaro straightened as best it could, arms upright and sure. "Will you marry us?"

Sam blinked, and barely noticed when her glasses slid to the tip of her nose. "Pardon?"

"The Gila monster and I want to marry, but we don't know how. Will you marry us together?"

Sam sat upright in her chair. "That's not really possible. You can't— It's just. I mean, you're two different creatures."

The top of the cactus' stem bobbed in something like a nod against the roof. Bits of spines fell to the floor. "Yes."

"Maybe you didn't hear me. You can't get married. You're a plant. This Gila monster's an animal."

Again the bobbing green nod. "Yes."

"It's not natural."

"That is why I have come to you, to make it natural. Will you marry us?"

Sam ran a hand through her hair. "You're not listening to me. I said—"

"I am hearing, yes. Will you marry us together?"

Sam frowned. After a handful of heartbeats, she took off her glasses. "I don't know. I'll have to think about it."

The saguaro bent in half, more a bow than a scrunch. "Thank you."

Sam levered herself out of the chair, wood and bone creaking with the effort. "Don't go thanking me. I never said I would."

"You never said you wouldn't." The saguaro bowed again. "That is your wisdom."

"Hmmm."

Sam walked the saguaro to the front porch and watched it skitter into the night, a shape to a blob, a blob to a nothing. Standing under the open sky where the sickle moon hung sharp and bright, every breath brought something new—coyote must, scrub oak, piñon pine from the heights. The desert night wrapped cold and dark around her, stirring memories she could have done without.

Against her better judgment, Sam followed the memories back inside to a Red Wing boot box at the bottom of her bedroom closet. She pulled the box out, settled onto the unmade bed, and removed the lid.

Memories lived in the box, dusty, musty memories that made her sneeze. Good ones, bad ones, other ones. Her first driver's license, Daniel's death certificate, the deed to the house and land. Her GED certificate, Daniel's 4F papers from the Army. Matching mother and infant hospital bracelets, a crumpled, white construction paper heart with LOVE U ALWAYS HPPY MOTHERS DAY!!! scrawled in red crayon. A rusty Band-Aid tin held Ma's silver locket with a picture of Pa from boot camp, a candy bracelet on an elastic string and a gold plastic ring from the state fair in Albuquerque.

At the shoebox's bottom? Sam paused, then pulled out memories banished to a plain manila envelope.

A marriage certificate. She'd married Daniel, a boy from the Pueblo, and lived alone with her husband on the other side of the bed. Sam refolded the meaningless piece of paper issued by the Taos County courthouse and set it aside.

Three black and white photos from one of those instant picture booths. Two young women, laughing, making faces, hugging. Tousled hair, turned up collars, eyes filled with stars and the lights of the midway. Herself and Dayline at the state fair, both sixteen years old with the world spread before them. The Sam in the picture didn't know a thing about the world. She set the pictures on top of the license.

A different photo, Polaroid, in color, two women in their mid-twenties, the white-capped ocean behind them, the wind whipping their hair into delightful tangles. Her daughter Kaitlin looked vibrant and lively; she had Sam's eyes, Daniel's unfortunate nose, and straight black hair cut in a bob. The other woman, blonde-haired and brown-eyed, was a stranger in all but her gap-toothed smile.

Sam turned the picture over. Written in blue ink on a piece of masking tape was a California address, and a phone number.

Sam returned everything to the box, and set the memories back in the closet where they belonged.

The Gila monster stopped by the next night while a pot of chili simmered habanero hot on the stove.

Sam ushered her guest inside. Light from the lone floor lamp near the rocker cast muted shadows along the lizard's colorful beaded back. PopPop Donner told stories of the Yaqui people's reverence for the skin's healing powers. PopPop told too many stories.

The lizard wandered around the room with a leathery egg in its mouth, searching out the small, hidden places. Its tail, thick with early summer fat, made a wide, lazy S along the dusty floor. Sam stood by the stove and let it roam as it pleased. A Gila monster in the house couldn't be any weirder than a cactus.

After exploring all four corners and everything in between, the Gila monster set the egg at Sam's feet. Its blue-pink tongue tasted the air, flick-flick. "I brought you a gift. Garter snake. Quite tasty."

Sam picked up the egg, careful to keep her fingers from the damp, venomous areas around the tooth marks. "Thanks. I appreciate it." She set the egg on the edge of the sink. "Mind if I sit down?"

The lizard laughed like sand blowing across an empty stretch of asphalt. "Go right ahead."

Sam gave the chili a final stir, then retired to her rocker. This looked to be another long night, and her knees weren't what they'd been thirty, hell, ten years ago. "What brings you out so late?"

Flick-flick. "The saguaro said it came to see you last night, and I wanted to speak with you myself."

"That's fine."

The lizard bobbed up and down on its front legs. "I want to marry the saguaro. It said you were very kind and would think on the request with your full wisdom."

Sam stroked her brow with a finger, wondering what she could say to make the lizard, the cactus, all of it go away. "Like I told to the saguaro, you really can't get married. It just isn't done."

Flick-flick, flick-flick. That tongue never stopped. "But why?"

"It just ... It isn't." Sam began to rock in quick, agitated bursts, her legs letting on when she couldn't find the words. "You don't have anything in common beyond, you know, desert things." Even to her ears, the argument sounded weak, but she straightened her shoulders when she said it.

"Yes, but our hearts want more." The Gila monster stepped back and forth in a strange little dance, black claws ticking over the wood floor. "It seemed so tall for a cactus, catching the sun as it went by. We started to talk and it turns out we both like morning dew, and the cool of sunrise, and the song of the black-throated sparrow."

As if to catch a stray thought, the lizard paused with its left foot in the air. Flick-flick. "The morning I sank my claws into its pleats and climbed through its spines to the very top of its stem, the saguaro asked to marry me." It lowered its foot, then its head. "My claws. In its pleats. It gave of itself to lift me up. No one had ever done that before. Watching the sunrise, so far above the ground yet still touching it through the saguaro's roots, I said yes. I would give my teeth if it meant we could marry." Flick-flick.

Sam listened, and hated herself even more than she hated the thick-bodied lizard at her feet. She bit off every word like a piece of sour lemon. "People marry to have kids."

"We are not people."

"Very funny. You know what I mean."

The lizard bobbed again. "Will you do this for us? We want to marry."

Sam's threw up her hands. "It's not always about what you want. Sometimes it's about doing what's right."

The echo of her mother lost itself in the wind beating against the windows, and Sam's anger drained away, leaving a fine film of guilt behind. She got unsteadily to her feet. The Gila monster skittered back, hunched with fear.

"No, no." Sam soothed the air between them with open hands. She stepped over the lizard and made her way to the window with the peeping tom moon.

When had she become her mother? The day she married Daniel? The night Kaitlin declared she didn't owe Sam a wedding or a grandchild, that she could love whom she chose, "right or wrong?"

She could still smell the cotton candy and fry bread, the roasted corn and Dayline's dime store cologne. After a dozen turns on the Tilt-

O-Whirl, the skitter of claws on the wood floor came from behind. "If you'll open the door, I can show myself out."

Early the next morning, Sam packed up her truck with her camp bag and plenty of water and headed out along El Camino Del Diablo.

She followed the highway west to Papago Well, then past the wildlife watering hole to slip on and off road the way PopPop taught her as a girl. When the sun had stretched itself orange and gold, and the closest thing to a road were the tracks of an occasional Sonoran antelope, she eased off the gas and looked for a place to lay camp.

A clearing surrounded by rocks and sage proved just the place. Sam laid out her blankets in the back, then built a small fire in the truck's shadow. Her one concession to age was the grinder and French press for her morning coffee. She had no time for that instant crap any more.

After a dinner of campfire biscuits and last night's chili, Sam propped herself against the camp bag and settled in next to the fire.

Sometime after midnight, she greeted the Milky Way. It stretched across the sky like an inverse of one of PopPop's beaded belts, bands and bursts of color nestled in a cradle of night. She hadn't beaded in years, had given it up right about the time she gave up Dayline and PopPop's old ways. PopPop hadn't said a word, but there was no escaping the disappointment in his eyes.

Nights like tonight, with only the stars and memories for company, she felt that disappointment all over again and missed her grandfather something fierce.

"You gonna finish that?"

Sam looked left and found a coyote bitch sitting at the edge of the firelight. The mangy thing was missing part of her left ear, and a thin scar caught the shadows along the left side of her muzzle.

Sam nudged the pot of leftover chili beside her. "What? This?"

The coyote nodded, eyes flashing orange in the firelight.

Sam pushed the pot towards her visitor. "Suit yourself, but it's pretty spicy."

"I lick my butt. How bad can it be?"

Sam snorted and went back to watching the stars. "Suit yourself, but I wouldn't do any licking after you eat."

The coyote laughed and helped herself to the pot, chasing it over the sand. Finished, the bitch settled on the other side of the fire, her tail curled around her legs. "What brings you this far into the desert?"

Sam kept her attention on the sky. She should have shooed the coyote away when she had the chance. "Peace and quiet."

Now it was the coyote's turn to snort. "Overrated, if you ask me. Give me a good story any night."

Sam uncrossed her ankles to ease her arthritic hip. "Didn't ask you."

"Sure you—" The coyote attacked the base of her tail before settling down again. "—did. That's why you came all the way out here."

Leave it to a coyote to complicate matters. "I was thinking about my daughter. I haven't talked to her in—what?—hell, I don't remember how many years."

Trouble was, she did remember, and the memory ate away at her heart.

The bitch snuffled the sand, licked her paws. "Why not?"

"Why not what?"

"Why haven't you talked to her? I hear my pups all the time."

"Because ..." Why hadn't she? The real reason, the one she'd kept at the bottom of a Red Wing boot box. The one that left her hollow inside without even the echo of her own tears for company. "Because I want what she has."

Sam waited for the cathartic rush of the admission, but nothing happened. Everything was the same—the sky, the fire, the damn coyote, herself.

She sat up with a grunt. "Me and Dayline fell out of touch back—"

"That's your daughter?"

"What? Oh, no. Kaitlin's my daughter. Dayline was my girlfriend." Sam frowned at her hands, waiting. When the coyote didn't say anything, she continued, "Anyway, me and Dayline kind of fell out of touch around the time Kaitlin moved west. We hadn't talked much for a couple of years before that."

The coyote yawned, tongue uncurling orange and black in the firelight. "So?"

Sam wedged a chunk of pine into the coals. Her eyes watered in the smoke. That's what she told herself. "Dayline died of lung cancer last November. I miss her, miss what we had. She used to wear Tweed. Folks gave her shit because it was supposed to be a dyke cologne, you

know?, but Dayline didn't care. We figured we'd be together forever—"
A jagged laugh made the word bleed. "—then I let my mom talk me into
marrying Daniel."

The bitch scratched her ear, licked the tips of her claws. "And that's
it?"

Sam cut the coyote a sharp look. "Yeah."

"What kind of story is that?"

"Hey now, I - "

The coyote stood. "You won't talk to your daughter because she's
happy and you're not? Big deal. You ever think maybe she won't talk to
you because you tell such lousy stories? You're selfish and petty, nothing
happens, the end."

"I am not petty."

"You gotta do something; that makes a good story. You don't even
burn your tail or learn a lesson."

"Hey—"

"Boring."

Sam balled her hands into fists. "Listen you—"

"Still boring." The coyote turned tail to the fire and wandered into
the night, its casual observation hot against Sam's cheeks.

"I'm not boring!" she called after the retreating shadow. She wasn't.
She'd done the right thing.

Hadn't she?

❧

Sam pulled up to the house and eyed the desert reception gathered
around her front porch through the dusty windshield.

The saguaro stood by the stairs, the Gila monster wedged in the
crook of its arm. Roadrunners, ground squirrels, and sparrows darted
about. A barrel cactus with an elf owl on top inched along on its roots.
A bobcat stretched out under the porch. A drove of dusty brown hares
grazed in her garden, while two tortoises and a clutch of Gambel's quail
kept to the saguaro's long shadow.

Sam set the brake, pocketed the keys. She rubbed her mouth with
the back of a hand. Finally, she climbed out of the cab. The early morning
sun beat down on her shoulders with a promise of more heat to come

later in the day. "Howdy."

The saguaro came forward. Tiny drops of water in the shape of the Gila monster's feet formed a dotted line up the cactus's pleats. It inclined its top. "Hello."

"Good morning," the lizard said.

Sam waved a hand at the gathering. "A little peer pressure, huh?"

For a moment only the wind spoke. Then the saguaro drooped, straightened. "We will leave if you ask it of us."

The plants and animals gave her their full attention. The hares paused in their forage, and the bobcat came out from under the porch.

Words warred for tongue-space in Sam's mouth. She scuffed her boots in the dirt. "I've never done a marriage before. I'm not saying I will, I'm just saying I haven't."

A hare laughed and whispered something to a tortoise. The tortoise tucked its head in its shell.

Flick-flick went the Gila monster's tongue. "We trust you."

Sam grimaced. "Not sure that's the best idea, but I suppose if you're still willing then I am, too. It'd make a good story to tell, tell my daughter someday."

Sam didn't have many stories. That had always been PopPop Donner's thing, all the old stories Coyote used to tell. Mom never believed the stories, said they were wrong, all wrong. Sam shushed the doubts.

She took to the front steps, and the animals arranged themselves behind the saguaro and Gila monster in the yard. She pushed up her glasses, then clasped her hands in front of her. "I've only been to a handful of weddings, and most of those at the courthouse, so I don't really know where to start." She cleared her throat. "We're gathered here. Um, we're gathered here today ... to ... Hold on a minute."

Sam hurried into the house. She found what she wanted in the manila envelope at the bottom of her memory box and returned to the yard.

"Is everything well?" the saguaro said.

"Fine, fine." She held out the Polaroid photo. "This is my daughter Kaitlin and her ... wife. I think. I'm going to call her when we finish up here."

Sam looked around, and brought over a rock the size of her fist. She propped the picture against the rock beside her on the porch.

She put her hand in the pocket of her dungarees and wrapped

trembling fingers around the strip of black and white photos. "Come on now, let's get this marrying done before it gets too hot."

She stroked the slick photo paper. Damn coyotes and their logic, but it did make for a better story. Sam hoped her daughter would agree.

Author's Note

"Telling Stories" was born around the same time as "Ink", inspired by the simple image of an older woman opening the front door and inviting a saguaro cactus inside. Yeah, okay, not so simple but you get the idea. I knew Sam was older and a lesbian, and that was about it. We had fun trying to figure out how she would manage to marry a saguaro and a gila monster. I wrote this before same sex marriage was declared legal and Podcastle published it after. A little complaint, but one I can happily live with.

My grandmother spoke often of her lesbian friends, and how none of them dared wear Tweed because it was a "dyke cologne." Funny how little details find their way onto the page.

Exchanges, No Refunds

"They wash ashore like moonbeams. I bring them in and lay them out to dry," the old man said from his stool behind the counter. The words lingered with hints of Latakia blend pipe tobacco. Dull yellow whiskers circled his mouth, those on his cheeks coarse and white. "Sometimes they're so tangled up it takes months to straighten them out. Folks should take better care of how they relationshipize. There's only so many to go around, you know?"

A middle-aged couple, her eyes soft and gray, his intense and brown. She frowned. He nodded. "We're looking for something different. Special," he said.

"Take your time," the old man said, and returned to cleaning his pipe.

Hand in hand, the couple browsed garters hung in colorful rows between displays of Pocky and salt-crusted hula dolls on weak springs. He pulled a strand from the display, blue with hints of summer sunlight—" I like this one." —and brought it to the counter, the middle-aged woman in tow.

"All righty. We don't take plastic, Mister. Cash in hand or nothing."

"Oh. Sorry about that." The man pulled a crisp green fold out of his wallet.

The old man took the money. "Wanna check the fit?"

She nodded.

"Nah, it'll be fine," he said.

And lowered her eyes.

"Suit yourself." The proprietor cut the tag.

The middle-aged man hooked one end of the garter through his heart and the other through the woman's. He smiled, eyes wide, seeking her approval.

She looked away, tolerant and distracted.

"Thank you," the middle-aged man said.

They returned a week later, garter unattached.

The old man still sat behind the counter, carving sea birds out of used Styrofoam cups. "Back so soon?"

"It was too tight. She wouldn't leave me alone, always telling me what to do but never what I wanted her to tell me." The middle-aged man frowned. "It's complicated."

"Yup. Them motherin' things are most times. Right knotty, too. There was one 'bout a month—"

"Do you have anything new?"

"Ayuh." The knife tip flicked bits of white in the direction of the display. "Found me some good ones down by the docks on Tuesday. Make an exchange if you like, but I don't do no refunds."

The couple took their time perusing possibilities, moving farther apart until fingertips were the only shared interest, and seldom at that.

The middle-aged woman stopped at the far side of the display, intent in her consideration. Her hand hovered between two silk strands: baby blue, cardinal sin red. She tentatively reached for one. "Maybe could we try—"

He held up black leather with silver studs. "This one looks good, right, hon?"

Soft gray eyes closed. She lowered her arm and shrugged with rounded shoulders.

He led her to the counter, rubbing his thumb over the studs in a rosary of anticipation.

The old man set the knife and coffee-speckled gull aside. "Found what you want this time?" He wedged a wooden toothpick between his teeth, rubbery lips positioning it just so.

"Oh, yeah." The middle-aged man fished out his wallet and threw money on the garter.

The old man eyed the money, shrugged, pocketed the bills. "Care to try this one on?"

The man answered before the woman could open her mouth. "I think we're good." He snagged the garter and then her heart, tugged to set the hook, threaded the other end through his own. "Oh, yeah. Plenty of play with this one. See?"

The middle-aged woman gasped and smiled cat pretty as she smoothed up to him, rubbing a calf along his leg. She whispered something in his ear.

"Have a good one," the proprietor said to the closing door.

Five days later, the middle-aged man dropped the garter on the counter. "There was too much play. She was more interested in away games."

"Ayuh." The old man sniggered and stuck the knife in the plank countertop. He swept the garter into a white plastic basket with a confusion of others. "Give it another try?"

The middle-aged man opened his mouth to speak.

"Yes, but I want to pick it out this time," the middle-aged woman said.

The middle-aged man frowned. "Um ..."

She did not hesitate, heading to the far end of the display without him, returning with the so very red garter clenched tight. "I'd like to try it on, please."

The old man nodded. "Sure thing."

The middle-aged woman secured her heart, then hooked the middle-aged man.

"May I?" she said, shoulders squared, and jerked the knife out of the wood. It came up in a curve that caught the middle-aged man clean and crimson in the throat. He dropped at her feet in a spray of red. The garter stretched but did not break.

When he lay still and moist red, the middle-aged woman unhooked her heart and took his wallet. She set two bills and the knife on the counter— "Thanks." —and out the door she went.

By the time the old man dragged the body out to the beach to feed the speckled birds, she was nowhere to be found. He pocketed the garter and went back inside for a tub of soapy water.

Author's Note

I describe writing as the act of pulling baubles and bits of life from the tiny drawers of an infinitely large medicine chest. This story came from the image of a Styrofoam cup a marine biologist had carved with a penknife and then taken with him into a deep sea submersible. Upon returning to the surface, he removed the cup from the bag and found it one-quarter its previous size, the beautiful carvings nothing more than slits in the hardened, compressed foam.

I pulled the image of the pre-dive cup out of its drawer and held it in my mind until I could see the knife nicking away at the foam, then the hands holding the knife, then the man, and finally the shop on the beach. The type of tobacco came from a friend who smokes a pipe, the garters from a passage in a book about 16th century French fashion. Writing is life broken down into its component pieces and tucked away until the next story.

How Toby Told Time

Toby was a boy who couldn't tell time, but he didn't mind. Time couldn't tell Toby, either.

"Hurry up or you'll be late for school," Time said every morning like clockwork. Tick-tock, tick-tock, tick-tock was the sound of Time's long finger tapping the hourglass. Out of bed, get dressed, eat breakfaster. Tick-tock, tick-tock, tick-tock. "How long does it take to brush your teeth?"

"That's a silly question," Toby said, making faces in the mirror. "It takes as long as it takes. Who wants to go on brushin' their teeth when their teeth are done bein' brushed?"

"Your mother is not going to be happy, young man," said Time peevishly, a tone it often used when common and sense were trumped by children and other small annoyances.

"Look. Watch me. I learned how t'make a face in the mirror and then hang it in the reflection so I can find it again in the bathroom mirror at school."

"Nonsense," said Time with a sniff of disdain.

"I mean it. Watch." Toby jammed his thumbs in his nostrils, wiggled his fingers on either side of his head, and stuck out his tongue. Mirroraculously, the Toby on the other side of the glass did the same. "Like that."

"Like what?"

"See it?"

"There's nothing to see." Tick-tock, tick-tock. "Stop wasting Me."

A diller, a dollar, a ten o'clock scholar!

At school, Mrs. Essex accused Toby of dawdling, which he supposed was something like doodling only not as much fun by the way she scrunched her eyes when she said it. "Everyone else has turned in their papers, Toby. I'll give you until three-fifteen to finish your test."

She pointed to the all-knowing clock above the blackboard behind her, declaring it to be precisely three-oh-nine, pay no attention to the red line chasing itself in circles.

Time craned its head from one side to the other in an attempt to read over Toby's shoulder. "What are you doing? You heard what Mrs. Essex said. You need to finish your work."

"I am," Toby said, drawing an airplane with the number eight as the propeller.

"That's not math."

"Is too." With a few thoughtful lines, the airplane eight flew through a forty-seven barn.

Mrs. Essex set down her red pen of teachership. "Time's up, Toby," she said and looked over her shoulder at the clock. "I could have sworn ..." She stood, turned her back on the class, and tapped on the clock face, giving Barry Lemmon a chance to pull Sarah Brick's hair and then scoot back to his seat as innocent as could be. "Hmph. It stopped. All right, Toby, I'll give you a few more minutes. Barry, keep your hands to yourself."

"Look what you made me do," Time said under its breath. "I hope you appreciate it."

"Did you know you got nose hairs?"

Time slapped Toby's hand away. "I do not."

"Do too. That one there curls like-"

Time covered its nose with a fold of its gray robe and kicked Toby under the table.

What makes you come so soon?

Toby's mother was a runner, running to the store, the post office, the library. She even ran to catch up with herself. "I made good time today," she said, gulping vitamin water and checking the watch clipped to the waistband of her leggings. She mopped the sweat from her face and neck.

On the other side of the counter, Time smiled proudly and tapped its hourglass, tick-tock, tick-tock, tick-tock. Toby's mother was very prompt.

"Did you see Mr. Olmeo's puppies?" Toby said as he shared his maple butter sandwich with his favorite stegosaurus. "He had them out yesterday. I saw them on my way to school."

"I didn't have time to look at puppies," his mother said and finished her bottle of water. She checked the pulse in her neck with two fingers, averaging heartbeats she could never replace.

"Very sensible," Time said.

"Gertie's flowers are coming up. She has red ones and yellow ones this year. Benji's parents put up a new trellis thingie in their garden. Howard's dad—"

"Mmhmmm. Listen, honey, I need a quick shower if I'm going to run to the drugstore before it closes. Be a good boy for Mommy and don't get into anything." His mother blew Toby a kiss and ran out of the kitchen and up the stairs.

"You could learn a lot from your mother," Time said sagaciously, but Toby was already heading for the backdoor, stegosaurus and sandwich in hand. "Hey! Come back here. I'm not finished telling you how you should be more like your mother."

"Let's go see the puppies," Toby said, hopping down the back steps.

"I don't want to go see the puppies."

Time followed in Toby's wake as the boy cut through the backyard, crossed the street not at the corner – startling drivers coming and going – and crawled through the super secret tunnel in the blackberry bushes on the vacant lot behind the Marvins' house. "What about your homework? You still have to clean your room."

"I will."

"You always say that, but you never do."

"I wanna see the puppies. There's one with a black patch of fur on his eye. He looks like a pirate."

"But you don't have Me to go see the puppies. You haven't even started your chapter reading. Young man, are you listening to me?"

"Uh-huh."

Mr. Olmeo was happy to let Toby play with the puppies. He opened the front door and out tumbled eight wriggling, squiggling, snapping, yapping bundles of energy eager to meet their new best friend. Toby wriggled, squiggled, and yapped with them, smearing maple butter and white bread with no crusts on their fur. He laughed in the face of their kisses without wondering where the puppy tongues had been. Mr. Olmeo smiled as he looked on. Time slumped onto the grass with the hourglass propped against its leg.

The pirate puppy crawled into Time's lap. It snuffled and yawned, its pink tongue a bubblegum banner unfurled, and promptly fell asleep. Time rested its far-reaching hand on the tiny thing. "I'm not petting him. I'm brushing the dirt off his back." Time glared petulantly at the old man on the front step while continuing to not pet the puppy. "Doesn't he realize he should be finishing his taxes?"

After puppies it was collecting ladybugs to take back home for the usual Daddy's home, set the table, eat dinner, clear the table. Tick-tock, tick-tock, tick-tock. Now. All of it. Don't dawdle. Toby doodled, drawing faces in the water rings left by the glasses.

Tick-tock, tick-tock, tick-tock. Get ready for bed.

"Do I really have nose hairs?" Time said, leaning in close to the mirror with its head tilted back to get a better look.

"Yahp." Toby gargled the foaming residue from brushing his teeth before tipping his head over the sink and letting it fall out of his mouth in sticky clumps and streams. Time sighed. Toby rinsed out his mouth and hung his brush on the rack.

"What?"

"I just noticed how gray my robe is," Time said.

"It's only dust."

"Only dust? What a horrid thing to say. Next you'll be telling me it's only ash." Time brushed at its right shoulder, gray smearing like memories on its fingertips.

Toby poked Time in the side. "C'mon. I got th'flashlight in my bedroom. We can shake your robe an'make a meatier shower in the light." So saying, he flipped off the bathroom light and hopped like a Ninja Turtle down the hall. Time followed more sedately, the hourglass hung loosely from one hand, rubbing the grit between the fingers of the other.

Toby's mother came back twice before taking the flashlight away.

You used to come at ten o'clock,

"You'll have to wait out here, Toby," said Mrs. Bernard, the school secretary, motioning to the accusation of uncomfortable wooden chairs arranged against the far wall. "Mister Nolen is running behind."

"Behind who?" Toby said, but the secretary was too busy with answering phones and triplicating memos to pay him any more mind. He retired to the center chair in the row.

"He's late," Time said, settling beside the boy, tick-tock, tick-tocking against the hourglass. "He's usually running late after his Wednesday lunches with Miss Chang." Time crossed its legs, pulling the hem of the robe over its sock garters. "You wouldn't be here if you'd finished your test."

"I did finish it." Toby traced a dark mark on the chair seat that resembled a lightning bolt.

"Finished it on Me," Time said in familiar refrain, yet the delivery was rote, lacking not only luster but conviction.

"There was a blue jay outside the window."

Mrs. Bernard looked up from her computer. "Did you need something, Toby?"

"No, Ma'am," he said, kicking his feet back and forth in time with a song he made up in his head.

"It's always something with you," Time said finally.

"Pete taught me to burp the alphabet. Wanna hear?"

Time looked around the familiar room and scratched its chin. "Might as well," it said without enthusiasm. "You will anyway."

Toby managed to make it to G before Mrs. Bernard said, "That's enough of that, Toby Riley."

"Now you've gone and done it," Time said. "I went skinny dipping once, didn't I? Did I enjoy it? I'm sure I did. So hard to remember anymore." The last was more afterthought than whisper. Time straightened the lay of its robe once— "Deucedly uncomfortable, that's what it is." —and then once again.

But now you come at noon.

"C'mon. Please?"

Time perched precariously on the foot of Toby's bed, a most undignified position for a Sunday morning.

"I don't know about this," it said, looking from the pile of well-loved cars to its robe and hourglass.

"Don't worry. It'll be fun."

"This is very serious work. After all, I am of the essence."

"Pleeeease?" Toby said. "I'll give you some of my comics." He pulled a handful from under his bed and set them beside the cars.

Hemming and hawing was beneath Time; it hawed and hemmed, instead. "Including the Spiderman ones?"

Toby chewed on his bottom lip as he gave the offer its due. "Okay, but not the ones with Doctor Octopus. He's my faiv'rit."

Time was not one to admit out loud it thought the Green Goblin could whip Doctor Octopus any day of the week. "Okay." It examined the toy cars. "Where are all your red ones?"

"I can't trade my red cars, those are my faiv'rits, too," Toby said.

"Hmph. And you'll still teach me how to make armpit noises?" Time said with a wistfulness typically reserved for old men and young lovers.

Toby nodded and stuck out a hooked pinky finger. "Deal?"

"Deal." Time crossed pinkies with the boy in the stick-a-needle-in-your-eye honest deal shake.

Time passed the robe and hourglass to Toby and accepted the comics and cars in return. "This, um, you know, this might actually be fun." It coughed, a gigglish sound. "I mean, I hadn't realized how heavy the hourglass really was, and the robe ..." Time waved a hand in a gesture denying any responsibility for the fashion sense of public service. "I might actually enjoy this, only for a little while, of course. Oooo ... Aunt May. She's still a looker."

Toby pulled the robe over his head. "How do I look?"

"Short. Now, how do you do that thing with your armpit?"

Toby showed Time how to make armpit farts and slobbery arm blows that sounded like really juicy farts, juicy enough to gross out the girls at recess. Then he took up the hourglass and went for a walk. He walked to the end of the drive and turned up the street to the convenience store where he bought a York Peppermint Pattie to eat beside the park fountain.

Tick-tock, tick-tock, tick-tock was the sound of Toby's fingers tapping the hourglass. He walked to Busch Gardens, it didn't take long, and rode the Loch Ness Monster sixteen times. He ate hamburgers and fried pickles and fruit cocktail with extra cherries for breakfaster. He made up words to the music in his head and sang to the pigeons at the zoo. Tick-tock, tick-tock, tick-tick-tockity-tap went his fingers against the hourglass, taking up the rhythm. Tick-tockity-tap-tap-tick.

Toby turned the hourglass on its side to tap hollow, and on end to tap deep. Tickity-tock-tock-tappity-tick-tock. Pigeons danced. Flowers unbloomed, shrank to seeds, and grew all over again. Butterflies flew still. People slowed down. They smiled. Tick-tock-tap-tappity.

Toby went off to find faces in the reflections of clouds.

Author's Note

"Where do you get your ideas?"

From conversations with my oldest son.

The scene. Bedtime on a school night, my partner and I in the living room doing parentish things. It's dark and cold outside, the wind whining to be let in. I call my oldest son upstairs to brush his teeth and get ready for bed. After the usual "I don't waaaaaaanna

...*" and "Do it anyway", he heads into the bathroom. And stays there.*

"Hurry up," I say.

"I am," he says back.

And doesn't come out.

Parents understand this next question: "How long does it take to brush your teeth?"

My oldest pokes his head out of the bathroom, toothbrush in hand, and says with minty foam lips, "That's a silly question. It takes as long as it takes. Who wants to go on brushing their teeth when their teeth are done being brushed?"

I tell you, some stories beg to be written.

Ink

A woman stood at the tattoo parlor's door. Small, damp from the storm, hair disheveled and slightly askew. Comfortable in her clothes, not her skin. The sight of her made Tiger's chest itch and his tattoos tingle. He turned down the stereo. "Can I help you with something?"

The woman looked at the shelves stuffed with pattern books, the posters of half-naked men and women displaying their tattoos and piercings. "Is this Stars And Stripes Ink?"

Her voice had a touch of falsetto.

"That's what the sign says in the window."

She brushed aside her bangs, tugging her hair back into place in a way Tiger supposed he wasn't meant to notice. "I would like a tattoo."

She smiled with suspicion and hope, an expression he knew well.

Tiger dog-eared his page and set the magazine aside. "What did you have in mind?" Like he had to ask. He stifled a twinge of jealousy and rubbed at the scars below his nipples, all that remained of his breasts.

Straightening her shoulders, the woman walked up to the counter and handed him a folded sheet of white paper dappled with rain.

Tiger spread the paper on the counter and considered the picture, a coiled Asian dragon with a lion's mane, pearl clutched in one claw, lightning in the other, vibrant colors and sharp, decisive lines. Hyper-masculine, all claws, teeth, and attitude. Not at all like her.

Tiger settled back on his stool and rubbed a hand under his chin, the stubble rasping over his knuckles. "How'd you hear about the shop?"

She blinked, hesitated. "From friends."

"That doesn't answer my question. Who?"

The woman looked at the counter, the posters, anywhere but at Tiger. Finally: "Gwen Winston. She said you did excellent work." She looked at him out of the corner of her eye. "I've never seen it. The tattoo, I mean."

The last came out in a rush.

"On Gwen? You wouldn't." Gwennie was good people, one of his first special customers when he opened the shop.

"I didn't mean to insult you. I just ..." She flushed. "Something that sounds too good to be true usually is."

"Gwen didn't think so." Tiger waited for that to sink in before he tapped the picture. "Where do you want it?"

She pressed her fingers to the Formica counter top until the tips were pale as bone. "My back," she said, cleared her throat, and added more assertively, "My upper back. How much?"

Tiger kept his gaze on her face, looking, seeing. She wasn't starving, but didn't have a lot of money invested in her clothes. Probably lived paycheck to paycheck if she could find work, lived off friends when she couldn't. Still, a guy had to eat, and he'd signed a new lease last month. "Two thousand cash. Twenty-five hundred if you pay by card."

The woman winced. "For a tattoo?"

He shrugged. "Cheaper than you'll find anywhere else."

She slipped her hand into her purse. "Do I need to sign anything?"

Do I need to leave proof that I came to a place like this? Tiger was used to that, too. "For a special request? Not unless you want to."

Her hands trembled as she pulled a flat, red wallet from her handbag and counted out a stack of tattered bills.

Tiger stuffed the money in his jeans pocket. "Why don't you take your coat off while I get things ready."

Prep was easy, normal. Tiger scanned the picture, and made a couple of copies at different sizes. He presented them on the counter, tapped the larger image. "This one's got the best detail with the fangs and the scales on the tail."

She reached towards the smaller image with wide, blunt-tipped fingers but didn't touch the paper. "This one looks almost cute."

"Yeah, but the detail on this one will really make it pop." He waited, fingers framing the dragon's head.

She swallowed. "How does it work?"

Tiger ran his thumb over the mane. "I tattoo the design, and it takes away everything you don't want."

The woman frowned; the expression did nothing to soften her jaw line. "Just like that?"

"Just like that."

"But how do you do it? I mean, that doesn't make any sense."

Tiger snorted. "I don't understand how a nuke bomb works, but they're real."

She crossed her arms over her chest. "I can ask a nuclear physicist how a bomb works and expect a full answer."

A challenge, a demand to know why she should believe him. Tiger put the money on the counter. "No hard feelings, have a nice night."

That caught her by surprise. She stared at the wad of green. He hadn't played the game. He should have balked, or sweet talked, or lied. His parents used to do it all the time.

The clock flashed from one minute to the next. The woman tangled her fingers in the front of her skirt, then smoothed out the wrinkles, a gesture straight out of a romance novel. "All right. I'm ready."

"Rock it. I'll make the stencil, have a smoke, wash my hands, then we're ready to go."

The woman tucked a lock of limp hair behind her left ear. "Sure. Okay."

Outside, the storm had blown itself out and the parking lot asphalt reflected the streetlights in twisted rainbows. The air was sharp with car exhaust and Mexican night from the beer pit two doors down. Tiger would have preferred a shop off the main drag, but he couldn't complain about the impulse business of anchors, and butterfly tramp stamps. Life in a Navy town made for good money after payday.

He leaned against the front of his pick-up and rolled a smoke. His tattoos shifted under his skin, expectant. One ink slid from over his right kidney to the top of his right thigh. The quadriceps muscle spasmed, and he dug a knuckle into his T-shot site until the tattoos settled their differences and the muscle relaxed. Crowded real estate down there, and damn tender when ink fought ink for display space. No big deal. He'd figure out who won later.

He lit the cigarette and inhaled. That first unfiltered drag burned wicked hot. An addiction, like getting a new tattoo. He took his time, watching the smoke curl up from his lips and unravel in the night. No hurries, no worries. Not yet, anyway.

Tiger pinched the butt, swallowed it, and headed back inside.

The woman paced in front of the Pepsi machine while he set up his work station – guns, line and shading needles, bottles of ink and small plastic cups, nitrile gloves, Green Soap and cotton pads. He put on Lou Rawl's Stormy Monday to clear the air and open his headspace, and motioned to the tattooist's chair laid flat beside his work area behind the counter. "Ready when you are."

She walked over and stopped at the edge of the counter. "Do I have to get undressed?"

He chalked the question up to her nerves. "I'll need to see your back."

She took a hesitant step towards the chair. "You never asked my name."

"I figured you'd tell me if you wanted me to know."

She frowned, then looked him in the eye with the same resolution that first brought her into the shop. "Liza Patton."

Tiger nodded and flashed a quick smile. "Tiger Hains."

She pointed to his left shoulder. "The reason for your tattoo? Or is it ink? Which is right?"

"Either's fine." He looked at the cut out collar of his black t-shirt and the wide orange head, with its bloodstained teeth and forked tongue, draped over his collar bone. The rest of the beast covered most of his upper back, the tail curling over his right shoulder. The equivalent of three months' rent to get it just right. He'd been so damn proud. His parents had disowned him. "This was my first."

"How many do you have?"

Not enough, never enough. Again he motioned to the chair. "I lost track a while ago."

Liza made herself comfortable on the center section. She reached towards the top button of her blouse. "I'd rather not take off my bra."

"Suits me fine."

Off came the blouse. She bundled it over her chest. "Will it hurt?"

Tiger noted the piss poor repair ink on her right shoulder, hints of a word under the bloom. He'd also noticed the two thin pink scars under the bangles on each wrist. He pulled on the gloves, smoothed the fingers in place. Will it hurt? Hell of a question. "Some people handle it better than others."

"No, I mean ... will it, you know ... hurt?"

No mistaking the fear beneath the words.

Tiger's tattoos twisted and twitched with memories. "That all depends on you."

"Did yours hurt?"

In more ways than one. "Like a bitch."

Liza nodded, and wrapped herself in silence.

"Roll your shoulders in. Lean forward a bit." He pulled the straps of her lacy black bra over her prominent shoulder blades. Moles dotted her back, some sprouting hairs like spiders trying to escape her skin, all low enough they wouldn't be a problem.

He washed her back with anti-microbial soap, and followed it with an alcohol wipe. While that dried, Tiger filled a disposable cup with rinse water and the ink caps with individual colors. The three S's: sterile, separate, single-use. His work area had the sex appeal of an operating room, nothing like the cool tattoo parlors he'd seen on cop shows growing up. That suited Tiger just fine. He preferred health and safety; he'd leave cool to the ink.

He smoothed lotion between her shoulder blades to help the stencil design stick. "You're shaking. You cold?"

Liza made a sound like a laugh. "Excited."

"Good." He positioned the stencil on her back and smoothed it with the edge of his hands. Slow count to ten and he pulled the thermal fax paper away, leaving behind the design in cartoon bright purple lines. Tiger leaned back to consider his work. He gestured with a hand mirror towards a mirror on the wall at the end of the counter. "Go have a look. Tell me it's beautiful, or I can move it."

Liza shook her head. "Whatever you think is best."

"That's not how it – "

"It's fine. I trust you."

Big words for a voice so small.

"You sure about this? It's going to feel kind of fucked up when things get going."

Liza nodded. "I've been sure for years."

The lady knew what she wanted. Tiger dipped the linework needle into the ink cap, tapped, the foot pedal, and drew black ink into the gun's reservoir. The tiger tattoo purred like the hammering rumble of the coil gun. All right then. He brought the needle to the topmost purple line of the mane and pressed the foot pedal.

He laid the ink one delicate, precise line at a time. People who didn't know tattoo work thought the needle injected ink into the skin, when it actually glided along and let gravity do the work. This part of tattooing, the linework that defined the piece, this was why Tiger learned how to ink. From the early childhood sketchbooks to the graffiti in his teens, it always came down to this moment, the stroke of ink on a willing body. Everything else was gravy.

The tiger tattoo watched him work, licking between its clawed toes.

Liza didn't move. At the first touch of the needle, she became stone for all that her heart raced beneath his hands. Only once did she make a sound, a whimpering sob the first time the needle passed over her spine. He refilled the reservoir as an excuse to pause. When she made no other sound, he continued.

Linework done, he rinsed out the black ink and swapped out for his rotary gun, lighter and better suited to shading. "How're you doing? Need a break?"

Liza shook her head.

"Walk it off a bit?"

"I'm fine." Her voice had lost some of its girlish charm. She coughed. "You can keep going."

"Okay."

He worked quickly without rushing, giving his full attention to the shadows sliding around the edges of every line. Add depth here, there layering. Wipe the blood away and repeat. He turned the sparse lines of the nose into a muzzle. Took simple diamond patterns on the body and created scales. If everything went right, any minute now he should see –

There. The dragon shook out its mane and turned its head to watch the tattoo gun.

Tiger slowed down, adding detail and gauging the dragon's strength with every refill of ink. He both loved and hated this part. From here on out, everything had to be perfect. Years ago he'd screwed the pooch on a special tattoo of a fancy tea cup and saucer on the shoulder of an older man, gotten so high on the inking that he ruined the design. The guy had stormed out in tears, refusing a repair, a second chance. Tiger often wondered what happened to the guy, if he'd gone back to living a lie. Wondered at moments like this, in fact.

He rinsed out the black ink and slid his palette of ink caps closer. "Hold still now. Shit just got real."

Liza let out a tiny, mewling moan, but didn't move. Maybe she was braver than she looked. Tiger sure as shit hoped so.

A darker green first to bring out the shadows. Tiger took a deep breath, and touched the color to Liza's skin. Sweet pain swept up his hands to his soul. Holy Mary, Mother of Jesus, the rush! The dragon rubbed itself against the needle, eager for color. Demanded all the attention, all the awe-struck wonder. It was the biggest, baddest motherfucker in the valley and Tiger liked it that way. Nothing mattered but the ink, always the ink, the way the tattoo shook its mane and twisted its tail. Dance, baby, dance. Another shot of scotch. A round for the house. He rode the colors and the high until a sound slammed him back to the table.

Sound? Crying. Who? Liza crying, muted sobs cradling even softer words: "No, no, no ..."

Tiger's hands froze mid-curl of blue on the dragon's tail. His tattoos crowded his forearms until his skin was matte black – more ink, MORE

INK – all but the tiger. It stayed on his shoulder, claws pricking tiny reminders of flesh and reason along his upper back. Tiger took a deep breath, clearing away the taste of scotch peat and bitter ink.

He rinsed and refilled the gun, pressed the back of his left hand against the squirming tattoo. Against Liza. "You still with me?"

She cringed at the contact, the sound of his voice. Cringed like he hadn't spent the past four hours getting under her skin, cringed like he'd hit her. Just because he couldn't see the scars didn't mean they weren't there. Tiger licked his lips. "How about a break?"

Still no answer, only the same frightened tears.

He set down the gun. "We're done here. Let me get you cleaned up."

That brought her out of it. Liza looked over her shoulder, pale and wild-eyed. "No! Don't stop!" She wiped her nose on her arm, leaving a glistening line. And softer: "Please. My dad would ... sometimes ... please."

Tiger chewed on the ends of his mustache. Was a tattoo the same as a punch? Time may have healed all wounds, but ink lasted until the end and with it the sting of guilt. He couldn't chance ruining another person's life. "I can't do this."

"Please." Liza curled tighter into herself as if offering more of her back. The dragon twisted like a cyclone knot. "I – " Liza coughed, cleared her throat. "Whatever you want. I can pay."

Her voice ran deep and ragged, the voice of living a lie.

Tiger stripped off his gloves. "It's not about the money."

"Please. I can't go on like this."

Goddammit. Goddammit! Tiger squeezed his eyes shut. Once upon a time, he would have given his imaginary left nut to swap places with Liza. He'd gone through his transition the old-fashioned way, hormones, scalpels, and all. The tattoos on his arms tingled with need, but this wasn't about them, or him, or his invisible scars. This was all about her.

She began to cry once more. "I don't know what else to do."

The tiger tattoo rubbed its head against the side of his neck. Tiger had seen what she might do on the inside of each wrist. He pressed his lips together until they throbbed with his pulse. "You sure?"

Liza nodded, a quick downward jerk of the head.

Tiger grabbed a fresh set of gloves. "Remember to breathe."

This time when the ink high slammed up his veins, Tiger wrapped the memory of Liza's tears around its neck and told it to sit the fuck down. He had work to do.

As if sensing the change of mood, the dragon flicked the tip of its tail back-and-forth in agitation. It threatened with lightning and teeth. It was the biggest, baddest motherfucker in the valley, remember?

Yeah, Tiger remembered. And he was the one with the ink gun.

Twenty, thirty minutes of electric sweat and the last of the color was laid. Perfect. One of his best. Tiger jammed the needle into the skin at the base of Liza's left shoulder blade and sliced her open bottom to top.

Liza's head came up. She inhaled a scream that came out of the dragon a roar.

Tiger dug his fingers into Liza's back and tore the skin away revealing muscle and the writhing tattoo. It smelled like beer and motor oil, gunpowder, sweat, semen. Manly man smells for manly men, not a girly boy who wore his sister's underwear and stole his mother's lipstick. The dragon whipped its tail around Liza's spine. She jerked upright, choking on her pain.

He grabbed the tattoo by the head. It sank its teeth into the meat below his thumb. "You little bastard, get out of there."

Tiger put his feet against the base of the chair and pulled until his ink knotted with the effort and his arms burned like a whitehot star. Now or never. Now. Or. Never. He took a deep breath and threw himself back against his workstation. The dragon's claws gave way, it screamed, and its tail came free.

Tiger pulled up the back of his t-shirt and slapped Liza's tattoo onto his lower back. The ink sank into his skin, screaming rage up his spine. The other tattoos rushed to greet the latest member of the menagerie. Muscles clenched, chasing the rage until it faded to sullen exhaustion. He slid off the stool to the floor, laughing and swearing. The best tattoos always hurt like a bitch.

He stayed on the floor until the spasms eased and the knots of ink separated into individual colors and designs, each content in their own stories. Well, almost content. Liza's tattoo flailed in the center of his back then slid down and to the right. Tiger rolled over and pulled up his t-shirt in time to see a scattering of butterflies rush up his side and the dragon's tail slide into his pants. The sharp heat of fresh ink settled around his T-shot site. That could get interesting come Sunday night when he did his injection.

When he could trust his legs, Tiger got to his feet and pulled down his shirt. He bandaged his throbbing hand in cotton and blue painter's tape. Liza lay on her left side on the chair, hair askew, back smeared with ink. A shame to wake her, but he was more than done for the night. He tapped her shoulder. "Hey, I need you to sit up. We're all done."

Liza rubbed her eyes. "Hmmmm? What time is it?"

Her voice sounded soft and in no way forced.

"Time to get you cleaned up."

She sat still and calm as a drowsing cat as he cleaned her back and rubbed in more lotion. Her skin was smooth and a touch red, but otherwise looked good. No ink, no blood.

While he worked, Liza touched her throat. She removed her wig. Her hair underneath was a light brown touched with gray at the temples, short but it would grow out. She ran a hand over her head. "Wow. I feel ... wow."

Tiger stifled a yawn. He pointed to the mirror on the wall. "Take a look."

Liza frowned and reached a hand over her shoulder to touch her back. "Is there ... ?"

Tiger passed her a hand mirror and nodded towards the wall.

Blouse still clutched to her chest, Liza stood and walked to the mirror. Her clothes fit differently over her narrower waist and wider hips. "There's no tattoo. Where ... ?" She turned to face the mirror. "Oh my God. It's real. It's ..."

Liza stretched the waistband of her skirt, looked inside. "The worm is gone. Get it? Worm? Wyrm? The dragon?"

She put a hand to her mouth and began to cry.

Guess she liked what she saw.

Tiger gathered his tools and inks, tossed the used cotton into the bio-hazard bin. He moved on automatic, drifting in and out of his post ink high. Needles in the autoclave, wipe down, pick up, a place for everything, everything in his place. At least he'd learned one good thing from his mother.

Liza dropped the blouse and pulled two silicone breast forms out of her bra. She stared at what remained in the cups, then met his gaze in the mirror. "I don't know what to say. Thank you. Oh God, thank you! Thank you!"

He retrieved her blouse, handed it to her. "Drop a tip in the jar if you want. I need to lock up."

"Sure, sure." Liza giggled. "I even sound like the real me. I feel different when I walk. And my throat ... Thank you so much!"

Great. Sure. Whatever. Tiger needed to get her out of the shop before his twinge of jealousy turned into bitterness and binge drinking when he got home.

Liza gathered her coat and purse, and he walked her to the door. Someone had scattered stars in the patches of clear night sky. Farther south, dogs complained about a fire truck speeding through the night. She turned to face him. "If you don't mind, I do have one question."

Most of them did. "Shoot."

Liza stared at the tattoos on his arms, a collage of masculine and feminine. "How many of those are your own work?"

"Twenty-two."

Her eyes widened. "Really?"

"Yeah." Not really. She seemed like one of those people with a need for numbers. He remembered the face and tattoo of every special customer. The numbers? Not so much.

"Where's mine?"

A few of the tattoos shifted to get a better look at her. Tiger almost hoped she noticed. "It's safe."

Liza searched his face, nodded. "I didn't leave a tip, but ... I can't thank you enough."

"It's all good." Tiger passed her a business card from his back pocket. "You know someone who needs work, send them my way. Male, female, anywhere or nowhere between, doesn't matter."

Liza dropped the card into her purse. "I will."

Tiger waited until her battered Ford Escort pulled out of the parking lot before he flipped the signs and locked the door. The tiger tattoo licked his chin with its rough, forked tongue.

Author's Note

I have been fascinated by tattoos since I was young enough to draw on my arms with a ballpoint pen (later graduating to colored markers and lipstick). I got my first tattoo in my early 20s, an uncomfortable experience on many levels. It wasn't until 2010 when I attended Clarion West that I got my second tattoo. In the years since, I have sat four more times to mark points along my personal journey. As I write this, the most recent tattoo is healing on my left forearm.

This story came from the question of the truths that tattoos can expose. From there it was a short step to imagining a tattoo artist whose work could strip away anything a person does not want, revealing the truth within. At first Tiger was a cis male, big, burly, a man's man, but as I pictured him working on Liza I began to realize that Tiger wasn't big or burly. He hadn't always been a man, at least not on the outside. The moment I understood Tiger's inner truth, the tiger tattoo looked me in the eye and whispered, "Write this story." So I did.

This was also my first deliberate attempt to write a "queer" story, one where the characters' genders were the focal point of the story, the truth nestled in the quiet spaces between the words. Listen close. Can you hear it?

The Hydra Wife

After Anya's troubles, Victor reinvents himself as her knight in shining armor. The morning Anya wakes and someone else looks at him through her eyes, he realizes her dragon is a hydra in disguise.

Victor reaches for her across the comfortable expanse of their king-sized bed. "Hey there. How you doing?"

She punches him in the mouth, and runs naked and screaming down the stairs. A frantic twenty minutes later, he finds her huddled behind the dumpster at the HandyMart two blocks away, sobbing like a child. She does not recognize him. The hydra laughs through her tears, two heads writhing from the stump of his wife's severed psyche. Their fetid breath—ammonia, bleach, rotting meat—pour over Victor in a mustard cloud, make his eyes water.

When the ambulance arrives, Victor coaxes Anya inside with promises that her mother waits at the hospital. He gives the store manager and responding police officer his contact information before locking himself in the men's room to strip out of his muddy armor and have a good cry.

"Dissociative reactions allow a child to create alters to hold unpleasant memories or feelings that might otherwise cause even more damage," says the therapist, a slight woman with fine smile lines at the corners of her eyes and mouth.

Victor frowns. "Alters?"

"Think of them as guards Anya created to keep herself safe from her uncle and cousins."

Curled in a fetal position, bound by pharmaceutical chains, the hydra sleeps in fits and starts. Blood crusts one nostril, all that remains after one head smashed against the door when orderlies removed Anya from the ambulance.

The hydra's breath catches in its throat. It whimpers, shifts, settles once more. Asleep, it looks delicate, fragile, like Anya on their honeymoon night. Victor's upper lip throbs. He rubs his face. "How long has she been a, a them?"

The therapist brushes a finger over the plastic identification bracelet secured around a cracked, black claw. "I can't say for certain, but I suspect since she was two or three years old, in the gray areas Anya can't remember." She uses a tissue to dab at brackish water pooled under the hydra and soaking the sheets, sets the sodden lump on top of a growing pile of tissue on the bed-table. "Some of her behaviors as a child were the alters' way of expressing her anger and hurt."

"But why now?" Victor scrapes his bottom teeth along his right thumb nail. The keratin comes away in small, damp clumps that cling to the tip of his tongue.

"They've always been there," the therapist says. "You mentioned during our second couples' session her lapses in memory? The sudden mood swings? The difficulties during sex?"

"But Anya was doing so much better." Scrape, scrape. "Wasn't she?"

"She is, and she'll continue to improve. This is another step towards mutual awareness. Something has changed in her internal landscape, how the parts of Anya's personality view themselves."

Victor reaches out and brushes the back of one of the hydra's claws curled in a fist on the thin hospital pillow. "My promotion?" he says in small voice. "I don't get home until late most nights. She can't sleep when I'm not there, says she doesn't feel safe."

"Possibly."

"There were times when she would look at me, or she'd say the strangest things, even when we were dating. She threatened to kill me once." Scrape, scrape. "Was that, was that one of these alters?"

"I don't know, but you have to understand this isn't your fault. You can't blame yourself for any of this. Anya is very lucky to have your love and support."

The words spill out in a petty rush that Victor only mostly wishes he'd kept to himself. "It's getting to be too much. I mean, I love Anya more than anything, but I don't know if I can do this anymore."

"I hear your concerns, I do."

Cultured, sincere words from a cultured, sincere woman. Victor watches the therapist out of the corner of his eye. How would it feel to run his fingers through her stylishly-spiked hair? To nibble her ears around the silver hoop earrings? What type of bra does she wear under her blue cable knit sweater?

He sighs and looks away. He has no real interest, passing fancies stirred by long, platonic nights, and now the thought of touching the woman he loves when someone else might respond. "What can I do?"

The therapist hands him a set of leather armor, a torch, a bow and quiver of arrows.

Beside him, the hydra snores.

The co-worker leans against the break room counter by the microwave, fluorescent lights highlighting the red in her hair. "How is she?"

Victor shrugs. His eyes feel gritty and sore. He fidgets with the leather straps of his armor. He wants to wear his usual slacks and button-front shirt, maybe a tie, but getting back into the armor before visiting Anya is its own sort of hell. "Doing okay, I guess. She wants to come home."

They are alone in the break room, the door closed against the whir and sigh of computers, the rise and fall of office voices.

She brushes her fingers against the back of his hand. "Are you okay with that?"

Her fingernails are peacock blue. Would her hand warm to the touch if she slid it under his shirt? Anya used to slide a hand under his t-shirt at night, her short fingers warming as they drifted to sleep together. "Yeah, I'm okay, I guess."

He is lonely, and frightened, and angry, but doesn't feel like talking about it. He tosses his half-full Diet Coke in the recycling. "I need to get back to work. Three days makes for a nasty backlog."

The co-worker nods. She squeezes his hand. "You let me know if you need anything, okay?"

His smile must look genuine. "Thanks."

The hydra peers at Victor with narrowed, rheumy eyes. Cheek spines flare, settle back. "I don't do dishes."

Sand and gravel, words trying to resonate at the back of the throat and diaphragm like a man's voice. The head wears one of Victor's sleeveless night-shirts and a pair of Anya's panties. It smells of his Axe body spray and brine.

Victor looks around the hydra's shoulder at the swamp of dirty dishes spread over the counter. He'd hoped for a morning off, a respite from doing everything himself. "That's fine. I can finish them tonight when I get home."

The hydra snorts and pours itself a second cup of coffee. Anya hates coffee. "Whatever."

Victor picks his way through the morass of mangrove roots to the counter. Moss hangs from the cabinet doors; a jellied egg-sack congeals beneath the oven timer. The reek of methane and sour milk curdles the air.

He pours himself the last of the coffee, adds a spoonful of sugar remembering that this personality likes its coffee strong enough to walk on its own. "How'd you sleep last night?"

The hydra gulps coffee and shrugs. It paces, steps stirring the shallow pools of algae in the low spots on the floor.

"The Roserem isn't working for you?"

"I don't like it, so I don't take it."

Victor inhales through his nose, exhales slowly through his mouth.

"You going to work today?" the hydra says as Victor spreads boysenberry jam over an Eggo waffle.

Victor nods.

"I said are you going to work today?"

Hot breath on his shoulder, and with it the stench of sulfur and rotting bones. Victor grips his torch like a club. "Yes, I'm going to work," he says, sharper than he intends.

The splash of liquid, the crack and clatter of ceramic against tile. The hydra screams and begins to cry. Victor turns to find the hydra pulling the nightshirt away from its body, a steaming brown stain spreading between its claws, the mug in pieces at its feet

"It's okay, honey. Here. No, it's okay." Victor gently takes the hydra by the shoulders and directs it a few steps to the right. He pulls the nightshirt over its head and drops it on the floor. The hydra clutches at Victor's armor; one head wails, the others hiss and thrash.

Splotches of red color the hydra's belly and upper thighs; a wide brown stain spreads across the front of the underwear. Victor pulls down the hydra's panties.

The hydra catches him on the side of the face with his own mug. "Get away from me!"

Victor drops to his knees, the world a mass of spinning, throbbing blood.

The hydra runs out of the kitchen and up the stairs, screaming for its mother.

The co-worker smiles, all bright eyes, small teeth, and a single, stable head. "What's up? You've been moping around for the better part of the day."

Victor's armor reeks of coffee, sweat, and aftershave. The hydra has not slept in three days; likewise, neither has Victor. They watch Disney movies and look at picture books when the hydra lets him near. He researches Dissociative Identity Disorder and downs Red Bull when it locks itself in the bathroom. He hasn't showered, afraid to leave Anya unattended. "Just tired," he says with the best smile he can manage. "What's up with you?"

She makes herself comfortable on the edge of his filing cabinet. "Stalling before I get back to performance reviews. Listen, do you want to grab a drink or something after work? I mean, we have to work late, anyway, and it's been a hell of a week for both of us."

The invitation has appeal. The therapist said he should take some time to himself; time to unwind. Anya would be okay. Maybe the extra time will improve things when he gets home. Maybe it will be Anya-Anya and not Anya-Someone-Else. He misses his wife with an ache that settles at the back of his throat, hot with tears.

His co-worker isn't Anya. "I think I'll take a pass. I'm wiped."

She nods, short, nervous jerks of the head. Her cheeks flush a cinnamon Victor can almost taste. "No worries."

"Thanks, though."

"Another time?"

He shifts around a pinch in the armor at his groin. "Sure."

Victor scrapes at his thumbnail, tasting blood and salt. "She slept through the night last night, that's a good thing."

The therapist nods, crossing her ankles. "Good."

"And she cleaned the kitchen yesterday. Swept and mopped, loaded the dishwasher."

Another nod. "Anya?"

Anya smiles at Victor, guarded, hesitant, arms crossed over her chest. She shifts on the couch, tucks her left foot behind his right. Her nails are ragged and uneven, chewed to the quick. "He didn't call the police when I hit him with the mug."

The therapist cuts a quick look at Victor. "What else?"

Anya frowns. The hydra twitches. A head curls forward, spittle oozing from the corner of its mouth. It wipes the damp line away with a ragged claw. Something dark slithers through the knot of roots at its feet. "What?"

A want-to-be man's voice.

The therapist slips on a leather mask and sets a coil of tarred rope on her lap. "I asked Anya a question."

The head cocks a boney eye ridge towards her. "About?"

The therapist loops the rope around the hydra's massive fore quarters, setting the knot without pulling it tight. "I'd like to speak with Anya," she says in a calm, even voice.

Water trickles through the moss on the walls, soaks the ruff of the couch cover. The edges of the carpet look like the floor mats of Victor's Subaru, unraveling green sprinkled with tiny white mushrooms.

The hydra rolls its shoulders and sits back. "I don't have anything against him, if that's what you're asking. He treats her good, which means something, y'know? I trust him most times."

"That's good to know." The therapist settles a second coil of rope over the hydra. "How does Anya feel about Victor? I'd like to hear from her."

Yellow steam rises from the water on the carpet. The hydra twists its head away from Victor, rubbing its cheek against the rope. Other heads and expressions writhe in the murky shadows. One head settles, squeezes it's eyes shut. "Did I miss something?"

The therapist unloops the rope from around Anya's shoulders. "What else has Victor done recently to show he loves you?"

Without opening her eyes, Anya reaches for Victor's hand. "He tells me he loves me, and I love him. I mean, it's hard to say sometimes, but he's everything to me. He came with me to the appointment. Not everyone would be willing to do that after all we've been through. And he washed my hair when I took a bath two nights ago."

Victor had dried her hair as well; it smelled like strawberries. He'd washed her hair on the first night of their honeymoon.

Anya squeezes his hand twice. Victor squeezes back.

A clump of moldering leaves drops on the couch between the couple. The hydra's claw twitches.

Victor pulled his hand away and wipes his thumb on his pants, frowning with abstract pain. The nail is almost gone.

A television above either end of the bar celebrates the sports' highlights of the day, picking apart the statistics to rebuild them for the next game.

A waitress brings Victor his fifth beer, his co-worker her third glass of wine. The bar crowd doesn't drip or steam; no claws gouge the wood floor. Victor has half the bottle gone before the waitress makes it back to the bar.

"I mean, it's not like I'm asking for a lot of time," the co-worker continues. "And it's eight months out, right? I'm going to check on my request Monday."

Victor nods without really hearing what she says. He runs his right thumb over her knuckles. After another late night at the office, he'd accepted her offer to go out. They'd started holding hands somewhere in the middle of his third beer. Anya would be fine for a couple of hours.

"Pardon?" he says, after another swallow.

She taps his bandaged right thumb. "What did you do?"

Victor looks at the thumb. "Cut myself. Listen, can we go someplace a little more quiet?"

She tips her head a certain way, smiles to match. "My apartment is a couple of blocks from here."

By the bottom of the bottle, her place sounds just fine.

Victor drives, not very well. They kiss in the parking lot, fumbling hands and nibbling mouths. She leans into his touch, sighs into his mouth. Her hands are cold.

Out of the car, giggling through the lobby, petting in the elevator like teenagers. She leads him to her apartment, fishing her keys out of her clutch. He doesn't want to wait. Before she can get the key in the lock, Victor presses her against the door, sliding his hands up her thighs and his tongue to the warm hollow of her throat. She tastes like cinnamon and wine, and not one bit like swamp rot. He fumbles with the bindings on his armor.

"Mmm ... Don't you, don't you want ..." She gasps, arching her back as his lips find her nipples through her blouse. "Right there, right, oh ..."

She grinds against his leg. Victor clutches her ass, drawing her to him. So good, it is so good to be alive, to feel again, to have someone hot and ready against him, the way it should be. It has been too long. Together they peel off his leggings, unstrap the cuirass. "Want you so bad, Anya," he whispers against his wife's throat.

She kisses him, giggles. "Rhonda."

A spigot opens and the beers drain out of Victor's head and into his gut, threatens to come right back up. He stares at her hand on her breast. Long peacock blue nails, slender fingers. Looks down at himself. "Oh, God."

"What? Don't let that stop you."

He tries to stuff himself back into leggings and falls back a step, slamming against the wall. "No. Oh, shit. I got to, uh, I got to, I am so sorry."

She frowns. "But I thought you wanted to, you know, come inside? Didn't you?"

Victor grabs pieces of armor. "No, no, I got to go. Have to go. I'm sorry, oh God, I'm sorry. Shouldn't have come."

He staggers past the elevator to the stairs, a stranger named Rhonda calling after him.

Victor strikes a spark with flint and steel. The torch flares to smokey life. He eases open the front door, stepping around puddles of muck. "Anya?"

Algae covers the furniture in a thin layer of slime. Moss hangs from the light fixtures. Dark water wells up from the carpet with every step, soaking his shoes. Shadows and a deeper darkness curl through the hydra's lair.

Victor eases the door closed. Maybe Anya is asleep, maybe everything is okay. He can clean up, even if only his thoughts, and then head to bed where he belongs. He'll call the therapist tomorrow, make an appointment for himself. Rhonda—oh, God, what he'd almost done!—doesn't have his home phone number. Work is tomorrow. His world on hold until tomorrow.

"Where have you been?"

Victor freezes. He doesn't recognize the voice, Anya's, yes, but which Anya? He peers through the hanging moss, searching for the hydra. Water dripps from the ceiling, trailing chill fingers down his back. "I had to work late," he says, edging around the hall closet towards the kitchen. The dark scoops up the torchlight and smears twisted shadows along the walls.

Above him, claws scrape over sodden carpet, tearing at the padding and wood beneath. The house sags in towards the beast's weight. The hydra slams into a wall. "You could have called."

Victor eases onto his knees and squeezes through the crawlspace into the kitchen. Languid drops of water merge in a perverse collision of identity along the walls. On his feet, he kicks away a clump of vines and loses his balance. His left knee pops, and Victor goes down in a starburst of pain. He squeezes his eyes shut, swallows curses and beer.

"Why didn't you call? Do you know what time it is? I was worried about you. You scared me."

Victor crawls to the counter, levering himself up with both hands and his right leg. "I'm sorry," he says around the pain.

"You. Scared. Me."

Victor hears the hydra on the stairs. He opens the refrigerator, stuffs a bottle of water under his right arm and twists off the cap. Half the water spills cold over his legs before he manages his first drink. Look casual. Act casual. Hands shaking, Victor sets the water on the counter behind him and brings the torch around again. Smoke makes his eyes water. "I thought you'd be in bed. I didn't want to wake you."

The hydra's shadow slips cold and black around the corner. Sinuous heads poke through the crawlspace, testing the air with great sulfurous snorts. "I didn't know where you were," they say as one, and the hydra steps into the doorway. Anya's favorite chef's knife catches a bare shimmer of light from the street. "I didn't—You were drinking?" One head darts forward, another back. "You fucking came home drunk?"

Victor recognizes this voice, the male voice, the protector. "I had a couple of beers with a friend. No big -"

"Who the fuck do you think you are?"

The hydra comes at him with the knife, takes him low and drives him to the floor in a tangle of gnashing teeth and acid breath. Heads and steel whip around him; the nightgown bunches in his face.

Victor pushes his wife off and rolls away, losing hold of the torch, catching the knife on the forearm with a hot flash of pain. "No! It's not like—"

"Keep your fucking hands off her! I'll kill you!"

The knife, the teeth, the claws, the anger multiplied in the eyes of every head. "Don't you fucking care?" it screams. "Can't you hear her screaming? Fucking drunk pervert!"

The hydra slams a knee into his groin and Victor gags. He manages to grab the hydra's wrists and wrenches the beast onto its back, straddling it in the stagnant water. He slams its hand down again and again until it drops the knife. "Stop it! Are you crazy? Just stop it!"

The hydra bucks and kicks. "You lying bastard!"

Razor teeth latch onto his arm, and he jerks away. "Fuck!"

"You lied, all the time lied! Goddamn bastard!"

"Just stop! I had a couple of beers with a woman, okay?, but I didn't do anything to her. Nothing." To Anya or Rhonda. "I was scared and lonely, and I didn't do a fucking thing to her. I need, I need to talk to Anya!"

"Fuck you!"

"Anya, you bastard! I want—"

A head thrusts out of the poisonous tangle. "I want my mom!"

Victor can't do this, can't take any more. Let the fucking therapists and doctors chain the thing up, dope it, gut it and leave it to bleed. "Fine! Whatever!"

He tears off the remains of his armor, grabs the knife, and throws himself off her.

"I want to go home," the hydra sobs, heads curled against its belly.

Victor tumbles into the water and retches until all he can bring up are his shoes.

Sometime later, the hydra says, "You came to the meetings."

Victor rests his head on his arms. The room won't stop spinning, swamp water sloshing against the walls. Every breath is a knife to the groin. He prays for a quick death. "What?"

"You came to the meetings with me." The hydra lays on its side in the still water, a low hillock, a clump of algae in the shadows.

It sounds like Anya, but Victor hurts too much to be certain. "I did."

Silence. Water drips, splashes. Victor braces himself, for what he doesn't know.

"Why?"

It does sound like Anya.

"Because I love you." Victor hopes he still means it; only time will tell. For now, he rolls onto his back, reaches out. "Because you're worth it."

A claw hooks around his hand, squeezes twice. "I'm scared."

"So am I."

Water laps at his ears, blending the sounds of the night and his breathing.

"Can you wash my hair? I feel dirty."

Victor pulls his hand away, levers himself up on his uninjured arm, then into a sitting position. The swamp surges with the rising tide. "I can do that."

Anya sits up, looks him in the eye. "It's going to take time," the hydra says in Anya's voice.

Victor makes it to his feet. He picks up bits and pieces of sodden leather and twisted metal. His thumb throbs beneath the torn bandage. He offered her his free hand. "I can do that, too."

Author's note:

I am a hydra. This is one story my partner has sworn never to read again.

Good Boy

Midgie sits on the blanket against the back wall of my cage, my prize for tonight's win in the pit. Dark skin, hair. Frightened. Angry. Resigned.

The dim kennel smells like old hay and unwashed bodies. Cages are wood on three sides with a chain link door. The Kennelmaster, a squat humanoid terrier with thick black claws and a scarred muzzle, opens the cage door and unfastens the lead from my stained leather collar.

"There she is, Pal. Go get her!"

A guttural growl, the words almost unintelligible, the meaning clear. They want winners. Dogs understand breeding, not six years of kickboxing competitions.

The door closes behind me with a rusty creak and the snap of a padlock. Not word one from the others, eleven humans in all. Talking is not allowed. The Kennelmaster wears a dozen or more withered tongues on a leather thong around his neck.

I despise my erection, would cut it off if I had a knife. I use spit to get her ready before another face floats to the surface of my memories. My body goes through the motions while I fly fish with my sister in Schuber Creek. Her sobs are the splash of water over rocks. When I climax, I shiver with the chill current rushing around my ankles.

Afterwards she licks my sweaty, bloodstained face and presses her lips to my ear before Kennelmaster opens the cage door to take her away. I stretch out my legs, knock over the metal food bowl to cover her whisper: "We have a plan."

Five Things I Do Not Allow Myself To Miss:

1)My family
2)Clothes
3)Soap

4) My bull terrier, Sigmund
5) My Before name

Sweat stings my eyes, runs down my neck. *Focus on the road. Be the road.*

My feet keep time on the hot asphalt. *I don't want to die; I don't want to die; I don't want to die; I don't want to die.*

Butch runs beside me, eyes straight ahead. Short, bulky, bad teeth. Brought back by rovers last winter. The Pitmaster took him for training. Someday the dogs will throw us into the pit together; only one of us will come out. I pick up the pace.

The Pitmaster runs beside us, our leads tied to his training belt. Head and shoulders above me, a hundred pounds heavier. Tall, sleek, brindle fur plaited down his back, missing half his left ear. Standard poodles were bred for hunting.

"Come on," he barks.

Had he been someone's pet before the change? A quick thought, murdered before it can escape my mouth.

We run along the weed-choked road that borders the field where humans tend pitiful plots. Heads down, no voices. Sticks and canvas bags the only tools to grow potatoes, pumpkins, and onions. Two dogs lounge in the cool dirt nearby, watch the humans work themselves to malnourished death. The dogs killed the fighters early, at least around here. Killed the old folks, too. If you can't fight, breed, or be trained, you're dead. I don't know about anywhere else. Four years captivity, six years since I saw a television broadcast, five since I heard the radio.

Or held my wife.

Past the fields and rundown farmhouses, battered hulks of abandoned cars, the elephant carcass of a semi on its side. Off the road to the river. Which river? No idea. Follow the Pitmaster down the slope through the brush to the green water running fast and cold. Spray scatters goosebumps over my skin. The Pitmaster takes us both into the water, washes us down with calloused paws. Fondles my junk— "I want a winner, Pal." —cuffs the side of my head, unhooks our leads.

Butch is the closest thing I have to a friend. We splash, wrestle on the slick rocks, are loud, raucous. He has the strength, I have the speed. Kickboxing was a hobby; the dogs have turned it into murderous entertainment. I never touch anyone anymore just to touch. Fuck or kill, that's it. Another time, another bath, Butch confessed he was gay. I confessed I didn't care. We touch as equals. We understand one another, and how it will end. I can't tell the difference between river spray and tears.

The Pitmaster watches from the shore. Cracks bones to get at the marrow. Human bones? Another murdered thought. The distraction costs me. Butch bulls into me, drives my head under the water, knocks the breath out of me in a burst of bubbles. I have leverage, he has weight. My chest tightens, hungry for air, before he rolls me up in a clutch, cheek to cheek. "Midgie talked to you."

He shifts and I break his hold, grab him in a headlock. "Yes," I say into his hair, soft as I can.

I drag him into deeper water, fighting the current, my fear. He grabs me around the waist and we go down in a tangle of arms and legs.

"They found antifreeze in a building on the forage trail," he tells me.

Panic claws its way up my spine to my animal brain. *Don't look at the Pitmaster.* Get my legs under me, grunt, "Poison."

Butch holds me close, hands clawing at my back. His uncut erection presses against my stomach. "You in?"

Jealous current tries to drive us apart. *Don't look at the Pitmaster. Don't. Look.* I hold on for dear life. "Yes."

Five Questions I Do Not Allow Myself:

1) What happened to my wife and children?
2) What happened to the dogs?
3) What happened to my world?
4) Is there an armed human resistance somewhere?
5) When will I eat next?

Dogs don't need us, but they like having us around. Don't know why. Ten thousand years of evolution, maybe?

I am tied to the trunk of an apple tree. Most of the pack and the well-behaved humans lounge in the shade of the overgrown orchard. Pups tumble and play on two legs, four legs, sniff, growl, hump, never stray far. Could be a dog park on a sunny day, but it's not. Four human children snuggle against pack elders, not allowed near their mothers except to nurse. None of them are mine. Thankfully.

The Pitmaster rubs the back of my head, pats my shoulders. "You're a good boy, you know that, Pal? I can always count on you."

Keep my eyes down. Focus on the withered vegetables and shredded raw rabbit in the plastic bowl. Shovel the food into my mouth with my hands, don't think about the taste. Try not to think at all. I am starving and still I eat better than the others.

Eleven human adults. Thirty-one dogs. Even the spindly Chihuahua could kill me.

"You're a good boy, yes, you are."

Tiny voice inside me cheers, "I am! I am!" I throw up in my mouth, swallow it back down. The acid burn isn't enough to drown the voice.

The Briarstreetmaster wanders over and drops beside the Pitmaster. Thick-bodied bitch, matted white belly and limbs, brown back, blocky head, lots of drool. Poppy, a filthy human girl, maybe three years old, climbs into her lap, burrows into the thick fur, finds a withered teat, begins to comfort suck. Watches me with wide, empty eyes. She looks a little like Midgie, a little like Earl. Her jaw is offset, lips swollen like someone shoved a claw in her mouth to tear out her tongue.

The Briarstreetmaster is alpha. The Pitmaster wants to be alpha. He does not acknowledge her fast enough. She shoulders into him, grabs his jowl in her teeth and shakes until he yelps, gives it one more shake, lets go. They sniff, she licks his muzzle, then looks at me. "When will he be ready for the pit?"

Dogs don't speak unless they want us to understand.

The Pitmaster pats my back. "Not tonight, but it won't be long. You want to get back in the pit, don't you, Pal?"

Tonight? Butch? Which of us will kill the other? I don't want to die. I lick my fingers to hide my shaking hands.

The Briarstreetmaster reaches across the Pitmaster, peels back my lips to check my teeth, presses her paw into my stomach. The Pitmaster gives the command to bow. Get on my hands and knees, forehead pressed to the cool earth. Feel her hot snuffle as she sniffs my ass, hefts my testicles. I want to smack her nose. Bad girl! No!

I bite through my tongue.

Growls, huffs, a low whine from the Pitmaster. One swats my ass, I can't tell who. The Briarstreetmaster walks back to her tree, Poppy close behind.

Tiny brown spider crawls up the left side of my forehead and into my hair. I grind my teeth, keep still. Moving before release earns punishment. Learned that the hard way. Stay in position until the Pitmaster slaps my thigh. I come back upright. He tousles my hair. "Seems you have a reputation, Pal. She wants your pup."

The words have teeth of their own. Can they hate now, too? Don't know, but I need him to understand. I don't want children for the dogs to raise or kill as they like. I forget myself, raise my eyes to look at him.

His ears go back, he bares his teeth, a remembering look, remembering the Before. Clothes and cars, scolded for snatching a chicken breast off the counter, hit by a car and left by the side of the road to die in pain. He could take my head off with one swipe of the paw. I drop my gaze, waiting for the blow. At least it will be quick.

He rubs my back. "We'll see about that. You're my good boy, aren't you, Pal? You know that, right?"

No matter how many times I yelled or spanked Sigmund, he always came back with more love.

I go limp with relief. I nod. I need him, hate him. Hate myself.

"That's a good boy."

The Pitmaster's paw finds and unravels a knot beneath my right shoulder blade. My traitorous body leans into the touch, curls on its side, rests its head on his thigh. His fur is soft.

On the other side of the clearing, Butch sits beside the Kennelmaster and watches me without expression. I close my eyes so I don't have to imagine his contempt.

Five Things That Frighten Me:

1) Dogs

2) Fighting in the pit
3) Dying
4) Being alone
5) Everything

We are smarter than the dogs. They are stronger, breed faster, but we are still smarter. We have to be, right?

Dogs are light sleepers. Two usually stay in the kennel at night, but tonight they join the rest of the pack at the pit on the far side of the dilapidated barn.

Rovers found two stray humans just after sundown. Normally I would face them one-on-one in the pit. This time, the Briarstreetmaster decides they should fight one another. Better sport. The winner will be added to the kennel; if they don't fight, they both die. I press back against a dim, small memory of my first time in the pit, the snap of bones against my feet, a woman's scream, the weight of a melon head busted open against a rock.

The realization I lost something precious.

The others are indistinct lumps pressed against the doors of their cages. I am a shadow of myself.

"Four jugs of Prestone, still sealed," Ruby whispers from his cage next to mine. "Uncovered them under a bunch of blackberry vines when I was picking berries. I didn't say anything."

"Fucking dogs," Rex says from his cage at the end of the row. He is the smallest shadow, stands just under four feet. The bitches pass him around like a cuddle toy.

"So it's poison," Carl says from the darkness on my left. "Not like we can—"

A human scream drowns in a chorus of blood-crazed howls. We hold our collective breaths.

"—can get them to, um ..." Carl's voice fades in the hot iron smell of blood.

Ruby fills the gruesome silence: "The more dogs we poison, the better our chances of escape. Someone gets out and kills a deer or something, or a bunch of rabbits, soaks the carcasses in the antifreeze or maybe ..."

Or maybe. A rush of low questions. What if they don't eat? What if it's not enough? What if they figure it out? What if it doesn't work? What if? What if? What if?

And then a question from the shadows: "Who?"

There. The real question. Who volunteers to be run down like an animal and have their throats torn out for disobedience? Who drinks the antifreeze and dies in agony if they can't find game? Who is the sacrifice so the rest of us can live?

"I'm in," says Midgie.

Silence.

I press my forehead to the cage door. It comes down to this. I have nothing to lose. The dogs have taken everything from me. Live on my belly or die on my feet? I say, "I can't live like this anymore. I'm in."

But it's not my voice. It's Butch.

"Tonight, while we still have a chance," he continues.

On the other side of the kennel, two cages down on the right. Hard, gentle, human Butch. "No," I say.

Butch grunts. He's doing something to the door of his cage. Metal grates against metal.

I clutch at the door of my cage, wire digging into my fingers. "Butch. Don't leave me. I'll go with you."

Say it again, louder. He can't hear me, none of them can. They're too busy thanking Butch and Midgie for saving them from their own cowardice. Even with the excitement at the pit, if I raise my voice the dogs may hear and investigate. Punish us for talking. Fresh meat for the pups, more tongues for the Kennelmaster's collection.

I'm a coward, a liar. I start to cry. Stuff my filthy blanket into my mouth to stifle the traitor sound. Crawl to the back of my cage.

Metal against metal. Sounds like Midgie sobbing.

Five Breeds Of Dog I Like The Most:

1)
2)

3)
4)
5)

The Briarstreetmaster circles the bodies while the pack waits anxiously near-by. Her ears are laid back, hackles up, tail still. Butch, Midgie, and a gutted fawn drenched inside and out with antifreeze.

Midgie and Butch are mottled, bloated, green-tinged foam crusted around their mouths and bloody hands. Midgie's dead eyes stare at the sky, defiant. Butch's head is tipped to one side like someone made a joke or asked him a question. Any minute now he'll take a breath, sit up, smile at me. We'll run to the river and wrestle.

The morning paints sharp shadows on the dusty ground. Going to be miserable hot. I sit at the Pitmaster's feet, his paw on my head. Breathe through my mouth to block what I can of the smell. Dogs find antifreeze irresistible. Used to find it irresistible.

The other adult humans cluster together under the trees with the children. Their thoughts are electric. *What is she thinking? Does she suspect? Will it work? Why don't they eat?*

My thoughts are numbers. *Thirty-one dogs. Nine adult humans. Four jugs of antifreeze.* Not enough antifreeze to kill the dogs even if Butch and Midgie somehow managed to use it all. Antifreeze isn't a quick kill, wasn't even in the Before. Either the pack eats and turns on us long before they die, or they discard the bodies and nothing changes. A surefire plot in the desperation of night disintegrates in the terrifying reality of day.

The Pitmaster looks at me. "What is it, Pal? What's wrong?"

I clench my teeth to keep from screaming.

No. The dogs will eat. I don't have to fight. I can strike out on my own. They can't catch all of us, can't kill all of us. We can still win.

Thirty-one. Nine. The numbers claw at my confidence, sink into my animal brain. I start to shake.

"Easy, boy," the Pitmaster commands.

His gaze presses down on me, smothers me in the heat. Poodles are one of the most intelligent breeds. Sharp eyes. Sharp minds. He knows.

Does he? Yes. No. My collar chafes at my neck.

Stop playing dead, Butch. Let's go down to the river, wrestle in the cold water. I can't do this alone. Please, Butch. He doesn't move.

The Briarstreetmaster crouches beside the fawn, pries open the gut, pulls back a paw slick with blood and antifreeze. She sniffs, licks, licks again. Buries her muzzle in the gut, pulls it back glistening red with a chunk of offal between her teeth. Her tail thumps the ground, and the four nearest dogs hurry forward to join in the feast. The others wag, prance, jockey for position.

I thought the dogs had taken everything from me, that I had nothing left to lose. I was wrong, so wrong. Ragdoll Midgie. Butch's stomach ripped open. The terrible rending, snarling, gulping. The squeals, snaps, grunts. The sound, oh God, the sound. They drag out my intestines. Rip off my arm. Crack my thigh to get at the marrow. They can't hear me scream because they've torn off my face. The last shreds of my humanity are devoured by the greedy pack.

"Stay," the Pitmaster says, and starts to move forward.

I lunge after him, grab the fur of his calf. He looks over his shoulder, raises a paw to strike. I look him in the eye and say, "Poison."

His eyes narrow. He looks at the feeding dogs and those waiting their turn, then back at me. He snarls.

"Poison," I say again. I don't care who sees, who hears. I don't want to die. I want to live, live, live, please, I'll do anything, I want to live.

"If you're lying ..."

I shake my head. "No, no."

An eternity later, he lowers his hand. Yips. The Kennelmaster looks at him.

Another yip, and the Kennelmaster heads our way, gathering other dogs with him as he goes.

The Pitmaster tugs on my collar. "Good boy, Pal."

I cling to his arm and begin to cry.

Five Things I Know To Be True:

1) I sleep in a cage.

2) I fight in the pit.
3) I win, I eat.
4) My name is Pal.
5) I am a good boy.

Author's Note

Shortly after Christmas 2016, we adopted a dog, Evan, a 70 lb. Abanian miniature moose disguised as a pit bull. He's fierce, he's ferocious, he'll lick your make-up off and snuggle like nobody's business. He burrows under the covers of a morning after we let him out to go pee, his "pack time." He also likes beef bones, and the sound of him cracking one in half with those pit bull jaws will give you chills.

"Good Boy" was inspired by a Tweet I sent as part of a horror fiction account that I follow (@tweetsthecreeps, check it out). 140 characters worth of an idea blossomed into a dark, weird, post-apocalyptic tale of humanoid dogs who treat people the way people now treat dogs. I've never written a list story before, so I experimented with small lists as a way to explore what has come before. My mother used to breed Labrador retrievers, so I had experience with the breeding attitudes. I watched how dogs interact at the dog park and researched dog pack behavior online. I hunched on my knees in the bathtub, imagining myself in a cage.

And Pal's name, the one he won't let himself remember? Take a guess.

Life Line

R yan queezed Patti's hand, doing his best not to disturb the cocoon of seemingly endless tubes. "Wha'd'ya need, babe?"

Patti smiled up at him through the bruises and bandages. "Help me sit up," she said, the words a whisper above the ticks and beeps keeping time in the hospital room.

"You got it." He raised the head of the bed, put down the side rail when she indicated she wanted to swing her legs over the edge. "Do you think you should be doing this?"

"I'm fine, Smoots. I—"

Ryan fussed with her hair, her hospital gown, seeking the reassurance of touch. "I talked to Deputy Delmore yesterday. He said the guy has lawyered up even though he popped twice the legal limit on the Breathalyzer."

Patti shifted and winced. "Later, Smoots. Listen—"

"Later, hell. I hope they—"

Patti scooted forward until her feet touched the floor. "Ryan, hon, I need you to listen to me for a moment, 'kay? I need you to book me on the next flight to Chicago. I don't care what airline."

Ryan had his cell phone in hand before he made sense of the request. "Wait. Chicago? What's in Chicago?"

"Are my pants still here?"

"Babe, you're not goin' anywhere. You lost a lotta blood when they put you back together. You got all these IV and transfusion tubes." Ryan's gut clenched around a momentary panic. "You do remember you're in the hospital, right?"

"Of course I remember." She pulled off the nasal cannulae, draped it over the pillow. "Use the VISA. The Master Card is tapped out."

"Screw the VISA. I'm not calling—"

"Yes you are, Smoots."

"Are you crazy?" Erica said in a low panic, easing the front door shut behind her. Cool night air chased anxiety in a rush of sudden goose bumps. She rubbed her arms, the porch creaking beneath her as she shifted her weight from foot to foot. "You can't just walk out of the hospital. What about your treatments?"

Quinn shrugged. "So I miss a couple of days. Big deal. It's not like I'll bleed to death."

"But your folks—"

He swallowed her words and thoughts with a kiss. He tasted of mocha and cigarettes.

"I really need your help, babe," Quinn said when he pulled away.

Erica blinked, savoring the memory as she tried to make sense of it all. "You're serious about this."

Quinn nodded. "Charlie Davis is dying, and I need to get to Chicago. Now."

"Who's Charlie Davis?" Marcus "Frito" Fernandez said, setting his traveling mug back in its holder on the dash.

The young woman who'd introduced herself as Becky at the Gas'n'Go an hour back shrugged like only a teenager could. "A friend."

"Ah." He cut a look at her huddled against the passenger door of the cab. Not so thin as to be stylish, not so heavy she had to rely on a nice personality. The tips of her spiky hair were a neon green, her jewelry roses and fairies. Tinker Bell fluttered across the front of her hooded sweatshirt. "He a good friend?"

Something haunted curled behind her eyes, a look both determined and vulnerable at once. "Yeah, I guess."

Frito checked his mirrors and eased off the gas to let a gutsy blue Corolla pass the rig on the left, then it was back up to speed, making time, making miles. I-70 rolled along in a wash of asphalt and Wyoming morning heat, greens and browns vying for dominance along the shoulder. With Stockton long gone and Denver still to come, it had the makings of a good run, the Lord and Jesus willing.

He noticed the way she eyed the half sandwich on the seat between them. "You hungry? You can have the rest of it."

She nonchalantly reached for the sandwich. "Thanks," she said, unwrapping it.

"It's grilled chicken. My wife gets on me about my cholesterol."

She picked off the banana peppers and had half of it gone before Frito thought to say, "There's water bottles in the back on the right."

Instead of crawling in back, the girl kept to her seat and reached around the curtain. Good. She had some sense at least. Thoughts like that led to others he washed down with a few more gulps of lukewarm coffee. "Mind if I ask you a question, Becky?"

The girl watched him from the corner of her eye as she picked lettuce off the paper. "Like what?"

"How old are you, really?"

"I'm nineteen," she said a little too quickly.

"Ah." Frito scratched the gray stubble under his chin. "You wanna reach in the glove compartment for me?" The girl's eyes widened as he knew they would. Frito kept his hands on the wheel. "Go on. It's nothin' bad."

Becky balled up the sandwich wrap and tucked it into the crack of the seat beside her. She leaned forward and popped the glove compartment latch.

"What's in there?" Frito said.

"A bunch of papers. A big tire gauge. A bible."

"Take the bible out and open it to the very back. That's a picture of my family—my wife, Carol; my girls, Andrea and Rosa; and the little guy with the finger up his nose is Patrick."

Becky's attention flickered between Frito and the picture. "They're nice looking."

At that he smiled. "Aren't they? I'm really proud of my kids. Andrea's eleven, and I figure Rosa's about your age."

Becky paled. "How old is she?"

He looked at her then, trying not to think about either girl holed up like a back row beauty at some state highway truck stop. "Sixteen."

Becky's shoulders slumped. Her hands trembled as she returned the picture and closed the bible.

"Do your folks know where you are?" Frito said when he figured she'd had enough silence.

"No." She twisted her fairy necklace around one finger. "They said I couldn't go."

"Ah."

"It's not like that! This is important."

He pretended not to notice Becky wipe the tears from her eyes. "It may be important to you, but I know I wouldn't want my baby girl hitching her way across country."

"What else could I do? They don't let me do anything anymore since I came out of remission."

The word brought Frito's foot off the accelerator. He caught the reduction in speed, returned his foot to the pedal. "Remission?"

Becky lifted her quivering chin in defiance. "Yeah. I have leukemia."

The father in Frito took a moment to cool down. He cleared his throat once, twice. "So, um, did you meet Charlie in the hospital?"

She smiled hesitantly, shyly. "Yeah."

"That's cool." A half-dozen mile markers passed before Frito allowed himself to say anything more. "Listen, we're gonna hit Denver by supper time. I can't take you any farther, but I'd really appreciate it if you let me buy you a bus ticket to Chicago. It's better than hitching."

Becky looked at her hands and took her time answering. "What do I have to do?"

"Say yes, and give my regards to your friend. And no more hitchhiking, okay? Ever." He probably had enough money in his checking account for a return ticket to wherever she called home. He'd text Carol to fill her in on the details when he had the chance.

This time Becky's smile wasn't as shy, although there were still tears. "Thanks."

"Not a problem. You want me to call your folks once I get you on the bus? That way they can't tell you to come home." He wouldn't tell Carol that last part.

Becky laughed through the tears. "I'd like that. I'm just worried I might not make it in time."

"In time for what?" Ned Emmett said. He set his lunch sack on the kitchen table. He'd expected dinner and the evening news when he got home, not the twins and Agnes rattling on about their daughter flying to Chicago.

Agnes handed each boy an oatmeal cookie and sent them outside to play. "No idea, but Wendy had to get to Chicago lickety split."

Ned went to the refrigerator. "Problem with a gallery opening, you think? Where's my Diet Coke?"

"In the back, where it always is. Maybe she's met someone special."

Ned grunted. He grabbed a soda, stood, closed the fridge door. "Mmmm."

Agnes pulled her stew pot out of the cabinet. "I wonder what his name is."

"And why can't you tell your parents about me, but you can run off to Chicago to be with him?" Andy said as he walked Lyric to the car.

Lyric tossed his overnight bag into the backseat. Neighbors across the street laid out the clutter of a garage sale while their ancient basset hound sniffed around the plastic containers. "I'm working on it." He settled behind the wheel. The engine turned over with a rumble and cough. "Charlie's important to me, okay? He helped me out years back."

Andy closed the car door, wishing he wasn't the jealous type. "I suppose you'll be staying the night with him."

The emergency brake popped, and the car rolled down the drive. "Yeah. He already has a room."

"Room three-oh-three, bed two," Helen said sotto voce, nudging Corona. "He comes in last night, no one calls or asks about him. Now he has three visitors in two hours."

The other nurse looked up from her suduko. "Hmm? Maybe they just got word."

"Yeah, but how? It took us forever to ID him. What's up with that?"

Corona returned to her numbers. "I dunno. I got no problems with 'em."

A fourth visitor ten minutes later proved to be the straw that broke

Helen's curiosity's back. She stepped around the nurses' station and went to the door, stopping at the threshold to the room, listening to snippets of conversation, platelets and clotting factor, not the typical bedside fare. An older man in jeans and a plaid flannel shirt, and a woman in a peacock dress, stood on either side of the head of the bed. A young executive and an elderly woman with gray braids stood at the foot of the bed.

Helen knocked lightly on the doorframe and stepped into the room. The quartet paused in their conversation and looked at her expectantly. "Hi. I just wanted to check Mister Davis's IV."

"Charlie," the man in the flannel shirt said. "He used to tell people Mister Davis was his father, and dead how ever many years."

Helen smiled. "Charlie it is, then."

The visitors waited in companionable silence as Helen checked the IV connection and took her patient's vitals, noting them in his chart. He remained unresponsive, withered and frail save for his distended abdomen. She brushed hair off his forehead. He didn't have long, but at least he was comfortable.

Helen stepped back. "Can I get you anything? Water? Soda?"

"A diet soda would be great," said Miss Peacock.

"Coffee, if you have it," said Wall Street Junior. "With Splenda."

The other two declined.

"Can do." Helen hurried to fill the requests, handing them out upon her return. "It's good to see so many people here. Most of our patients and long term residents don't have as many visitors as they'd like."

"Charlie's a great guy," said Miss Peacock, holding the old man's hand as if it were spun sugar. "He saved my life. Did you know he landed with D-Day, and fought at the Battle of Hurtgen Forest?"

"Did he?" Helen smoothed the blankets. "A war hero and a life saver. Did he help you in an accident?"

Miss Peacock answered Helen's question, but her eyes never left Charlie's face. "Nothing so dramatic. My last pregnancy ended with an emergency C-section. I'm told I lost a fair bit of blood, not that I remember any of it. Charlie was one of the donors."

Miss Braids nodded from her place at the foot of the bed. "I was the one in an accident. Charlie was there for me when I needed blood." She took a tissue out of her handbag and dabbed at moist eyes. "Charlie was a dog man. He used to volunteer at the veterinarian's office when he was a boy because he wasn't allowed to have a dog at home."

"And birds. He loved birds, too," said a voice from the door. Helen looked over her shoulder as a young man in baggy jeans and a stretched out Atlanta Falcons jersey strode into the room. His arms were tattooed tapestries of color and meaning.

The newcomer continued, "That bothered him when he lost his house, 'cause he didn't have no birds no more."

The others nodded and made room around the bed for the newcomer. The older man in plaid held out his hand, the young man gripped it. "Plasma after my liver transplant."

"Blood transfusion after I got shot."

Introductions with no names? Helen looked from one to another. "You must all be local, then."

They shook their heads no amid various declarations of "Atlanta", "LA", "Littleton", "Decatur", and "Clearwater".

She frowned, turning the improbabilities over in her mind. "I didn't realize there was a donor identification program available for transfusion recipients."

Stan shrugged. "There isn't. We know Charlie because he's, well ..."

"Charlie," Miss Peacock said for him.

Rikki nodded, rubbing Charlie's leg through the blankets and sheet. "He's a part of us, right man?"

They nodded. Miss Braids brightened. "Do you remember that time when he was, what?, six or seven, and he decided to run away from home because his dad ..."

Helen allowed a nurse call signal to take her out of the room before the conversation became even more confusing.

Later, grabbing a last cup of coffee in the kitchenette at the end of her lunch break, Helen turned to find the older man in jeans and plaid standing in the doorway, two travel mugs and a Styrofoam cup in hand. "Some of the folks were wondering if they could get a refill."

She stepped away from the coffeemaker. "Sure, go ahead."

"Thanks."

Helen leaned against the counter. "I'm sorry. I never got your name."

He smiled. "Stan Marks."

Helen carefully swirled the coffee in her cup. "Charlie's a popular guy. People were spilling into the hall before we told them they had to wait in the lobby."

"Yeah," Stan said as he pulled the lids off the mugs. "I'm expecting a lot more people to show up." The corners of his mouth turned down in a distracted frown as he poured the coffee. "I hope they get here soon."

Helen raised a cautious brow. "Just how many more are you expecting?"

At that Stan smiled. "Can't say, really. Charlie had a twenty-five pheresis pin, and a fifty gallon donor pin."

"You're kidding, right?"

"Nope."

Helen blanched at the thought of hundreds, perhaps thousands, of extras from *The Twilight Zone* filling the halls, streaming out the front door, getting in the way if there was an emergency, all because of one man. "You realize how crazy that sounds?"

Stan fit the lids back on the mugs. He stuffed his pockets with packets of sugar, sweetener, and non-dairy creamer. "Yup. When he came back stateside after the war, Charlie took to thinking of donating blood as another way to serve his country. So did Edith."

"Edith?"

"His wife. She died just about a month before I received Charlie's transfusion."

Helen sipped her coffee as she tried to fit the pieces of a puzzle together in the dark without a picture for comparison. "Okay, so you did know Charlie before your transfusion."

"Nope." Stan's voice was as easy and small town as his smile. "I'd never met him before this morning."

Helen searched the craggy features for a hint of deception. "Things like that don't happen. There is no mystical connection to blood donors."

At that Stan laughed, a low, dry rasp. "If someone'd tried to tell me all that last night, I would have said the same thing. Kooky, huh?" He took the cups and headed out, greeting a young woman with spiked green hair hurrying past, "Plasma."

"Platelets during chemo ..."

Helen could not hear the rest of the young woman's answer. From the kitchenette door, she watched them turn into room three-oh-three.

Helen asked around towards the end of her shift, and the answer was always the same. Charlie Davis saved their lives one blood component at a time. A war hero who loved animals, and once saved a child from being hit by a trolley car in San Francisco. He lived a widower's life in his later years, lost his home and savings to a bad investment, and now drifted above the pain of tumors killing him one cell at a time. Not one of the growing crowd claimed to have met Charlie Davis before that morning, yet each knew when they took him into their lives through an IV needle.

At shift change, Helen briefed the incredulous charge nurse, taking care to give updates on every patient and not Charlie Davis alone.

"I just don't get it," she told Corona, slipping on her sweater.

"Get what?" her shift mate said, rooting through her purse for keys.

"Them." Helen waved an arm to take in the flow of people in and around room three-oh-three.

"What's to get, girl? He has a lot of friends. That's a blessing in this place."

"Yeah." Helen chewed on her bottom lip as she watched the crowd rub elbows with itself. "You have a good one. See you tomorrow." She grabbed her purse and went off in search of Stan.

She found him at the foot of Charlie's bed talking to a handful of new faces she didn't recognize. This was just too much. "Hey, Stan. Can I talk to you a minute?"

"Sure." He followed Helen out of the room as people filed slowly through the door to replace him. "What's up?"

Feeling decidedly silly, Helen forged ahead before common sense won out. "I wanted to let you know that I really appreciate all that you're doing for Charlie. Not just you, but, y'know, all of you."

"We should be thankin' you," Stan said, hooking his thumbs in his pockets. "You took Charlie in and made him comfortable so he could rest easy at last. We really appreciate that."

Helen blushed at the compliment, wondering why it seemed more genuine than most. "Yeah, well, VA hospitals aren't glamour houses, but our patients are people, too."

Stan smiled like a child with a new toy. "Charlie would've liked you."

"Yeah, about that ..." She stepped into the door of a temporarily vacant room, suddenly self-conscious. "I don't believe what you were telling me earlier about the, um, the whole blood donor thing. I mean, it just doesn't make sense."

The older man shrugged. "It doesn't make sense to me, neither, but it's true."

"It can't be, don't you see? Even red blood cells only last four, maybe five, months. After that, they're broken down by the spleen. There's no way any of you could think Charlie is still a part of you, unless the treatment was very recent. That's just crazy. Why not say you have some strange connection to all of the donors?"

"Maybe they weren't afraid of dying alone and forgotten."

Helen stopped, stung and ashamed by the gentleness of the words. "I didn't mean for that to sound the way—"

"I understand, Miss. The way I figure it, no one wants to die like that. Maybe it scares Charlie more than most folks. He didn't have anyone else, so he needed to remember himself. We're all supposed to be the same under the skin, right?"

Helen took a deep breath, let it out slowly. "Yeah. Anyway, I wanted to say that I may not believe any of it, but I'm still glad you're here."

It took her a moment to realize that Stan no longer looked at her, his attention now focused over his right shoulder. In fact, the entire crowd had stopped what they were doing to look in the same direction. A near-by woman in a gray pinstripe suit reached for Stan. He took her hand, and, as Helen watched, one by one a chain of hands stretched from room three-oh-three, down the hall, and disappeared around the corner.

Maybe it was the extra hours, or the stress of handling the crowd, but Helen suddenly wished to be a part of such togetherness, to become a link in the silent chain, instead of the reasonable outsider looking in. How far, she wondered, did Charlie Davis reach?

Author's Note

I tend to be a very linear writer in both process and form. I am a creature of rigid boundaries, defense mechanisms that have come to define my life. Don't get me wrong, there is a certain beauty to angular, sharp writing with clear definition and color, but sometimes I wish I could write with the same swirling, stylistic beauty other writers manage so well, the subtlety of color and form, the exquisite prose that reads like poetry and leaves me breathless and wanting more. So, what do I do when am hungry to explore? I throw myself out of my writing box and try something new.

"Life Line" was my first attempt at a different sort of writing. There is no single point-of-view character, and the main character never says a word. Every last line of a scene ties directly to the first line of the next scene, a conversation of miles and moments. Does it work? I think it does, and in the end that tiny spark of confidence will light my way until the next time I start eyeing the sides of the box, looking for a way out.

Scarecrone

Papa put Mama's Sunday dress on the scarecrow, and nailed her buckle shoes to the base of the pole. He screamed "Whore!"

And "Don't need you no how!"

And "Fucking Injun bitch!"

Mama used to say Papa drank because he couldn't keep a steady job after fighting the Germans. He'd been drinking real hard since Mama left.

That night, I snuck out my window and found my way to the scarecrow by moonlight and memory. The way the scarecrow's sack head flopped to its chest, I could barely make out the stitched eyes, but I liked to think it looked at me like Mama used to. I hugged the scarecrow tight; it smelled like old mattress ticking and Mama's finishing powder. I said "I'm sorry you went away, Mama. Please come back."

And "I miss you."

When I woke the next morning, I found a glossy black feather beside me on the pillow.

At breakfast, Papa grabbed the coffee pot before I could pour his first cup and wash away his bull temper. His eyes were angry red, and he had a chin full of whiskers. He smelled sour with beer.

Sunlight came hot and dusty through the open front door, telling about the puny corn and withered beans and lean pantry. In his highchair, Will Junior ate biscuits crumbled with the last of the eggs from the charity basket at church.

I turned back to the sink to finish the dishes. Papa grabbed my shoulder and spun me round. He stared at me hard with them red-rimmed eyes, whiskey and beer eyes. He said "Where you get that, Dolly?"

I touched the feather I'd tied into my hair with a bit of ribbon from Mama's sewing box. I didn't let on that he was hurting me. Only made it worse if you showed pain. I said "I found it on my pillow."

Papa narrowed his eyes and said real low "On your pillow?"

I nodded and said "I thought it looked pretty."

Papa ripped the feather out of my hair, and I cried out. Will Junior gave a start at the sound and began to cry.

Papa threw the feather to the floor and ground it under his boot.

He said "How many times I got to tell you you ain't no Injun?"

Will Junior started crying harder. I said "But Mama—"

Papa's hand cracked across my cheek and snapped my head back. He yelled "Don't you talk to me about your mama! You want to be an Injun like her? Huh?"

He slapped me again. I tasted blood.

All spit and fire Papa said "You ain't no Injun. I don't got no Injun children, you hear me?"

Will Junior started screaming loud as the thunder ringing in my head. Mama always said I should be proud to be Zuni, that it wasn't nothing anyone could take away from me, but I kept my eyes down like Mama always said to do and said "Yessir."

Papa pushed back his seat and stood over me like Goliath from the Bible. He said "You shut him up."

Then he stomped out of the kitchen, and all I could see was that bright, glossy feather with the pretty ribbon, now all crumpled and broken.

Late that night, while I lay in bed and watched the moon coming up over the few stalks of corn, I heard a cough and something like a knock. Papa said "You awake, Dolly?"

I rolled onto my side and looked at him standing in the doorway, the dim light from the kitchen making him glow a little from behind. He didn't seem angry, but I pulled my sheet up to my chin all the same. I said "Uh-huh."

I said it soft so I didn't wake Will Junior sleeping in his box at the foot of my bed. I didn't want him to cry and make Papa mad.

Papa crossed and uncrossed his arms, stuffed his hands in his pockets. He said "I, uh, I wanted to apologize for this morning. The feather, I mean."

My heart felt funny like it did every time he apologized. I said "That's okay."

Papa said "I wasn't feeling too good and let my temper get the best of me."

And "I didn't mean to hit you. You know that, right?"

I guess I knew that. I said "Uh-huh."

He kept quiet a long time, and I wondered if he'd fallen asleep leaning against the door, then he said "All right."

And "You get some sleep now."

And "I love you."

I said "Love you, too, Papa."

He walked back into the kitchen. Patsy Cline came real soft over the kitchen radio. I heard Papa open the refrigerator like he always did at night.

Christmas Eve last year, Mama gave me a Mister Franklin half-dollar as a secret special present. We talked about school and dresses, about fry bread and being proud to be Zuni no matter that Papa didn't like it much. I said "I'm going to Hollywood and be a movie star, and marry Cary Grant."

Mama braided my hair like the way she said Hotda Annie used to do for her and said "I love you so much, you silly bird."

I said "Even more than you love Will Junior?"

Mama laughed and said "There's room enough in my heart for both of you."

I said "Even room for Papa?"

She said "Of course. He was quite a gentleman to me when we first got married."

I tipped that Mister Franklin half-dollar back and forth in the moonlight. His face was so smooth he almost didn't have no hair no more. I said "Yeah, but do you got room for him tonight?"

Mama never said nothing to that.

The next morning I found another feather on my pillow. I touched it with my finger. The feather felt almost alive, like petting a crow. Out in the garden I could see Mama's dress dancing round the scarecrow in the wind, flapping and flirting in the morning sun.

I put the feather in my cigar box, then gathered Will Junior up from his wood box. I said "You see a crow in here last night?"

Will Junior made happy sounds, patted my face with his slobbery hands. He had blue eyes like Papa, not brown like mine, and his hair was soft brown gold instead of black.

I cleaned him up and took him to the kitchen to find something for his breakfast. A stack of nine empty beer cans sat on the dish board by the sink. That explained why Papa wasn't around; he must have gone into Holbrook real early. He did that sometimes when he was looking for work or needed more beer. I set Will Junior in his highchair and said "We don't have much for breakfast. You think Papa's going to talk to Reverend Tibbet about another charity basket, maybe?"

Will Junior burbled and laughed the way babies do.

I gave him the last of the corn flakes and shared a can of government baked beans between us. Will Junior kept trying to take the spoon. I said just like Mama "You're enough of a mess already, young man. Open your mouth, here comes the train."

After breakfast, I washed and hung out Will Junior's diapers and clothes, swept out the house, and threw Papa's beer cans in the pile by his old blue truck. He got the truck from Grandma Thurston when Poppy Thurston died and always said he'd get it running again someday, but he never did nothing with it. Now it didn't have a floor no more, and rabbits made nests in the wheel wells. I once caught a rat snake in the cab and would have kept it for a pet if Papa hadn't killed it with a shovel.

The day before she left Mama tossed Papa's empties on the pile and said "Two piles of rust that never did anyone any good."

She never answered me why she said that.

I kept busy with my chores and playing with Will Junior. He liked it when I played peek-a-boo and when I made funny faces. It was easier doing things without Papa around. I could take my time and get them done right without being scared he might yell at me or go after Will Junior. I loved him—he was my Papa, I had to love him—but sometimes, when he'd been drinking hard and hit Mama, he scared me. I never told anyone, not even Mama.

We shared another can of beans for lunch, then I put Will Junior down for his nap and went to the garden. Mama always said it didn't amount to much, but we had to take care of it so it could take care of us. I pulled a piddling few weeds and drew water from the well to soak the plants as best I could. Mama used to talk about planting the three sisters way, corn, beans, and squash all together, but Papa never let her.

The scarecrow watched with its stitched eyes while I worked, Mama's dress flapping around the post. Kind of looked like one of Hotda Annie's kachina dolls. I talked to it like I would have talked to Mama, about how we didn't have much food, and the coyote I saw in the front yard the day before. I said "I finished my math book, so I'm going to do it again. I can add numbers in the hundreds column now."

And "Will Junior had a dirty diaper after breakfast. We don't have much soap left, but I scrubbed all his clothes extra long to make sure they got clean."

And "Why didn't you take me with you, Mama?"

The scarecrow didn't say anything back.

Finished with the watering, I did my best to wipe the dirt off her shoes with the bottom of my dress. They were my favorite of all her shoes, red with gold buckles and tiny heels. When I was little, Mama'd let me wear them and I would pretend I was a Zuni princess, though Zuni don't got princesses. Besides, no one would ever call a Zuni princess a half breed.

I stood up and hugged the scarecrow with all the love I had inside me. I said "I love you, Mama. Will Junior loves you, too. Papa, he ..." I wiped my face on the front of the dress. The lace alongside the buttons made my nose itch. "Please come home, Mama. I miss you."

The wind shifted and the dress flapped around my legs, hugging me back. Spiders skittered along the sides of my dirty red sneakers and up over the tops. I tried to stomp them off, but my feet wouldn't budge. I pushed away Mama's dress and saw there weren't no spiders. Tiny brown roots grew out of the base of the post, picking their way over my shoes. The roots grew over the laces, held me snug like two big hands. One twiggy finger brushed my right ankle. It scratched me like a cat, and blood followed where it led. I screamed, tumbled back, and my feet tore free. Mama's dress billowed up in a sudden wind, and the scarecrow's head whipped side to side.

I got up and ran for the house.

I hadn't been to the schoolhouse since before Mama left. Papa said I had to stay home and take care of Will Junior instead of riding the bus to the Pueblo. I sort of wanted to go back to school. I missed my friends, and having a hot lunch when there wasn't no food at home. I didn't miss the ruler across my knuckles when I wrote with my left hand, or being called a half-breed, though.

Papa said I should be white like Will Junior, then I could go to the school in Holbrook. He would threaten to cut my hair and make me white. He always apologized the next morning, but on nights like that when he'd been drinking heavy, Mama used to hide the shears and knives.

I avoided the scarecrow as best I could after that. First thing in the garden each morning I'd water and weed near-by, then I'd hurry off to take care of the rest of the rows. I didn't say anything to Papa. He would have hit me and said I was stupid if I had.

One night I got up late to drink some water to keep the hungry down, and through my window I saw Papa in the moonlight standing by the scarecrow. He unzipped his pants, pulled out his wiener, and peed on Mama's shoes. Without a wind, Mama's dress hung dishrag limp on the post. I didn't sleep much more that night.

For eight mornings straight I found another feather on my pillow. I saved every one of them in my cigar box. They made me feel beautiful like Mama, like a Zuni princess even without the pretty shoes. Sometimes late at night I'd lay them out on my quilt, glossy and black in the moonlight, one eye on the feathers, the other on the scarecrow in the garden so still and waiting. I didn't know for what, but I knew it waited and that scared me more than Papa ever could.

On the eighth night, with Papa passed out at the kitchen table and Will Junior fast asleep in his box, I pulled out the crow feathers, nine perfect, one broken. The moon hung full in the sky like my Mister Franklin half dollar. If I squinted just right, the scarecrow almost looked like Mama, head tilted to one side, arms stretched wide.

I found more ribbon in Mama's sewing box and tied all the feathers in my hair, even the broken one because it was the first and most special. The wind picked up and came through my bedroom window, playing with the feathers. I could have gone into the bathroom to look at my reflection, but I didn't dare wake Papa.

It didn't matter. In the middle of my room with only the moonlight for company, I lifted the hem of my nightgown and began to dance. I curtsied and dipped like a Zuni princess would if they had a special dance. I twirled in slow circles, dancing with Cary Grant. I hugged the moonlight and flew past the stars on my way Hollywood to star in a movie with Rock Hudson or John Wayne. I would be so beautiful up there on the movie screen.

Someone grabbed my shoulder and spun me around. Papa glared down at me and said "Wha'd'ya think you're doing, girl?"

That's when he noticed the feathers in my hair. He slapped me upside the head. He said "What the fuck are those?"

I put a hand to my hair and said real soft "Feathers."

Papa said "Feathers? What'd I tell you about that?"

Will Junior started to cry.

I got cold scared, deep down in my bones scared. Papa smelled drunk and mean and his eyes were crazy in the moonlight. I said "I'm sorry, I didn't mean—"

The wind picked up and began to blow hard through the window, bringing in dust and sand and the sharp smells of night.

Papa slapped me again, hard enough to make my ears ring. He said "You wanna be a stupid Injun? Is that it, huh?"

I said "No, Papa, I was just—"

Papa grabbed me by the hair, screaming "You're just like your mama. Just like her!"

I cried and begged and screamed. I grabbed hold of his wrist. He wouldn't let go. He dragged me out of the bedroom and into the kitchen. On the kitchen table beside a tumbled stack of empty beer cans sat a framed picture of Papa and Mama on their wedding day, all smiles and happy, him in his Army uniform and her in her best dress.

Papa went straight for the knife block and grabbed the kitchen shears. I tried to kick him, to run away, and he punched me in the face. My nose snapped and my head exploded in stars.

Papa started cutting my hair off in big hunks, jerking my head around, screaming "I'll show you!"

And "I'll show you what we do to stupid Injuns!"

And "I said hold still!"

My head got lighter and lighter until it didn't feel like anything but the blood running down my upper lip. I flew up high above myself and saw my ragged bald head, all my hair and pieces of feathers tossed around the kitchen floor. Saw the blood coming out of my nose, my right eye starting to swell. Saw Papa stagger to the sink, crazy and crying. Saw myself get off my knees and run as hard as I could out the front door.

I tumbled down the stairs and kept going. Now I knew why Mama left. I was Mama running for her life, terrified that Papa would find her and use more than his fists. I heard Will Junior crying over the wind, but I couldn't go back. I couldn't never go back no more.

The wind howled my name like the angel of death, dark and terrible. I heard Papa right behind me, felt his breath on my neck. He clawed at my back with beer can hands, wanting me back so he could hit me again, the stupid Injun.

Somehow I made it to the back of the house and into the garden with its whipsaw leaves and tumbled rows of desert rocks. There stood the scarecrow, tall on its post, head whipping back and forth in the wind. It wasn't near as scary as Papa. I fell into Mama's dress, wrapped my arms around that old scarecrow and held on for dear life. I said "Save me, Mama! Save me!"

The scarecrow said "Hush, you silly bird. No reason to cry anymore."

I buried my face in Mama's dress, blood smearing the dusty folds. I said "He tried to kill me."

The scarecrow wrapped its arms around me and pulled me close. It said "I know. He killed me, too."

The wind went away, and the night grew so beautiful still. Mama's twigs grew up around my shoes and over my arms. She passed me up with her love until I hung on her like Jesus on the cross, and when the twigs pierced my skin it hurt just a bit then I felt her love move all through me. My hair grew long and thick with mattress ticking and feathers. Mama kissed my cheeks, my lips, my eyes. She slid her dress down over my head, and her finishing powder made me beautiful.

I slid off the pole and into Mama's shoes, a real Zuni princess. Me and Mama, we made our way back to the house to see Papa one last time.

Author's Note

"Scarecrone" came to life fully formed from the moment Papa put Mama's dress on the scarecrow to the final line with nothing to say. It came from certain childhood terrors, and the fear that I might someday grow up to be my father.

This is another stylistic experiment, forsaking the expected punctuation and dialogue structure, trying something new. I wanted Dolly's voice, the voice of someone without much in the way of formal education. I found it.

Parting is Such Sweet Sorrow

"We don't serve your kind here, Willy Shakes," the bartender said. I picked at peeling varnish along the edge of the wooden bar. "That is the short and the long of it?"

"What?"

Typical. Words without thought never to heaven go. "Zombie-wired or deadhead?"

The bartender pulled a baseball bat with the handle wrapped in worn electrical tape from under the bar and set it in front of me, bony knuckles clenched tight around it. "Smart asses."

By the look of his pallid, sunken cheeks and humorless expression, he'd honor his hospitality more in the breach than the observance. Big surprise, I was unwired, the only deadhead in the place.

"Oh, that kind." I gave the dim room a once over. Zombies crowded the tables, wires streaming from the tops of their scabrous heads, emaciated bodies in ill fitting, sometimes dusty, clothes. Slack-jawed, eyes rolled back when not in use. Sucking at pouches of Vita-juice and talking to one another in slurred, guttural voices when uploaded. *Terminals* the uploads called them; *zombies* by any other name. I found the right zombie at a table in the far corner— "Well, then you can serve me over there." —and didn't waste any time.

I gambled that the bartender wouldn't bother following me, not with a full house and customers raising empty pouches for refills. He stayed behind the bar, and I slid into an empty chair without a fuss.

Alas, poor Siam Johnny, I knew him. Quite the sight slumped unoccupied on the other side of the table. Remnants of glossy black hair now brittle as dead grass, cheeks sunken and pocked with sores old and new, egg white eyes, the once hard body dressed in a disposable jumpsuit. Smelled like bread rising and the sidewalk after a strong rain.

Four wires—blue, black, neon yellow, brown—snaked from the back of his head to the table port. Hard to find a better lockman in the D.C. Metro before he opted for terminal wire. "Nobody squats in their own flesh anymore. Uploads are the now, and I want a piece of it," he'd said the last time I saw him in his own body, saw him in any body. He had the eyes, and the slide, and the honeyed skin I craved in silence because Siam Johnny only strutted with femmes.

"Thought you walked the deadhead talk."

"That was before Cecil offered a test upload. Life at the speed of thought, no, faster than thought." He went dreamy for a moment, then flashed his trademark smile. "Deadheads are old time, Willy. You got the cred, you pay for someone to take care of your body for you, not like the lowball zombies around here."

He came in close and jabbed me in the solar plexus with a long red-lacquered nail. My mouth watered with the whiskey pull of his breath. "Upload with me. Think of the biz we can scam when we go terminal."

That was, what?, eight, maybe nine months ago, and now the golden boy of Siam was as withered and wasted as the rest of them. My Brutus brain punched me in the nose with the memory of his whitehot rut after a shower, and I got a potato-finger. Maybe if I'd had my chance at him. Maybe not.

I keyed my prompt into the table unit and leaned back. No sense burdening myself with a heaviness that's gone.

The zombie twitched, sat up straight. The eyes blinked, crossed, focused on me. The upload smiled, sneered more like it, and said in a hollow rasp, "Willy Shakes, my favorite bard still in the flesh."

"Long time no see, Cecil. How's tricks?"

Cecil B. DeMillionaire raised Siam Johnny's arm and motioned for a waitress. The zombie in a mini-skirt, proving zombies should never wear mini-skirts, stumbled over her own feet and delivered a Vita-juice. Her wires fed into the spring-reel attached with surgical staples to the back of her head, keeping them untangled and out of the way.

"Can't complain, can't complain," the upload said, breaking the pouch seal. Gray cheeks sank in further then ballooned like tumors with the first swallow. He craned the neck, flexed the elbows, brushed a hand over the front of the jumpsuit and rubbed the dust between bony fingertips. "Looks like Johnny hasn't seen much action lately. Boy had better arrange for more hosting or he'll have to disconnect and take himself to a med stack."

I didn't let on that I'd noticed the same thing, or that it bothered me. Must have showed on my face.

Cecil laughed Vita-juice and morning breath. "Still the diehard deadhead, eh, Willy?"

Cecil blew hard about funding the first one-hundred uploads and how he followed them into "our brave new reality" when the process proved viable. Word had it he was behind the current body swap craze, allowing the chronic uploads to spend their hard-earned creds living the high life for a few hours in better fleshed zombies instead of their own wasted husks. DeMillionaire pulled in good cred in interest from each hosting lease, and the swap craze strapped a whole new monkey to folks' backs.

I shrugged. "What can I say? I'm all for the sins of my original flesh."

"Deadheads," he said, and snorted. "Pathetic."

The Vita-juice had lubed the zombie's pipes. Cecil still sounded hoarse but enough like himself that I couldn't hear Siam Johnny any more. My potato-finger went limp fry. "If I'm so pathetic then why'd you set up the meet?"

"Because you're bacteria, Willy boy, and I need you for the shit work." He thumbed the table unit.

My handheld buzzed. I pulled it from my inside jacket pocket, keyed it to accept the download. Two seconds later, I scrolled through the file. "Mona Twelve-fifty? An upload?"

Cecil nodded, neck popping, skin flaking to dander on the shoulders. "Yes."

I set the handheld on the table. "Too slick."

Cecil cocked a brow. "Pardon?"

A case of he knew I knew he knew all this, but he wanted to play big man. "What's the angle? A snatch-and-grab on an upload means a total disconnect, otherwise when the zombie—"

"Terminal."

"—drops unconscious the upload dumps failsafe back to the net. I'm left with a body and no brain. Immobilize the zombie, the upload dumps back on its own and it's the same thing."

Cecil curled those cracked lips in a smile all his own. "Which is why I want you to disconnect her and hold her incommunicado until we find her terminal and can meet for a closed system download."

I worked the numbers. If this Mona 1250 was downloaded to someone else's zombie and I disconnected her, that started the timer flashing not only on her original body but on the body she inhabited. 72 hours max a zombie could manage disconnected before it flatlined. Same for the upload without its original body on the other end, something about coding limits, or physio-neural dependency, or withdrawals. Uploads talked about the holy grail of permanent uploading and leaving the body behind. They also talked about paying someone to change their sani-pants. Both smelled as sweet to me. "I don't do wet work."

Cecil drained the pouch with a slurp and the crinkle of foil. "I only need you to hold her until my marks bring her terminal for the download."

"And what about the other upload, the one linked to the zombie she's hopped when I disconnect her?"

"So long as you do what you're told, the terminal will be reconnected and no harm done."

Some biz complicated things, made life sticky with damn spots that wouldn't out. Still, I needed to eat. I read the file again. "How much?"

He named a figure. I courtesy countered. We settled where expected, half up front.

I spent the next two days scoping the locations and arranging the snatch. Spec had her moving regularly between three zombies: one in the back room of an abandoned tenement in the White sector; another in a crack ward cum day spa where uploads could treat themselves to deep tissue massage; the third in a tool shed in the processing district. Cecil's marks put her in the tool shed on snatch day, but no timeframe for when she hopped. Damn. No way of knowing if the zombie would be occupied before she got there, and the failsafe wouldn't allow her to hop if I disabled the zombie before she arrived. The rest of the spec looked solid, but I worked all I could on each location just in case.

I also scoped Mona 1250. An odd one, her. One time neuro-programmer, gave it up when her younger brother died from sepsis after a bad port repair. After that she lobbied for standardized zombie healthcare for hosting leases and purchase packages, enforcing age requirements for uploading, and dismantling mandatory coding that "shackled personality to flesh" and "interfered with freedom of identity". She'd even spoken up for improved deadhead employment opportunities. A real martyr for the cause.

The sleepy grooms now smeared with blood, I hit a sweat crib with a deadhead pretty boy who smelled like orange blossoms and hemp, and looked nothing like Siam Johnny.

Snatch day, I paid extra for another go with the pretty boy to work out the tension, cleaned up, checked my feed. No new updates from Cecil, so I slotted a tip and headed out.

I left early enough to take Metro Trans, arranged three re-routes to throw any possibility of a tail. Didn't think it would be a problem, but it never hurt to be too careful with down low biz.

Lots of seats to choose from. I took one near the front. A dozen or so riders, deadheads focused on their handhelds or dozing in their seats. Fewer of us these days, fewer people to appreciate living in the world instead of wire-dreaming the experience. Never understood the allure of wiring, myself. I'm a body man even with all the creaks, aches, rumbles, and farts. Give me the medicine that quickens a stone and makes me dance canary.

The processing district didn't process and wasn't so much a district anymore. Five blocks of squat brick buildings from back in the days of cheap energy now served as storage for mom and pop corporations and uploads not yet ready to relinquish all their material worth. Even the graffiti had seen better days, now nothing more than dull streaks of color beneath layers of dirt and soot.

I took my time on the approach, eyeing for cameras, dogs, or other impediments requiring a zapper. Rusted chain link fences hung with battered CAUTION HARZARDOUS WASTE signs sectioned off the storage yards behind the buildings. All clear this early. I didn't need a key code or cred check; old time picks, a muffler cloth, and a boot heel to the gate latch did the job.

I eased the gate open far enough to slip inside then wedged it shut. I played it safe and stayed close to the walls. Mona 1250's shed stood by the east fence, more an impromptu shack with mismatched block and plank walls, windows painted black on the inside. As before, I caught the low hum of a generator coming from that direction but didn't see any sign of a solar feed. Carbon fueled? Couldn't be.

I slipped to the side, listened, the white noise of the generator too loud to make out any movement. Not only that, a deep breath confirmed the generator ran on carbons. She left no tracks on the energy net. Seemed Mona 1250 had deeper pockets than I thought. One more reason Cecil wanted her out of the way?

The paint job blocked any possible glimpse inside, and reflected any reading so I couldn't get a heat signature with my handheld. I tried a reading through the wall, same result. Well, well. I put the handheld away and eased the air pistol out of my back holster. I preferred a knowledgeable shot, but it wouldn't be the first time I'd gone in blind.

Keeping low, I eased around the corner and set my fingers on the door handle. A cleaner spot in the center suggested regular, if not recent, use, whether from my target or another person wasn't clear. Would she be alone? I would have to chance anyone inside also couldn't hear me over the generator. I'd have time for one shot, maybe two; the neuro-blocks would keep an upload from hopping or a deadhead from moving. My heart kicked it up a notch, and I pushed open the door.

A dark room lit by dull indicator lights, the walls painted the same black as the windows. The bite of carbon fumes enough to make my eyes sting. A quick look in the space between door and frame revealed no one behind the door. A single gaunt figure in a baggy shift leaned over the generator, wires streaming out of its head to a unit on a table behind it. I pumped two quick shots into its neck, and the zombie fell onto the generator.

Figuring it best to weigh the upload more mighty than it seemed, I went in low, hit the bio-feed port safety, and unlocked the zombie's wires. As they snapped back to the spring reel I hadn't noticed, the zombie grunted and slumped. I pulled it off the generator, gently laying it on the floor.

The zombie's eyes rolled in their sockets before focusing on me. "Wut?"

The word came out hollow and slurred from the block, yet with an unmistakable feminine inflection through male pipes. Had to hope it was Mona 1250. The arms spasmed, hands coming up clenched tight. I grabbed both and wrapped them together in plastic filament.

Male. The zombie had a slight build, better fed than some but still undernourished. Could have been nice looking before the wire job. The eyes darted back and forth. "Whu?"

I secured the feet. "Cecil sends his regards."

The entire body twitched. "Nooo."

"Yes." I flashed a penlight in both eyes to check for pupil response. Good. A quick physical exam. The skin rough and papery, zombie reek, two spots of blood on the neck after I removed the darts, no other injuries.

Satisfied she wouldn't go anywhere, I made a thorough search of the shack. An array of scanners, sensors, and other who knew whats arranged on the table with the zombie unit, all attached to a power cable that ran to the generator. A box of freeze dried Soy Joys and pouches of Vita-juice stashed under the table, and beside it a smaller box containing a Match-15 flechette pistol with four extra cartridges. I took the pistol and cartridges. A pile of blankets that smelled like cat piss and rotten onions by the generator, next to that a carton of sani-pants. A knee-high refrigeration unit holding a six-pack of Budrich beer cartons, and a partly-eaten vegan kelp wrap. Not much to look at.

I keyed Cecil on my handheld, signaling all secure. He responded YOU'RE LATE. in blocky red on the screen.

Pretentious bastard. Let's see him make a snatch in his zombie deluxe.

I settled beside the zombie, my back against the cold box. "Hey, Mona. How's tricks?"

"Pleez ..."

"Sorry. We're in this together until the crew gets here with your body."

She turned the head away. Much to my surprise, the upload cried with the zombie's eyes.

Mona 1250 smacked the zombie's swollen lips. "How much is he paying you?"

I named the figure.

"You know he's going to kill me."

I did, but felt it impolite to agree with the dead. I fed her the last piece of Soy Joy. "If he'd wanted to kill you, why not ice your body and leave you to unravel on the net?"

She mumbled the concentrate between stubby teeth. "Because he wants what I know, and when he has it he'll make an example of me to the others."

Thirteen hours in, the hot air of the shack reeked of zombie stink, carbon fumes, and piss. Between the uneven purr of the generator and the poor lighting, I had a proper skull-ache and my skin felt too tight.

I'd positioned the zombie, still bound and in clean sani-pants, sitting up against the wall beside the refrigeration unit.

I held up a Vita-juice. She shook the head, no. I crumpled the empty Soy Joy wrapper, and stood to walk off the cramps.

I'd worked the numbers again since disconnecting Mona 1250: about her brother; her shadow files, a few anyway; other habits; her contact with some of the survivors of the Moscow digital killjoy a few years back. The new data came on the down low, taking particular care to keep Cecil deaf and blind.

She watched as I rolled my shoulders and rearranged thoughts. She'd mentioned Cecil's interest before, some kind of wiring tech I supposed; she'd refused to answer the one time I'd asked. Others, though, first time she'd said anything like that. "Others?"

"Like me, who believe we're ready for the next step."

The wistful tone so familiar, my chest ached.

I paced the measure of the shack, my world's stage and myself a player of many parts. Yeah, I'd worked the numbers, and I didn't like how they added up. What to do? Sit quiet and dumb for the cred, or confirm I was the wise man who realized he was a fool. I took a chance, opened the refrigeration unit. "Want a beer?" Held my breath.

Mona 1250 stared at me. "I don't drink beer."

Of course not. She didn't drink beer. Cecil met me through Siam Johnny's zombie to get me on his side because everyone knew Willy Shakes saw biz through to the curtain call whether or not he liked the production. I looked from the wrap in the refrigeration unit to the zombie's mouthful of rotting teeth. This zombie couldn't have taken those bites. "How many others?"

She hesitated. "Enough." And with surprising passion: "Not labels or classes, but people no matter how they choose to live."

A big production, indeed. "You unlocked the coding for permanent uploads. That's what Cecil wants from you."

Mona 1250 stared at me, zombie eyes fever bright if such a thing was possible.

"You want to offer it up for a smaller cut—"

"For free."

"Oh, that's even better." I slammed the unit shut hard enough that its stabilizer blinked in protest. "An upload with a conscience. Talk about an improbable fiction." I laughed, an ugly sound. "Give it away and then what happens?"

"People live better lives."

"Better? You, you think so?" I would die a beggar, and not a comet to be seen. I couldn't stop laughing, the sound echoing inside my head. "You and your band of merry thieves even stop once to think about what you're doing? Do you remember what it was like when people first uploaded, how hard it was then? You ever think what this wiring miracle will do to the world, how many lives you'll destroy, or were you too busy wallowing in your own good intentions?"

Mona 1250 nodded the zombie head. Nodded at me, damn her. "You're right, it won't be easy at first, but in the end the coding will allow people the freedom to work, live, and exist as they choose whether in their own bodies, as temporary uploads, or permanently on the web. Or beyond."

Gear lights blinked, the generator hummed, wind whistled through the crack under the door. I hated her calm, even tone, how reasonable she made it sound. Hated Siam Johnny for leaving me. I looked anywhere but at the zombie. No wonder Cecil wanted her out of the way. Nothing more dangerous than a fanatic with a noble cause.

My handheld signaled incoming. Cecil. I cued for audio only. "Willy."

"Where are you?" Cecil said from the black screen. Did I hear echoes of Siam Johnny in those pipes?

"Busy. What's the word?"

"Is Mona Twelve-fifty with you?"

"Not right now. She's inside. I'm taking a dump."

"How poetic. We have her body. ETA four hours."

I glanced up at the zombie. "Please," she said without sound.

"I'm good. Remind them to bring clean sani-pants." I terminated the connection.

"What's it like?" I said when I could speak without putting a three punch of flechettes between the zombie's eyes.

In spite of the upload's fear, the zombie's expression softened, the eyes unfocused. "It's like ... flying, only better. No, not flying. Like flying in your dreams, only more substantial, an encompassing reality. You don't do, you are. I've ... gone other places beyond ..."

I'd seen that expression before, seen it and wished I could be the reason. "Faster than thought."

She came back from the description, back to me, the shack, the disconnected zombie prison killing her by seconds. I didn't do femmes or zombies, but could have kissed her just then.

"Eighty-eight thousand, one hundred twenty-three people died last year as the result of improper implants, post-surgical or terminal health complications," Mona 1250 said. "Four-thousand sixty of them were under the age of twelve. An additional twenty-eight thousand, nine hundred people were diagnosed with severe psychological trauma and irreparable harm resulting from disconnects or med stack diagnostic error. Over two million total since the first uploads eight years ago. My coding will also serve as the platform for better terminal status monitoring and care. I may not be able to save them all, but I can't sit back and do nothing."

Cecil B. DeMillionaire, millions earned, millions burned. His payout would taste like Siam Johnny's zombie, twigs and sandpaper in my mouth. I put my back against the refrigeration unit, rubbed my face. "I bet you can quote the statistics for every year since your brother's death."

No answer. I didn't need any.

When I could speak, I didn't know what to say. When I knew what to say, I didn't want to. "You were predictable, a closed loop with at least two other uploads if I figure right. Each one of you in a different location, working a different angle. That's how Cecil found you. If they've timed it clean, Cecil's marks disconnected the other zombies about the time I hit you."

A sharp intake of breath from behind, a softer sound of despair.

Tasting honey sweat and whiskey breath, I slipped my snapknife out of my back pocket. I rolled to the zombie and came up on my knees. The eyes were wide. Fear for herself or the realization that idealism could be worse than merely fatal? "The fact that no one's come to check on you after the disconnect is a good sign that he has any local deadheads incommunicado or worse. I don't expect he'll take too fondly to me once he figures things out, but I plan to trip away and make no stay."

I cut the filament around wrist and ankles.

Mona 1250 brought the legs up, tried to stand. I made it to my feet first and gave her a hand up. The zombie's palm was dry and cold, the grip strong.

"I expect an advance mark before your body gets here to scope you out." I jerked my head towards the table. "Do you need any of that?"

Mona 1250 drew back, looked at the table, shook the head. "That's for back-up. The original computations are—"

"Somewhere else, fine. Help me with this."

Not that a zombie could do much, but together we managed to drag the generator to the center of the shack and tip it over. I unscrewed the cap, then skipped back as carbon fuel poured out.

Mona 1250 moved the feet out of the way, not quickly enough to avoid the splash. "What are you doing?"

"How long until you go online with your code?"

The eyes blinked, the expression cagey for a moment, then a quick nod. "Less than twenty-four hours. We need to secure the server and—"

"You have four, six at the most."

"We can't—"

I jerked a length of wire from the reel on her head, released the port safety, and plugged the zombie in. "Tell Siam Johnny Willy Shakes asked how's tricks."

Mona 1250 turned the lips down in a frown, opened the mouth to ask, but something of my expression stopped her. Good, because I no longer had the voice to answer.

The zombie nodded, the eyes rolled back in its head, and it collapsed in the spreading pool of fuel.

I'm an honest Puck. I made amends to the fellow who's body burned with the shack. Maybe he'd like life as a permanent upload.

Good luck, Mona 1250. Good night, Siam Johnny. I'd say good night until tomorrow.

Author's Note

Confession time. I hate zombies. Books, movies, television shows, comics, costumes, all of it. What began as a specific cultural reference has been warped into a twisted, stunted version of itself. Zombies are now a way to blame something outside ourselves for our own shortcomings. Nukes, super bugs, mob violence, racism, sexism, environmental pollution, all of it. Zombies made us do it. Beyond enjoying the campy game mechanics of the ZOMBICIDE board games, I could happily leave zombies by the side of the road to starve for lack of their own popularity. So what did I do? I wrote my own sort of zombie story.

Should you ever be so inclined, I highly recommend the Horrible Histories British sketch comedy show (2009 – 2013, worth tracking down, seriously, I mean it). The show explores the dirtier, sillier, harder to believe truths of history, "gory, ghastly, mean and cruel, stuff they don't teach you in school" and it is a hoot! One of my favorite skits is the William Shakespeare song where the Bard sings some of his best known quotes. A touch of cyberpunk, a few zombies, a dash of Shakespeare, and walla! Willy Shakes was born.

Just Be

It was a muggy, porch sitting Saturday afternoon when the stranger came northbound along Rural Route #16. He was clean and well put for a man, save for the dust and sweat of the road. He touched the brim of his weathered hat and set a booted left foot on the worn step of Burt Mitchum's storefront. "Howdy. You fellas know where I can find the Levendis homestead?"

"Levendis? You mean the old Levi place? Up the way two miles or so." Partridge Maycomb pointed north with his sweaty bottle of RC Cola. He noticed the stranger's eyes, goat's eyes, but didn't say nothing as it wasn't his business.

"Out on behind the poplar grove on your left as you go," Seth Blovett said, and spit chew juice over the railing. He saw how the man's ring fingers were longer than the middle ones, but wasn't one to say so.

"Ain't much to the place. Run down. Been some time since folks lived there." Carl Mays took in how the fellow's ears were pointed, but figured it wasn't his place to speak out.

The stranger brought his boot back to the dirt road. "Thank you kindly."

Bubba Maycomb, Partridge's half-wit son, watched the stranger walk on. "Pa, hey, Pa, you see that fella's—?"

"Never you mind, Bubba," Partridge said, and finished his RC.

Near on two miles up the road, the stranger turned left at the crown of summer poplars. The house was small and not much to look at, but he didn't see it run down at all. The windows were whole and the door clear of high grasses. The plank walls wore fresh whitewash. An apple tree with low branches promised good pickings come fall. A patchwork quilt of asters, goldenrod, and ox-eye daisies made up the front yard. A comfortable place, not so much lonesome as content to be alone. He pushed his hat back and strode up the dusty drive and around the house on the left.

He found what he was looking for past a march of poplar on the far side of the backfield. A golden-haired boy squatted in the thick mud alongside a tumbling creek, faded overalls rolled up to his knees. With a crooked stick, he turned rocks over a splash at a time.

The stranger came along side and hunkered down. The mud dried up and cracked around his boots. "Howdy."

"Howdy," said the boy without looking up.

"What'cha hunting?"

"Mudbugs. Or treasure, sometimes."

The stranger picked up a smooth black rock and tossed it into the water. He breathed in the heat of the day, the cool of the stream. "What sort of treasure?"

"All kinds. I found this yesterday." The boy reached into his right front pocket and pulled out a ragged tube of woven paper-thin strips of wood once red or green, now faded and dirty. "Hold out your hands."

The stranger obliged, and the boy slid one end of the tube over each of the stranger's first fingers. "Now try to get loose," the boy said with a smile. His eyes were blue as the sky, with sunbeam lashes.

The stranger moved his hands apart; the tube tightened until it was snug around his fingers. "Well."

The boy picked up his stick. "Some trick, huh?"

"You could say so."

A shape scurried out from under a tipped rock, and quick like the boy picked it up for a closer look. He turned the mudbug this way and that, its legs and claws going every which way, then set it back in the water.

The stranger eased his hands together and freed his fingers, left, right. He set the tube on his left knee, smoothed it flat. "You always let them go?"

"Yup."

"Good of you."

There wasn't no wrong in the silence that settled between them, but soon the boy sighed and scrunched up without moving. He put himself more inside his skin, like as if he didn't want to say what had to be said. "I like it here."

"So do I," said the stranger. "Real nice place."

"I don't got to rush none, or worry."

"Yup."

"You ain't going away, are you?"

"Nope."

The boy poked his stick in the mud. Two twigs near the top stood out crosswise. "It's not fair."

"C'mon now." The stranger's words were gentle. "Deal's a deal. We take turns, here or anywhere, that's how it's always been."

The boy's shoulders sagged low as his frown. "It's so hard. All most folks want me for anymore is for wanting. Round here, I can be myself like I used to, even have my name to myself again. It's all peaceful."

"I know. No demands or foolery. No deals." The stranger stared straight on at the sun, unblinking. "We can just be."

They touched hands and kept company with the creek until the boy sighed and made his feet. "All right." He rolled down the legs of his coveralls. "You take care of the place, 'kay?"

"Always do." Mud oozed around the stranger's boots. "Take your time comin' round again."

The golden-haired boy headed towards the house. He looked back once, only once, as a dark-haired boy with two left feet unlaced his boots so's to feel the cool mud between his toes with no one around to call Old Scratch out for doing it.

The yellow-haired stranger headed southbound towards the bend in Rural Route #16. His overalls was faded but clean, and he wore a John Deere ball cap far back on his head. He smiled bright and friendly— "Howdy, fellas." —as he walked straight into Burt Mitchum's, and equal friendly when he walked out with a frosty RC Cola and fried bologna sandwich and went on down the steps.

Bubba Maycomb watched the stranger walk on. "Pa, Pa, you see that fella's—?"

"Never you mind, Bubba," Partridge said, and took another swig of cola on a muggy, porch sitting Saturday afternoon.

Author's Note

This is one of my gentle stories, one of the stories that would surprise people who love my longer work. There are no monsters or struggles, no trauma or even crazy slapstick, only a brief moment between two friends seeking shelter before heading back into the storm. This is my favorite of my flash pieces.

Samaritan

At the sound of hoof beats, I came around the corner with my courage and my axe. The last white riders didn't like no free black man working his own land. An axe couldn't do much against a gun, but I'd cut down as many as I could before I let them set a hand on my skin, and God have mercy on their souls if they put an eye on my baby girl.

A single rider came in fast, his horse foaming and streaked with sweat and west Texas dust. Not a thing came behind him. I put myself between him and the house, ready to call him out, when I caught sight of the horse's horns. Two of them, long, sharp, jutting out front of its head and made pretty with silver rings dangling from the tips. In all my years, I'd never seen a horse with horns.

The rider pulled to rein. I thought about taking a step towards the animal, thought twice about not. "Howdy," I said when I could.

The horse tossed its head. Them rings sounded like far off church bells on a cool spring morning. The rider turned to me, head bowed beneath the wide brim of his dusty hat so as I couldn't see his face, but I could see his long, white hands that never worked a day. He wore a trench over dark britches, and a shirt stained fresh red across the belly. I looked from the stain, to the horse, to the wide-brimmed hat. That's when the rider fell out of the saddle and onto his face.

I dropped the axe and run to him. The horse whinnied and scampered back when I called out, "Ruth, come quick!"

My girl come running onto the porch. She stopped cold at the sight of the horse. "Da?"

She sounded scared. Couldn't say that I blamed her. "Get the bucket and bring water from the creek."

As I talked, my hands worked up the rider all on their own. His hat came off to show hair bright as the sun, and a wicked gash over his right eye. He smelled like fresh cut hay and the hot copper of new blood. I looked up at the horse, those horns. The rider was white, but he weren't from around here.

Ruth stood stone still on the porch.

"Get on now!"

She done moved at that. I shouldered the rider up the front steps and into the house. I expected to work under him, but he weighed next to nothing for a fellow his size. The Devil's voice weighed me down more, saying I should leave him in the dust. What did I owe some man who would sell me and my kin soon as look at us? For all my fear, I kept hold of the truth of the Good Samaritan and put the Devil and his wicked tongue behind me.

I stretched the fellow out on my rickety bed; his feet hung over the end. At the sound of those rings, jingling like far off church bells, he groaned and opened eyes the swirling green of leaves in a stream, calling out something I didn't understand.

"You're gonna be just fine, mister," I said, working his arms out of his coat.

I can't say as he heard a word I said, but he closed his eyes and went limp. A hand on his chest made sure he was still breathing.

Ruth come back in with the water, and I had her put it on the fire to boil the way Delilah would have done before the Lord called her and baby Matthew home.

Ruth twisted the bottom of her blue sack dress in her hands. "I can give the horse water, too, can't I, Da? A little water won't give it no colic, right?"

By then I had the rider's shirt pulled up and his belt undone. "You're straight on smart, baby girl. A sip or two won't hurt none. Just set the bucket in front of it. Wake up the fire and set the dish rags in the water pot to boil before you go."

A smart girl, my Ruth, smart and pretty like her momma. I sure could have used Delilah's's hands beside mine. She'd always had a way of nursing body and soul back to health, but she was in Heaven not quite a year now and I had to make do on my own.

The gash on his forehead bled some yet weren't so bad as the cut in his side, all jagged like someone took to sawing him in half and stopped after a stroke or two. A few bruises, some scratches, the backs of his hands sliced ragged. I plastered his head and hands with brown paper and witch hazel, and cleaned up his belly with the dishrags after they boiled a time. Then I got my sewing kit and set to stitching his side with thread soaked in a little Sunday sipping whiskey. He grunted with the push of the needle, but didn't make no other complaint.

I took my time, did my best, all I could do. There weren't much light except for what came through the door and the chinks in the mud daub between the logs. I studied his skin, pale as moonlight on milk.

And his ears. I brushed that sunlight hair back over those strange double points on top, and the fine gold hoops and chains on the bottoms.

I took the water off the fire, set the soup pot back over the edge of the coals.

Ruth kept her eyes to the stranger like she was curious but too afraid to get near. "He gonna die, Da?"

"That's for the Lord to say. Get on out now."

Sitting at bedside all day only ate up sunlight, so I headed out after her to see about the rider's horse. That strange beast nosed the red dirt near the water bucket like it was looking for grass that just weren't there, like it were a real horse and didn't have no horns. Ruth watched from the porch as I come down the steps slow and easy. The horse looked up with swirling eyes like the rider's, bright silver instead of green.

"What you gonna do?" she said, tugging on her dress.

"Don't rightly know. Hey, there." I kept my voice low. I figured if horses liked such talk, chances was a horse with horns would too. "You're a big fella, ain't you?"

The horse shook its head, pranced, twitched its tail. Were that some kind of horned horse talk? Did it understand me?

The horse let me set a hand on its neck. It had a strong pulse under the chestnut hair, not so fast at all. It smelled musky like a horse, but of growing things, too, like the rider. Close up, I eyed the sleek lump of the saddle, the two small saddle bags on the rump, how the bridle weren't that much different than ones I'd seen before even though the beast's teeth were coyote sharp.

The horse sighed, shifted a mite. "Good boy," I kept up softly. "Good boy. Come on, now."

A bucket of water hadn't done it no harm, so I told Ruth to sit tight and led the horse to the creek south of the house. Right away it dipped its head and began to drink. When I tried to lead it away, the horse stayed solid put until it had its fill of the muddy water. Seemed the beast knew what it needed.

With no rains for well on three months, it was a wonder the creek run at all. That set me to thinking again about packing up, selling off the acreage to the railroad men. Rumor had it they was coming through and paid good money for land, maybe even to a black man like me. I could take the money and move to San Fransisco, get on with a good job, maybe find my baby girl a new momma. After the war, Delilah and me headed west before anyone could tell us otherwise. Our own land, freedom, a family. Now her memory and two graves were all that kept us here, and memories didn't feed hungry bellies come another winter.

More of the Devil's tricks. I tore up handfuls of dried grass and brushed the horse down. When it were finished drinking, I led it round back to the lean-to where I used to keep Julius before I traded him for eggs and flour.

The saddle didn't look heavy, but I couldn't let the horse suffer under the weight in the heat. I had the kit-and-caboodle on the ground when I caught eye of a green glow coming from the nearest saddlebag. Had it been glowing before and I just now noticed it? I looked around. The horse stood quiet, and Ruth weren't nowhere to be seen, so I eased open the flap thinking I'd close up whatever were open then head on back to chopping wood.

Inside the bag were some dried fruit and a small box, like some sort of woman's keepsake, with that green glow seeping from under the lid. Knowing it were a sin, but too curious to tell the Devil to mind his own matters, I lifted the lid to peek inside. Out shot every color of spring like a rainbow of birds. Reds, yellows, greens, blues, all of them come together smelling of tart green apples and cool water. The light spilled up over my face and onto the uneven lean-to planks. A peace come over me, so profound that I lost myself in its ease.

I stayed like that on my hands and knees until the horse nuzzled my shoulder with its cool damp nose. I closed the box and the glow went away, though the ease lingered, and with it a touch of fear because I wanted with a powerful wanting to open the box again. Maybe the Devil knew something I didn't.

I checked on the rider before midday. Sleeping fitful, calling out in his dreams, words I didn't know. I wiped his face and chest with a wet rag. Those swirling eyes drifted open without seeing much, then closed. I set the rag on his neck with a prayer for his health and peace in the Lord. I didn't have no idea if my Lord were the same as his, but a prayer couldn't hurt.

Come afternoon, I was shucking a pitiful few ears of corn from my withered garden and thinking about that wanting feeling when a rider came in from the north, riding easy. A small, sun-dark man on a thick-bodied dun, bedroll strapped behind him, no gun that I could see. He looked road-lonesome, but I could tell from the squint that in his eyes his whiteness was still better than my blackness.

He stopped a neighborly distance away. "Howdy, boy."

Made my neck prickle, the way he said it. I didn't look away or wring my hat. This was my land. "Howdy yerself."

Odd to have two riders on the same day. And I wondered at how he looked at everything but me, like looking for something that weren't found.

He tipped his head to see around the back of the house. "Name's Jed Bothell. Looking for work. I'm handy with an axe and saw. I can put up fences or push a barrow."

"Strong working man is always a good thing, but I got no work for you nor money to pay if I did."

His eyes told me he didn't like straight talk from colored folk. I kept shucking my corn.

"Not for pay," he said after a while. "A good meal and a place to rest my head is enough for me."

Those words didn't sit well. Maybe how he said them, or the way he hitched his lips when he did.

"Can't help you there none, neither. Widow Carson a mile or so west of here—" I pointed that way. "—she can always use an eager hand, and she's a right good cook."

He squinted his eyes at me in deep and sour thought. Then he smiled, tight-lipped. "Thanks kindly, boy."

Weren't nothing kind about him. "My name is Solomon Hatchett and this is my land."

"Apologies. Solomon." He put a finger to the brim of his hat. "Nice to know folk are looking out for their neighbors."

"Yup."

He watched me for some little time. "That corn there lookin' kind of puny."

I picked up another cob, tearing open the husk with a green sound and smell that brought on thoughts of the rider. "Yup. Eats puny, too."

He shifted in the saddle. "Been a while since I had me corn so fresh I seen it shucked."

"Widow Carson put up some fine corn relish last summer. Ask her for some with her biscuits."

"Oh." Jed looked again towards the back of the house. Two fingers of his right hand fiddled with a thing in his vest pocket. "It's sure on hot. You got a place I could set Martha out of the sun, bo – Solomon? Maybe I could step inside the house for a sip of cool water?"

I had a sudden longing for my shotgun, and not only cause I'd seen his kind before. "Didn't need the lean-to so I cut it up for kindling, and there's cooler water in the crick if you can find it through the mud."

I saw it again, that sour look. It cleared as quickly as it come. "No matter. I'll ask on with the widow."

Jed turned his mare around and headed off a few steps, then stopped and fumbled at his chest. He held out his hand, slowly moving it this way and that, stopping finally in the direction of the woodshed and lean-to.

"Problem there, Jed?"

He moved his hand to his chest, like to put something back in his pocket. "Just getting light enough to check the time. Eyes ain't what they used to be and all." Jed looked over his shoulder, tipped his hat. "Have a good evening."

Would have been easier to believe him if his shadow weren't long towards the woodshed.

I stayed put until Jed Bothell was mostly out of sight, then brought the corn inside and put it on the table. The rider lay eyes closed and quiet on the bed. I went over to check the plaster on his head and he grabbed my hand in one of his. He opened them eyes, stared up at me hard as flint, then croaked out something I didn't understand. He made the same sounds again. I tried to pull my hand away, but his grip kept me to him like a shackle.

A terrible rage come on me then. I weren't no animal for him to grab. I earned my freedom from President Abraham Lincoln! Lord help me, I raised my fist against that strange rider and the Devil laughed in my face, laughed and called me out as a coward if I didn't name myself a man and strike that rider down.

God Hisself stopped me. God said, *Son, look at him, give him all your eyes. Look at him, see him, see the man hurt and alone in a strange place. Fixing to get beat because he different.* Because he talked best he could and it sounded all gibberish to me.

Lord above, Lord above. That's all I could think for the longest time. Lord above.

I uncurled my fingers, drew a hard breath, and set that hand on top of the rider's trembling fingers. "I don't know what you're sayin'. You speak good American, maybe? Or Mexican? Habla español?"

He pulled me down and hisself up until we were close enough that I could feel his breath warm against my cheek. He said whatever it were, more slow without much breath, eyes tight on my face.

"I'm sorry, mister. I don't ken to what you're telling me."

He sagged and let go my hand.

I made him comfortable, fetched a wet rag to mop his face. A sip of water dribbled more down his chin than in his mouth. He lay his head back.

"A stranger come and went. Is that it? He wanted to look around, but I called him off. Lord only knows what he were after, but I made sure he didn't see nothing about you or your horse."

Should I say something about the glowing box? Best not. "I need to check my stitch work. Can I do that?"

The rider turned his head away and closed his eyes.

The stitches looked healthy, smelled like fresh grass with no hint of blood at all. The rider didn't say nothing else, didn't take no water when I offered. In time he fell back to sleep.

That night after a supper of soup and the last of the cheese, Ruth asked, "Why you cleanin' your gun?"

My little girl played with her rag doll. The rider slept sound on my bed.

"I thought I saw a rattlesnake." I kissed the top of her curly head. "You go on and wash your face, and get on to bed."

The Lord helps those that help themselves. I figured it were better to be ready for help and not need it than need it and be waiting for the Lord in vain.

Dark shapes eyed me from the trees. Leeches with great, heavy chains and swirling gray eyes dragged me under murky water, biding on my last breath, watching, waiting...

I gave a little scream and sat bolt upright from my pallet by the fire. Ruth stirred beside me, and I peeked under her blanket to make sure there weren't no leeches or chains. Nothing but her rag doll. I let out a shaking breath, covered her back up, and looked to the rider.

In the faint red light of burned down coals, I saw him at the end of the bed, head bent over cupped hands. Sounded to me like he whispered a prayer, but that might could have been the wind. Maybe he had the box? I eased forward, hoping to have another peek inside.

"You all right?" I said real soft.

He poured whatever were in his hands into a bag. The mess of things sounded heavy and a bit like metal. He stood real slow, then staggered with his bag of something over to my shotgun by the door. Lord help me, I had some unchristianly thoughts.

He brought the sack and gun to me, and offered them up. For a minute, I didn't know how to think of it, but I finally took them with my held breath. The sack was filled with shotgun shells. I breathed out. "What am I gonna do with these?"

He didn't bother talking this time, just pointed to the bag, the gun, then me.

I looked at him standing there, a milk pale magic man, eyes aglow. "These ain't for normal men, is they? You did somethin' to them because there's, there's somethin' else comin'. Lord above, what kind of man are you?"

The rider all but fell back on the bed. He drew a deep breath and freed it in a sigh, pulled his blanket around him, and turned on his side, away from me.

I fished a handful of shells out of the bag. They glowed like some faint star, high in the sky, so soft the light barely brushed my palm. Most went into the pockets of my dungarees, but for two I cracked the breech, slipped them in, and closed it up with a snap.

I stirred the coals, and went to fetch me my Sunday whiskey, in need of a sip for all it were Wednesday. The box didn't feel so needful anymore when all I could think on were leeches and chains and dark night fears.

I hadn't meant to sleep, but the next thing I know my head came up at the sound of hoof beats in the early morning light steaming through the walls.

Ruth raised her sleepy head. "Someone comin', Da?"

Lots of someone by the sound of it. The rider weren't nowhere to be found. Righteous fear wiped away any sleep in me, fear for what might come for the rider and find me and my baby girl in his place. "Nothin' but a dream. Close your eyes and go back to sleep."

Strange drowsy like, she laid her head down. I took up my gun and made for the door. Outside rode up four horses from the direction the rider come yesterday morning, three riders on chestnuts with long, slender horns, and Jed Bothell on his dun.

I come down the stairs easy like, the gun down but ready. "How you come on with Widow Carson, Jed?"

He hitched his shoulders in a sort of shrug. "Wouldn't know," he said, not bothering to hide his hate for me. "My friends here are looking for someone and think he might be here. They aim to have a look around."

He didn't have no sidearm that I could see, but the other three had jagged swords under their long coats. My fingers tightened on the gun. "You tell them there ain't no one here that has business with them."

The other three riders looked me up and down. Their eyes swirled dark gray beneath wide-brimmed hats. They had that same milk pale skin like the green-eyed rider before them, the same smooth, long hands. Could have been brothers for all I knew, but the wind made dust devils behind them, and brought me the smell of rotting leaves and dead things.

One urged his horse forward and talked at me in those different words. I somehow expected he'd sound like a rattler's tail, but his words had preacherful grace. He touched a hand to his sword's grip. That weren't grace.

They could have been a righteous gathering, those gray-eyed riders, but their smell and their eyes said they wasn't to be trusted. Jed Bothell, he didn't look shamed or scared or nothing, just sat there like a cat waiting for Lucifer hisself to pour a bowl of cream. And they was looking for a man I doctored up in good faith.

I pulled back the hammers. "I don't right know what he said, and don't much care to, so it's best if you all turn around and—"

From behind the house come a scream that curled my toes and brought my gun to bear. Faster than spit, the first rider come around the back corner, dug his heels into his horse's flanks, and jumped the beast right over the one closest to me. An unshod hoof caught the gray-eyed rider in the face, tumbling him into the Texas dirt. That quick, the first rider came down on the other side and wheeled around, hair wild and green eyes full of burn.

One gray-eyed rider gestured. Black vines erupted from the ground and twined around the legs of the first rider's horse. The horse screamed again, and the sound knocked the surprise right out of me. I opened up with both barrels at that same gray-eyed rider, and caught him high in the chest. He flew back off his horse, and the vines turned to dust.

The rider on the ground near me come up on his knees, sword in hand, and hissed words at me through his bloody mask.

My heart clenched tight and I screamed. I couldn't breathe, couldn't think, dropped the gun and to my knees as pain fired my whole body. I felt my heart take its last beat. Sweet Delilah said my name.

The world turned black all around, hoof beats came at me hard. Jed Bothell yelled something. I heard another scream—mine?—and my chest swelled with light. The Lord stood me right up and pushed me out of the way as the first rider, off his horse now, pulled one of them swords out of the chest of the gray-eyed rider on the ground.

I took up the shotgun and slapped two shells home. Fast as that, I fired at the last gray-eyed rider, catching his horse in the neck with both rounds. The beast went up on its back legs and fell over. That rider twisted out of the saddle quicker than I've ever seen a man move until the first rider leapt even faster and drove him to the ground with the sword between them.

Another reload. I pinned Jed Bothell in my sights. "Don't move."

Jed held his hands out wide and empty, his face pasty white and afraid of a black man like he'd never been before. "I-I ain't raised a hand against you. Don't go doin' nothin' rash."

Both hammers came back. The Devil whispered temptation, *shoot him, shoot him!*, but I kept God in my heart. "That's right, so you get offa my land before I decide you need a good scratchin'."

He wasted no time riding back the way he came.

It was done. The first rider scrambled off the last gray-eyed rider, leaving the sword sticking out of the sumbitch's chest. Fresh blood slicked the first rider's shirt beneath his coat and a scorch mark covered where a man would have a heart.

He staggered to his horse, tore open his saddlebag, and pulled out the keepsake box. I thought to feel that strong need again, but it never came. I'm ashamed to say I felt a mite sad at that.

The rider opened the lid a bare bit. A rainbow lit over his face, and he let out a sigh more like a sob. He closed the box and set it real gentle back in the saddlebag, whispering grace-filled words. That's when he turned to me and smiled, and we understood one another just fine.

Ruth slept right through. I don't know why I woke up, maybe on account of being responsible for my land.

The rider gathered up the horses on a lead behind his own. They didn't mind none, nor when he spoke words over the gray-eyed riders and they turned brown and crumbly at the touch of his hands. He stared at the remains for a time, writing green fire letters with a long finger through the piles. The fire faded, leaving dark mounds reminiscent of good earth. He swept the piles into his hat with the side of his hand, favoring his left side as he went.

"Let me have a look at them stitches," I said. I wasn't sure what could be done about the burn.

He ignored me until every bit of brown was scooped into the hat, then stood and gestured at me to follow him to the paltry garden beyond the house. I did.

I stood by as he scattered fistfuls of remains over the rows. "We got to be eatin' that," I said.

He smiled at me and threw out another bunch. That smile said whole books worth, but I'd no idea what it meant beyond good will.

The sun was full over the horizon and promising Texas heat by the time we walked back to the horses. He didn't speak against me when I gave him a hand into the saddle. I pointed to the saddlebag. "You take care of that, you hear?"

He smiled again, pointed towards the garden, and I liked to think said the same. I looked over my shoulder and shook my head to clear what I saw. Couldn't be. New green spread over the cornstalks, plumped the beans.

I turned back around. The rider and horses were dust on the other side of the clear running creek.

Author's Note

I am a fat, white, genderqueer, pansexual, disabled, mentally ill, mother of two special needs boys, married to a wonderful partner with their whole parcel of other identities to juggle. We have friends of all ages. African American, Latinx American, Asian American,

Pacific Islander American, and any flavor of religion. They extend across the range of gender, preference, and sexual identity, and span the political spectrum. Mentally or physically disabled, some survivors of abuses from their childhood and adult lives. When my world is filled with such beauty and horrors, why, then, would I limit my stories to those involving straight, cis, white folks? I want to see myself in stories. I want to see my friends in stories. I want to read the stories my friends write. I want to cheer them on so they can fill the world with their incredible stories.

Representation matters. I don't always get it right in my stories. I've gotten it horribly wrong and more than once been called on the carpet for it. So I learn, and next time I try to do better. And when I fuck it up again, I know folks will be there to hold me accountable for my words. Good.

/climbs off soap box until the next time

Curtain Call

The technician buffed my face, swapped my blue eyes for green, and lubed my joints. She polished my chest and used the reflection to touch up her make-up. "There you go, Ms. Starlight. Wha'd'ya think?"

I pranced and dipped in front of the mirror on the back of the dressing room door. "I think it's show time, baby cakes!"

I grabbed my wrap, and headed out front.

Onstage, Big Eddie Flashpoint did me right in that lady-loving baritone of his: "Luscious Ladies and groovin' Gentleamps, it's that time again, time for fast beats and slow heat. Put your hands together for The Joystick's Stainless Steel Siren, Miss Gina Starlight!"

Bright searchlights swept over the audience, catching neon silk suits, the chrome curve of bare shoulders. The boys came in on three, and I exploded onto the stage in silver and gold. I opened my arms and owned the house, every last erg. "Twilight Madame," "Gearing Up For Love," "Spark and Shine, Be Mine!" Sal Ballastern, bless his faulty pump, would have cried himself rusty to hear "Sweet Silver Sassy" for my second encore.

Benny Gracenote, the club owner, waited in my dressing room after the set. "Gina! Sweetheart! You were terrific!"

He came at me arms wide, all puckered up.

I wasn't having none of it. I gave him a palm to the chest. "Hold it right there, grabby gears. We need to talk."

He bumped against the vanity table, rattling my polishes and oils. "Talk? What? Huh?"

"I want a new chassis."

Benny rolled his eyes. They clicked and popped in their sockets. "Gina, sweetheart, we've been over this before."

"I want a new chassis."

"Times are tough all over. Money's tight."

"Don't you give me none of that money's tight malarkey. I pull them in six nights a week, pack the house, double the drinks, right? Right?" I crossed my arms over my chest, better to show off the goods and hide them at the same time.

"Well ..."

"You know I'm right."

Benny dropped his arms and looked away. "About that."

He started in. Fewer customers, fewer receipts at the end of the night, tough times all around. I stamped my foot and demanded to know who did he think he was? Who did he think he could get that could sing half as good as I could? It's not like I was ever going to be—

"Replaced?" My hair snarled and rerouted. I pushed him into the vanity again. "What are you talking about? When? By who?"

Benny reached for me and his handkerchief at the same time. "Gina, listen, sweetheart, it's not what you think."

I brought my four-inch heel down on his instep. "Who?"

"Ow! Patsy— ow! ow! —Patsy Bellbottom."

"That factory knock-off?" I sat down, cleared my throat. Benny hurried to push in my chair. "What's she got that I ain't got?"

"Gina, Gina, it's not what you ain't, I mean, don't got, it's just that Patsy is, you know ..."

"Lighter? A newer model? Has bigger heat sinks?"

All the above.

Patsy had a spiff new composite chassis that needed less bracing under the stage, which meant lower insurance rates. Her heat sinks, well, word had it they was something to see.

"I was thinking of expanding and wanted, you know, fresh oil to liven up the place. And with your contract coming up, I just figured you might want a break, and the audience might want—"

I gave him my angry profile. "A body so tight it's got the plugs for the plays?"

"—something new."

I sniffed. I fingered a bouquet of copper carnations on the vanity, a gift from a sweetie in the audience. Sal used to bring me flowers after every show until his wife found out he was rewiring me on the side. "After all I done for The Joystick, that you should treat me this way."

"Sweetheart, don't be like— "

"I signed on when this place was nothing but a plank bar and a fistful of stripped wires. I'm what keeps the customers coming back."

"Well, now—"

I grabbed my comb. "I done you a real favor, you know? All I'm asking for is a new chassis."

Benny put his hands on my shoulders. "It's business, Gina, nothing personal, you know that."

I made like I didn't know I was leaning against him. "Big deal."

"And, hey! I got great news. Me and some friends, we put our heads together, and I got a new opportunity for you."

I sat a little straighter. New opportunity? I loved The Joystick, but Benny knew some big names with bigger marquees. Maybe an upgrade, my name in lights. Maybe his way of making up for being such an insulated jerk. I combed the sparks into my hair. "Where?"

"The Cathode Ray!"

That was my last wire. I threw him out on his ear.

I was so mad I couldn't see straight, and not sure who I'd shoot if I could. Has-beens and never-beens begged for scraps at The Cathode Ray.

Yeah, I had a cross-seated seam here and there, and my heat sinks were loose. My left knee froze sometimes, and I'd snagged a couple wires under one arm. Didn't mean I hadn't done my good turns. Early on when I needed a back-up so's I could update my voice box and digitals, Benny asked if I could maybe do with a discount neural suite instead of going to a shop and I said sure. Sal had taught me some tricks with neural suites from his days in the upgrade industry, so I didn't mind too much. I'd even taken a pass on my share of the box some nights just so's Benny could pay the band.

He wouldn't really drop me for Patsy Bellbottom, would he? I mean, I was the Stainless Steel Siren.

Saturday afternoon, Benny's girl sideboard pinged me on my way out the door to The Joystick. Said Benny was giving me the night off, that I could take it easy, maybe scope the Cathode Ray and chat up the band. Said he had someone else lined up, not to worry about it. Catch you later, toots.

I blew a gasket. That lout. That lousy, two-bit heel with a gap-toothed gear for an operating system! I stormed back up the stairs, made for a quick change of clothes, and headed back down to hail a cab.

Some new guy with a brass weave worked the door and let me by without a fuss. Maybe it was the hat and veil, or maybe he just pretended not to recognize me.

I found an out-of-the-way table. It took three tries before a waitress came my way. "Forty-weight and tonic, straight."

Five minutes later, she finally made it back with my drink. "Took you long enough," I said when she dropped my change on the table.

She shrugged, rolling back and forth on one of those new wheel upgrades. "Sorry about that. We got a new act tonight, so it's a full house."

I packed the house, too, but nothing like tonight's wall-to-wall. The quick headcount and crappy service ground my gears. "Do you know who I am?"

She didn't bat an eye— "Should I?" —and rolled away.

Life sure looked different from the audience pit, not near so's luscious and bright. No one noticed me. I wanted to shout, "Hey, you rubes! I'm over here!"

It didn't work.

I sipped my drink and tried to forget the waitress's smart mouth. Tried not to think about the postage stamp stage at the Cathode Ray.

When the lights finally dimmed, Big Eddie Flashpoint stepped through the curtain, all smooth silk and sleek chrome under the spotlight. He snuggled up to the microphone. "Ladies and Gentleamps, we have a special treat for you tonight. She is sweet, she is smooth, and she's here for what we hope is the first of many shows. Put your hands together for the luscious Motortown Songbird, Miss Patsy Bellbottom."

The room went dark and quiet. The boys came in on four with a low, honey-sweet bass and a cymbal sigh. A single spotlight, my spotlight, pierced the gloom center stage and there she stood, Miss Patsy Bellbottom, in a green sequined gown that hugged her curves like a factory floor lover. Copper hair, polished skin, tight chassis, heat sinks out to here. No one said boo, not a one, then she lifted her head and began to sing.

The Motortown Songbird, that's what Big Eddie called her. She melted the room with Carter Bulbwright's "Turn Me On, Baby," then set the night moving with "Overcharged." "Little Copper Hen," "Gearshift Boogaloo," "Sparkler." She tied the tunes up in a bow and gave them to the audience. Her voice shot through the roof on its way to the stars. It dipped itself in the shadows and painted mercury kisses on every cheek. She had my voice from twenty years ago, modulated in ways I could only dream of anymore. She only stopped singing long enough to let the jackhammer applause die down, then went right back to it.

Me? I sat and watched. I couldn't do nothing else. Who needed the Stainless Steel Siren when the Motortown Songbird owned the room?

I caught sight of Benny stage right, all smiles and glad eyes. I wasn't being replaced, I was being sold for scrap.

Of course they'd set her up in my dressing room. I waited until all the factory boys went back up front for drinks, then I turned the knob and walked right in like I did after every set. I could have used the old service corridor that opened into the back of my closet, but the Stainless Steel Siren don't take the backdoor for nobody.

There were flowers everywhere—on the shelves, the vanity, tucked in the coatrack. They'd even tossed the pillows off the couch to make room for more bouquets.

Patsy didn't look up from applying her jeweler's rouge. "Listen, I'm about to go on again, so if you don't mind—"

"Hello, sweety."

She dropped her make-up brush and whirled around on the chair—my chair—eyes wide. "Oh! Miss Starlight."

I gave her my stage face, all smiles and bright eyes. Never let them see you leak, that's what Sal always said.

Patsy stood, smoothing her dress over her hips. "Sorry about that, I didn't, um—Come in, come in." She cleared off a space on the couch, setting the flowers on the floor. "I mean, this is your dressing room and all so I really shouldn't tell you what to do."

"Thanks, but I'm not staying long." I straightened the wire-link doily on the edge of the couch. "I saw your show."

"You did?" Her eyes didn't have none of her smile.

Neither did mine. "You've got quite the chops on you. Nothing like mine, of course, but you could make it big someday."

"Of course." Her hands fluttered at her elbows, around her hair. "The Joystick's a big step up from the Cathode Ray, but Benny says the stars the limits. He said I was going to be a regular here."

That grimy, loose-chained, two-faced rat Benny. I locked my lips in a smile so's none of that slipped out. "Mmmm."

My lip lock must not have held, because she ducked her head and added, "Of course, we'd share stage time for a while."

So's that's how it was going to be. I smiled again without so many teeth and made myself comfortable on the couch.

Patsy perched her pretty little self on the chair. "So." She let the word out slow like a low whistle. "You liked the show?"

I set my hat and veil beside me on the couch. "'Little Copper Hen' was nice. 'Overcharged' wasn't bad, could have been a bit tighter."

Her smile faltered. "I have some of my best tunes coming up." She looked at my clock ticking its tock on the dresser.

"Yeah, but you got to wind them up tight right off so's they'll stick around."

That put a dent in her ego. She pursed her lips and swiveled her sleek little shoulders. "Benny swears I'll knock 'em dead."

"Sure you will." I'd show him knocking someone dead. "How'd you meet Benny, anyway?"

Patsy must have figured I wasn't that much of a problem. "He started coming to my shows at the Cathode Ray and we hit it off. One night he bought me a drink, and—"

A sharp knock, and the door opened. "Patsy! Sweetheart! Two—" Benny caught sight of me on the couch and all that schmarm went right out his tubes. "—minutes."

Benny stepped inside, closing the door behind him. He straightened his tie. "Hey, Gina. Wasn't expecting to see you here. Thought you'd be home, you know, resting."

I wanted to rest his face against the wall, the lousy cranker. "Resting or at the Cathode Ray?"

"The Cathode Ray's not that bad," Patsy said quick like. "You'll love it. They've got a great band."

Benny gave her a look, then turned back to me. "Now, Gina, don't be like that. I just thought you'd want a night off is all."

"That's all, huh? Funny—" I cut a look at his new pigeon. "—I thought I was going to have to share a stage."

This time they gave each other looks.

I stood and picked up my hat, giving Benny a good look at what he was letting go. When I came up, I could tell he'd liked what he'd seen. Patsy's pout told a different story. I said, "I'll see you tomorrow night, right?"

Benny cleared his throat like an engine with a bum ignition. "Well, I thought Patsy might stay on for the rest of the week."

All the good will I'd ever had for Benny filtered right down the drain. He must've seen it in my face because he brought his hands up like so's to make amends. "Gina, sweetie, don't be like that, huh? It's business is all."

I brushed by him on my way to the door. "Yeah. Business."

Benny never pinged to apologize. Not once, the lout. After a couple of days, I got a little tight in the head; I started to believe he was right. I mean, I was just a rundown singer, right? He handled the business.

One morning, I took a taxi downtown to drop in at the Cathode Ray for a looksee. The cabbie pulled up to the curb outside the club. "Here you go, lady. You want me to wait?"

"Sure." I set my hand on the handle, but couldn't open the door. Rust, broken bottles, and bits of wire littered the sidewalk. The marquee had chipped enamel and missing bulbs. The shops on either side had been boarded up, the walls covered in Technicolor binary.

The cabbie looked at me in the rearview mirror. "You getting out, lady?"

"What do you care?" I said back, my face pressed against the window. "The meter's running."

An older model in a trench coat huddled by the front door, a sign propped against the stump of his third arm: WILL WORK FOR WASHERS. I could smell the desperation of the street, like smoked metal and burnt insulation. I knew that smell from way back.

That's how Benny wanted to play it? Fine. Back in the day, Sal made his bankroll in the upgrades industry, pretty pennies and patents to burn. I didn't know business, but I knew enough other things. Time to show Benny how we did things on the other side of the cabling.

I sat back against the seat. "Take me home."

The cabbie shrugged and pulled away from the curb.

That night, I stopped off at the florist for a bouquet of gold-rimmed daisies, cheap like Patsy. I had the cabbie drop me off a block from The Joystick, and hoofed it through the back alleys to the service door.

The dumpster smelled like an oil pit, and a load of empty cans was set out beside it for the morning recycle. A look at my watch said Patsy should be on stage another five minutes, seven tops. I'd have to work fast.

I eased the door open and slipped into the dimly lit sink room. Busy kitchen drilling and clanging came from the door straight ahead, but the door I wanted was tucked behind the push brooms and mop buckets on the right. Quiet as I could, I moved everything to the side and jimmied the latch. The hinges creaked, and I locked, listening. The kitchen clatter didn't stop. I opened the door a bit more and slipped inside.

The corridor smelled like dust and dried metal polish. A bare bulb above my head showed the grease and skids of what had been The Joystick's start and now wasn't nothing but forgotten.

I hurried to the end of the corridor, and put my ear to the small door that opened into the dressing room closet. I listened hard. Nothing. I listened harder. Still nothing. Good.

I slipped into the closet, and eased the door shut behind me. Dresses, shoes, boas, doodads, none of them mine. I pushed to the front, listened again, then cracked the door. It didn't look like my dressing room no more. My clock, my shoe rack, my widgets, all gone. Didn't smell like mine, either, all cheap synthetics instead of my imported lubricants. Patsy lived there now. Benny had better not have dumped my things or I'd show him a thing or two about being dumped. I checked my watch and headed out of the room.

The hall was showtime clear. I made it to Benny's office, knocked on the door, and slipped inside before anyone saw me. Benny looked up from his cast iron desk, and blinked in surprise. "Gina? What are you doin' here?"

His office was cozy with fancy chairs and cabinets. He was alone, just him and his ledgers. I clutched the strap of my bag, gave him my best smile, and shut the door behind me. "Heya, Benny. Long time no see."

Benny sighed and closed his book, marking his page with a scrap of aluminum. He came around his desk without so much as a smile. "Yeah, you're lookin' good. Have you been by the Cathode Ray? Dickie's been expectin' you."

I kept it cool. "I've been busy, you know, thinking and stuff." I held out the daisies. "I wanted to apologize."

The words stuck in my craw, but I said them with a smile.

Benny eyed the flowers like he expected a bee or something. "Listen, Gina, don't do this, okay? You don't got to apologize for anything."

"Sure I do. Last time I had my wires in a twist, and that ain't no way to say good-bye. This is good-bye, right?"

He didn't look so proud anymore, but he didn't look sad like, either. "Yeah, yeah it is, but no hard feelings, right? It's business is all, and I think you'll be a good fit for the Cathode Ray."

I set the daisies on the desk, and palmed a glitcher out of my bag at the same time. "I figured as much."

He looked at my shoulder bag. "What do you have there?"

"I need to get rid of some things to make ends meet. Maybe you'd be interested, you know, for Patsy." With my free hand, I reached for the clasp.

His lips curled in a quick smirk, then settled back into a frown. "That's fine, but maybe you should be going."

I brushed my hair behind my ear, setting the electrode between my fingers. "Is she doing okay?"

Benny locked a moment. "Fine."

"That's good." I took a half step towards the door. "She's a good kid, you know? Stage work can take a lot out of a girl."

"She's fine. Listen, I really do need to—"

"Tell her to flash a bit of thigh every once in a while. That'll hold 'em for the next set."

"Fine, fine. Listen, you need to go. Talk to Barry at the bar, tell him I said to give you a free drink. Two drinks if you want, huh?"

He brushed by me on his way to the door, and I pushed the glitcher against the back of his head. Benny twitched and fell into my arms before he even got his hand on the knob.

I locked the door, jammed a chair under the handle so's it wouldn't move, then dragged him to the center of the room. Voices in the hall and a look at the clock said the first set was winding up. I didn't have much time.

The neural suite came out of the bag, and started up with the sharp smell of burnt circuits. I bought it used years ago. It was an off-brand and way past its warranty, but I couldn't afford to be choosy now. I might not get another chance.

Still, I had a bad case of the what-ifs. What if the magnetic leads reversed and crunched my processor? What if someone broke down the door and pulled my plug before I finished? What if? What if?

I stared down at Benny with his big money suit and upgraded shoulders. He owed me big time for all I done for him. With a body like that, I could do what I wanted. I wouldn't have the music, but I'd be the one shining the spotlight. I'd show Benny the business all right.

Took a bit to find his pop-switch so I could get at his processor. I searched under his hair, down his back, and finally found it behind his left eye. One press and I opened Benny's head. I poked around with a bobby pin to suss out his wiring. Leads, crossovers and splits, inputs and feeds. His processor flashed like crazy, but he couldn't so's much as bat an eyelash to stop me.

I struck gold at the bottom of a copper crease, or I hoped so anyway. I never got good with figuring blueprints. I set the bobby pin against a tiny silver plate and leaned over so's I'd be the last thing he ever saw. "Bye-bye, Benny-boy."

I pressed the bobby pin against the plate until I heard a click. Benny's body gave a ten-second jerk, then the light went out of his eyes as I purged him from his own system, easy-peasy. I could hear Sal laughing all the way to the bank.

Now came the tricky part. I wired myself to the neural suite and did the same to Benny. The connections didn't want to seat in his sockets so I hammered them in with my shoe.

Someone knocked on the door. "Mister Gracenote? We're out of solder, and there's none in stores." Knock-knock-knock. "Mister Gracenote?"

Of all the lousy—!

I made the last connections with a kiss and a bit, then stretched out on the other side of the box. I could feel my pump in the soles of my feet, I was that tight.

"He in there?" another voice said.

"I thought I heard something, but nah. Probably out front."

Footsteps, then nothing.

My pump chugged right out of my chest. I hoped this worked. It had to work. It would work. I threw the switch.

The world tucked and curled down the tubes. Spinning, spinningingingingspinning. My toes got sucked through the white noise of my head into my time pump exploding out my fingers along the roof of door sole of my feet tumbling hairing my hear my hairhear where wear—

Knockcrickocking. A voice slar-away, far and a dayway: "Mushtor Greezhot? Buzz?"

Two hands lifted, mine?, which?, mine? Backforward which? Process slowing. Processing, process ... ing ... pro ... cess ... ing ...

I ripped the wires out of my head, and the world went black.

I came to with all my fingers and toes in the right place, and not.

Someone knocked on the door. "Benny?" Rattle-rattle went the knob. "Benny? You okay?"

Patsy Bellbottom. The Motortown Songbird.

"Is something burning?" Knock-knock. Rattle-rattle. "Open the door."

Burning? Insulation. Old circuits sharp like a knife carving me a new nose.

I turned my head to the door, and stared at a slab of metal dressed like me on the other side of the neural suite, wires streaming out of its head.

I lifted my hands, cleared my throat. "Hold on." Benny's throat, Benny's voice. My voice now. I could've burst out singing. "Hold on."

"Okay."

I got to my feet with no problem at all. In fact, I felt right at home. Lucky thing, too, because I had to do something with my old body. I picked it up and gave it a long look, crossed seams, bum knee, and all. So long, Gina Starlight. Hello, Benny Gracenote.

"Benny?" Patsy sounded kind of sulky on the other side of the door.

"I said hold on." I pushed the neural suite under the desk with my feet, then eased the old me into the oil cabinet without popping any cans. I set a pin through the handles to be safe. I'd dismantle myself later. Weird thought, made me kind of kinked. I shook it off and headed for the door.

Patsy gave me the side eye and her bottom lip. She wore a gold sequin shrug and not much else, hot from the stage. "About time. What's that smell?"

I stepped out of the office like nothing was wrong, pulling the door shut. "My book press went hinky."

"Is that why you weren't there after the set?"

A pack of admirers waited a few feet down the hall, ready with their flowers and smiles and compliments. Let them wait. I was in charge now, I was the one running the show. Maybe they didn't need the Stainless Steel Siren no more, but they needed Benny Gracenote because I had what they wanted. I had the Motortown Songbird.

"Yeah." I pulled her to me, and kissed her cheek, put an arm around her waist. I'd learn the books and maybe show her the ropes. I could get used to this. "No worries, baby cakes. It's business is all."

Author's Note

I love reading science fiction. Writing it? Not so much. Not that I don't like a challenge, but I recognize that it's not one of my strengths. That could be why I keep trying.

While on a working vacation in Las Vegas (nowhere near as glamorous as it sounds, believe me), I treated myself to a facial and massage. Much to my surprise, the facial technician buffed my face with a Dremel tool. Buffed my face. I mean it. And all I could think of at the time was "Is she going to change my eyes out, too?"

A story was born. After a tuck and polish, I submitted it to my writing group who then savaged it, and rightly so. Sexist, ageist, insulting, belittling, privileged, etc., etc., not at all my intent behind the story. The only kind word was "You did robot noir really well." I limped home and nursed my ego for a few days before returning to the tattered manuscript. As much as I hated to admit it, they were right, and their critique helped me turn an okay story into a high-polished extravaganza at the mike. It's business, after all.

The Vessel Never Asks For More Wine

Eileen didn't realize she'd stepped off the curb until the horn's shriek brought her back to the moment. A sharp jerk on the back of her collar sent her tumbling into a nest of hands and anxious voices. The bus reached the corner and turned out of sight.

She brushed bits of nothing from her coat to keep her hands from shaking. Catching her breath, Eileen turned to the man behind her. "Thanks. I didn't even see it coming."

"Wasn't me, lady." He jerked his head to the left. "It was that guy."

She looked through a gap in the knot of bodies and saw a slight figure in a dark brown overcoat hurrying away against the pedestrian flow. "Excuse me, please," she said to crowd, and to the one hurrying away: "Hey! Hey, wait up!"

The retreating figure glanced over his shoulder and picked up the pace.

"Mister! Wait!" Eileen pushed through the crowd, desperate to keep him in sight.

He was halfway down the block before Eileen caught up with him. She clipped her leg on the bumper of a sedan pulling away from the curb, but made it to the walk with a smile and a breathless, "Listen, hi there, I—"

The man managed a hasty step back, raising a hand to defend against her presence. "I'm sorry," he said in oddly accented English. "I have to be going."

He hunched his shoulders and turned away.

"No, wait." Eileen put a hand on his arm, drawing back as he flinched from her touch. "Sorry. I didn't mean to scare you."

"No, no, you are fine. Good-bye. Thank you."

"Yeah. I just wanted to thank you, y'know?" She offered her hand. "I'm Eileen Adelman."

Face to face, Eileen understood why she'd had a hard time following him through the crowds. He didn't appear much older than her own twenty-four years, was barely over five feet if she had to hazard a guess, and the sort of thin her Bobe Uma called "two bones and a hole". A mop of coarse, brown hair a shade darker than his skin framed sunken cheeks and a sharp nose.

The only remarkable feature in an otherwise plain face were his eyes, the right slightly larger than the left, and the caramel gold that edged a desert dune at sunrise. Ashes and the shadows of memories lingered in the creases around those eyes, unexpected in a man his age.

The slight man peered intently at Eileen and then her hand. He reached out and accepted her offering with care. "A pleasure to make your acquaintance. I am Borgio Yilmaz." He released her hand and returned both of his to the sanctuary of his pockets.

The air was chill enough that Eileen did the same, telling herself there was no reason to feel slighted. "Pleased to meet you, Mr. Yelmez."

He hesitated and then nodded once. "Borgio, if you please."

Eileen smiled. "Borgio it is. That almost sounds Russian."

The corners of his mouth turned up in a brief, tight smile. "Turkish actually," he said. "My surname, it has a loose English translation of 'never gives up.'"

Eileen tucked her hair behind her ear. "Okay. Well, I don't mean to take up so much of your time. You must have, like, a thousand things to do today, y'know, running around, saving other women."

Borgio tipped his head to one side and considered her with those startling eyes. "Not really."

"Oh. Well, um, thanks again. You have a good day." Eileen tossed off a quick wave and turned to leave when he called her name. She turned back.

The little man shifted nervously from foot to foot. "If you please." He pulled a worn leather planner from the inside pocket of his coat and extracted a business card. "My card. Perhaps we can do you for lunch. No, no. Have lunch together?" He flushed and dropped his gaze.

Eileen paused and then accepted the card. He reminded her of a small dog desperate for attention yet terrified of being noticed. "Sure. Why not?"

The little brown man smiled shyly. "Thank you."

"Not a problem. It was nice meeting you, Mr. Yelmez."

"Borgio, remember?"

Eileen slipped the card into the front pocket of her wallet. "Borgio. Right."

She found the card three days later while cleaning out her purse.

Eileen examined the heavy cream cardstock under the light of the desk lamp, delighting in the weight and texture. Gold embossed letters spelled out *Borgio Yilmaz, Literary & Technical Translations, Paris/ Prague, Member ALTA, FIT, CLTA*, with his attendant contact numbers and email. She turned the card over, running a finger against the grain of the paper. Deciding it couldn't hurt, she picked up the phone and made the call.

They agreed on a late lunch of dim sum and that Friday.

The Star of David that hung from a fine gold chain around her neck fascinated him. "Your father is Jewish."

The off-handed statement caught Eileen by surprise. "My whole family is. Is that a problem?"

She kept the frown from her face, but not the words.

Borgio's eyes widened. "Should it be? I am sorry. Speaking the English is—"

Eileen waved away her pique. "Sorry, I used to get flak about that when I was a kid. Never mind."

"Ah."

Borgio smiled over the rim of his teacup, his gaze following her chopsticks from the small blue and white ceramic bowl to her mouth and back again.

They finished lunch with small bowls of mango ice cream. Borgio insisted on paying for the meal. Eileen agreed so long as she left the tip.

The day outside was warm enough to make a body think spring had not completely abandoned the Windy City. Eileen moved a few steps to the right of the door and rummaged through her purse for her cigarettes and lighter.

The color drained from Borgio's face. "What are you doing?"

"My bad." Eileen checked the direction of the wind and took a step to the left. She tipped out a smoke, returned the pack to her purse, and cupped her hand over the end for a light.

"How long have you been smoked?" the little man said.

Eileen returned her lighter and exhaled away from him, hoping he wasn't the preachy sort. "Smoking? I started in my junior year in high school. My dad smokes, too."

The man who had made her laugh with his oddly worded puns retreated into himself as she watched. "No, no, not him as well. When did he start?"

"No idea. In the Army, I guess."

"Of course. A nineteen-seventy-one enlistment."

Eileen frowned around her cigarette. "How did you –?"

"And you. That is, what? Seven years? Eight?"

"Yeah. About that," Eileen allowed slowly, wondering at his earnest dismay. "Listen, I can put it out if you're allergic."

Borgio's expression was tense as he focused beyond her. "The average lifespan for women in developed countries is seventy-nine years, perhaps as long as eighty-four years depending on the study. Women who smoke in their mid-twenties to early thirties shorten their lifespan by as much as seven years. I didn't know you smoked. I should have. I should ..."

His voice trailed away, words unraveling until only the accent remained. And then he untangled himself from the dark place and found Eileen once more. "Yes, please put it out. Put it out and never start again. For my sake."

The little man ducked his head and all but ran from her until swallowed by the crowd.

"For my sake?" Eileen's mother said, wiping crumbs off her fingers with a napkin. "What kind of come-on is that?"

Eileen poured herself another glass of Merlot and settled back on her mother's leather couch. Girl's night meant wine, hummus, and other naughty treats forbidden during the calorie counting workweek. She swirled the wine, summoning a chorus of colors and warm oak notes. "I don't think it was a come on. He looked really upset. It was weird."

Her mother scraped the last of the humus from the side of the container with a pita chip. "I still say you shouldn't have gone out with him. And what's he doing following you around like that?"

Eileen took a drink to hide her sigh. "He was passing by the deli when I sat down. Maybe he was hungry."

"You're hungry, you go inside and order something. You don't stand outside and bolt when the victim of your dreams sees you."

Eileen rolled her eyes and reached for the wine. "I'm hardly a victim, Mom."

She wasn't, was she?

Two days later, Eileen didn't answer Borgio's call. He left a message. She deleted it unheard.

In her dreams, he watched her from slumbering shadows while she searched for her Star of David in a box of Cracker Jacks. He wept sand when she took a puff from a bubble-gum cigarette.

It was his voice and not her mother's that Eileen heard when her mother called to say that two pack a day Uncle Bernie was going in for a CAT-scan because the doctor found a spot— "A spot, you hear me?" —on the bottom lobe of his left lung.

Maybe her mother was right. Was he behind the newspaper at a window table across from the Picasso? What about the dun figure in the knot of people waiting for the light to change across the street?

For six days what-ifs crouched in the center of her chest, the fear of the unknown, of the second-guessed. She had Borgio's contact information; she could call the police. She was angry with the happenstance stranger for his odd concern, angry with the what-ifs and imagined bullies.

Enough was enough. Ignoring what her mother might say, Eileen cradled the phone against her shoulder, lit a cigarette because she damn well wanted to, and retrieved the business card from the top drawer of her nightstand. One ring, two rings, half of a third, and then his voice with its warm, peculiar accent: "Good afternoon."

She wondered if there wasn't a hesitation when he answered. Did he have caller ID? Was her number programmed into his phone? Eileen looked the bully of her fears in the eye. "Hi, Borgio. It's Eileen."

"Hello there. It is a pleasure to hear from you again."

It took five minutes and a second cigarette before Eileen could work up the courage to ask him out. Meetings with publishers claimed his attention all weekend, but Borgio agreed to a late dinner at his hotel the following Monday. "I look forward to it," he said with a nervous joy.

Eileen was surprised to discover she was also looking forward to seeing Borgio again. All the same, Monday night she charged her cell phone and brought her pepper spray.

Eileen changed her mind about the dinner with the lights: confident neon; fluorescent street lamp introspective; flashing pensive with the walk sign. Back and forth, good idea, bad idea.

Three blocks from the Affinia Hotel, she heard, from behind an alley dumpster, the moist crack of anger striking flesh. Slurred words rode voices fueled by fear and cheap liquor: "Fuggin' buddis-muslim piez o'shit."; "Fuggin' yew-ess-aye, towelhead muthafugga."

Eileen clutched her purse and quickened her step, one of the pedestrian herd averting her eyes and heart, until a familiar voice begged the men to stop. Was it the lunch companion or the stalker? She smelled grass and heard schoolyard laughter as her own bullies knocked down the scrawny Jewish girl.

Eileen grabbed her pepper spray and dashed into the narrow alley. Two men kicked the writhing man at their feet. "Get away from him!"

They turned on her with blinks and staggers. "What?" said the first. His cheap nylon jacket was smeared with garbage and oil.

"You heard me." Eileen kicked him in the knee and caught him in the face with the pepper spray. The man howled and went down, clawing at his eyes.

A bloody and torn Borgio levered himself out of the filth. "No."

Pain exploded white and coarse against the left side of Eileen's face. She staggered against the dumpster.

The second man raised his fist and brought it down again in drunken outrage. "Wha's you doin', huh? Huh?"

His buddy writhed in the muck and slush. "Gahdam! My eyes, gahdam!"

Eileen tasted hot iron and tears. She brought her arms up to shield her face, the pepper spray dropped and forgotten in the sudden *what was I thinking?* fear. She gagged and managed, "Leeb'im 'lone!"

She tried to kick the man away. He grabbed her foot, jerked, and her head hit the pavement. The pain tore through her, bright shrapnel slicing behind her eyes.

"You some kinda crazy lady? Paulie, she crazy—"

The man fell back, and Eileen thought she heard two screams. Three sharp cracks, a wet snap. She rolled to her side as Borgio came up from all fours and leapt at Paulie still screaming against the far wall. The young woman couldn't close her eyes fast enough; she witnessed the violence she heard seconds before, and was sick.

The brown man did not stop until Paulie lay limp.

Out of the gray, small hands gently gripped her upper arms. Someone that looked like Borgio leaned over her in the dim strobe of passing traffic. "Come with me."

"I really should be going," Eileen said into her cup of hot tea.

Borgio nodded. "Not until you finish that, if you please."

The hotel room was well appointed in tasteful earth tones. A navy soft side suitcase and matching carry-on were neatly arranged on the bench beside the bureau. Eileen sat at the foot of the king-sized bed, wearing a bathrobe. Borgio, in a clean shirt and khaki slacks, sat on the far side of the room, in front of the window with curtains drawn. His face was a bruised and swollen caricature. A makeshift icepack melted slowly on the desk beside him.

Eileen realized with a distant, impersonal calm that she was in shock. She stood outside herself, critically examining her reflection in the mirror: the swelling bruise under her left eye, the split lip, the short, dark curls still damp from the shower. Shock.

The silence between them echoed with sounds and other things she wanted to forget. "This is good tea."

"Thank you." Borgio set the icepack to his face. "The hotel selection was very poor. That is why I went out." He gestured to a rumpled, dirty plastic bag on the corner of the desk. "I am particular about tea."

"Oh. The doorman was ... I'm surprised he didn't say anything. When we came in."

"I've learned in my time that the best doormen appreciate the price of discretion."

This was it. This was where he admitted to stalking her. "So you do this often?"

"Goodness no. This evening was ... unique."

Eileen stepped back inside the woman at the foot of the bed and glanced at the little dog she'd kicked to the curb. Borgio looked pained in a way the beating could not manage. "I'm sorry," she said when she could do so without laughing, or crying, or both. "I'm still a little ... you know."

"Of course." He looked at her and then away, scraped fingers nervously plucking at the icepack washcloth. "Would you like some more tea?"

"No. I'm good." She sipped at the tepid brew, her attention wandering to the red and white NO SMOKING sign on the nightstand. "Thanks."

"I am particular—"

"You already said that."

"Ah."

A dull, insistent throbbing settled behind her left eye, feeding the headache stirring beneath the shock. "So, those guys ..."

"Thought I was some sort of terrorist," Borgio finished with a slight, sad smile.

Eileen drew a steadying breath and got to her feet. She walked to the hotel room door and back to the bed, counting the steps to a question she needed to ask. "You didn't defend yourself against those guys, did you?"

Borgio refolded the washcloth around the plastic bag of ice. "No," he said with quiet resignation.

"But when the guy went after me, you ..." The memory rose buoyant with her gorge. Eileen took a sip of tea. "Why?"

The little man with caramel eyes took his time in answering. He set down the icepack. "Sit down, if you would," he said, getting to his feet. His left hand gestured to the bed; his right arm stayed close to his side. "Please."

Eileen sat on the corner of the bed closest to the door as Borgio moved with slow, uneven steps to the carry-on on the bench. He rummaged through the center section and pulled out a small worn leather notebook secured with a piece of heavy black yarn. "My name," he said as he held out the book, "is not Borgio."

Eileen accepted the offering. The covers were tattered and creased, the edges of the pages worn to fine fuzz without definition. "Okay."

"My given name would translate as Borga, son of Purgin, brother of the black ear and son of the mountain. The translation is incomplete."

"Because it's Turkish?"

"Because there is no one left but me to translate."

The world's loneliness flittered through that single sentence and to Eileen's surprise her heart ached to hear it.

There was no picture worth his hesitant, sepia words that night. They were faded and worn smooth, bits and pieces of once-upon-a-times in lands far, far away. Borgio told her of growing-up as the oldest of ten children born to the senior of his father's three wives. It was a good life, not easy, but they were free to live as they pleased. He spoke of his people, the People of the Mountain, those who paid homage to Allah and Inanna, who followed the herds of black-faced sheep down to the valleys in the winter and back up the mountainsides in the summer.

"So you're not Turkish?" Eileen said, afraid to believe she knew the answer.

"I was born in the Taurus mountains that would become Turkey, but not Turkey, yes."

Eileen struggled to remember what she could of high school history. "You can't be that old. That was, like, right after World War One."

"Turkey's boundaries were established at the Conference of Lausanne. My people were a memory's memory long before the Ottoman Empire."

Eileen clutched at the leather notebook, an anchor to the hotel room and Chicago. "That's old, like fantasy, not real old."

Borgio parted the curtains to peer through his reflection at the night. "It would seem that way, yes? It is hard, the remembering. I wonder, sometimes, what I have twice forgotten that I once remembered."

In the quiet moments between now and then, he told of foraging for eggs in ground bird nests and drinking sheep's milk warm from the teat. He shared the ache of losing his fourth sister to "the bending fever," and the night The People of the Mountain were laid low.

"They came quickly with spears and ropes," the memories said— Eileen could see that Borgio had gone away and only distant memories remained, reciting an old tale from a book with yellowed pages. "It was a hard winter and our baskets held more than theirs. They cut us down, men and women. I crouched in the remains of my father's ..." The memories searched for a word. " ... tent, and cried as my mother bled out beside me."

Eileen had discovered the hole in his tale. "That doesn't make any sense. Why didn't they kill you?"

The little man turned from the window, the curtain shutting out the night once more. "Perhaps they did. It is not always clear. But I survived then ... and now."

"Survived?" The impossible clutched at Eileen's heart, seeping like ice water into her veins. "So, you're telling me you're a vampire?"

Borgio blinked and then laughed the same shy laugh of sharing dim sum. "No. Vampires, vampir, they are the not real."

"Then what are you?"

Borgio hesitated. "Old. I heal without scars from every wound, though not as quickly as I might like. I cannot make magic out of my eyes, and I have no great strength. I eat and sleep and am a man, merely old."

"I think," he continued thoughtfully, "that I lived because they died. The years that they would have lived became my own. And the years of my people who married into other tribes, if they died of accident or hate before those years were over, those became mine as well. And the years of their children, and children's children, throughout what is now history."

Eileen noted that he was making sense in an odd, distant way and the realization bothered her. There had to be a question she could ask that he could not answer, a way to force a lie from the truth so she could laugh and walk away. "Like you sucked the life out of them?"

"Not that, I think. I take up the time without meaning to, the time my family and blood could not use so it is not wasted." Borgio pursed his lips to catch thoughts in a net of words. "It is like yawning. When you yawn and there is a sudden hic where you take in more air, yes? You feel it. That is how I know. It is the breath of their years. I feel it sometimes when I breathe. Once many years, centuries, ago, it happened four times in one day." He looked away after that and did not speak for some time. "There it is. I am the, the vessel. Receptacle?"

Eileen chewed on her bottom lip. "Can you ... die?"

"Everything dies; I am no different. I take in more years than I need and let them out slowly. I hope to die of old age someday when there are no more years left in me. Disease and injury are passing acquaintances." He smiled sardonically. "You could say I am in excellent health for a man my age."

Eileen thought about the paperback books her father devoured with the devotion of imagination, stories about fantastic people and realities that stretched beyond the glossy covers. "Do you have all of their memories, too?"

"No." His answer was flat, abrupt, and final. It spoke more than Eileen wanted to hear.

Borgio rose stiffly and crossed the room to the coffee pot on the counter outside the bathroom. He set a tea bag in a cup and filled the cup with hot water. "I could hope for loose leaf, but this will have to do. Are you sure you would not like another cup?"

She sloshed the remains at the bottom of her cup. "I'm sure. You realize I don't believe a word of this, right?"

His laughter this time was gentle and more refined. "Not believing makes little difference in the truth, but I understand."

Eileen waited until Borgio had settled in his chair before she dared the next question. "So why tell me all this?"

Borgio shifted, grimaced. "Normally I would not, but I chanced your unwitting involvement when I agreed to meet you for lunch, and feel you are owed an explanation." He gestured with his cup to the book in her hand.

Eileen examined the book more closely. The yarn was worn smooth and the knot simple.

"The bottom of page seventy-one," he said.

The pages were compressed with years. Eileen flipped through half-seen names and numbers recorded in a precise hand in blacks and blues and browns until she came to page seventy-one, where at the bottom she read:

Eileen Adelman, March 8, 1984, 0253, Allegheny Hospital, Pittsburgh, PA, USA, daughter of Lawrence Adelman.

And the entry above that:

Lawrence Adelman, May 10, 1960, 1212, homebirth, Harrisburg, PA, USA, son of Ira Adelman.

She closed the book, marking the page with her thumb.

Her mother told her to get out, now, *forget your things and get the hell outta there.* Eileen looked up at Borgio sitting as far as he could from the door, asking only that she finish her tea before running screaming into the night as any proper gentleman would. He watched her through the thin veil of steam from his cup, small, brown, and alone. She opened the book and moved her thumb aside.

She read until she couldn't take any more. Nine pages, forty-seven entries, cousins, uncles, aunts, second cousins, her father's side of the family captured in the same tight hand. Names she did not recognize, some that her father might not recognize, family flung far and wide, reaching back, possibly, frighteningly, to the oldest of ten children born to the senior of a man's three wives.

Eileen carefully closed the book, retied the knot, and set it beside her on the bed. "That's quite a read. It's not, um, not what I expected."

She sought something to do with her hands, her thoughts, with the list of names and relations he could not possibly know. "Is that why you came to Chicago?"

"No, I do have business here but decided to check up on you while I was here."

Eileen laughed at the irony. "Mom was right. You were stalking me."

Borgio managed to blush beneath the bruises. "That was not my intention at first. And then ..."

Eileen picked up her tea. "You pulled me back from the bus because you didn't want any more time. Same thing with the smoking."

"Yes."

"And the guys in the alley?"

Her savior twice over winced. "They couldn't cause me any lasting harm, but you ..."

"Thought so. Did you know it was going to happen? The bus, I mean."

"No. I was following you from your apartment to perhaps see where you worked, and then planned to find my way to my own business for the day." He dropped his gaze. "Things did not go as I planned."

Eileen nudged the book with the tip of a finger. "Is this everyone?"

Borgio adjusted the icepack against his nose. "Of your line to current, although you may have a new relation in China. There are at least four other lines I have discovered. Research of this nature takes time, and the modern information age is not as efficient as some might believe."

"That's a lot of people."

"And years."

The words were so quiet Eileen nearly missed them in the beating of her own heart.

Eileen gestured towards the book. "I guess you can't really Google something like this. Even after all this, I really don't know what to believe, y'know? Jews are into guilt, not ..."

Borgio gave a bruised, lopsided smile. "I would feel the same way in your position."

Eileen finished her tea in silence. "I think it's time I head home."

Borgio set the icepack aside and stood. "I will get your clothes."

Eileen looked away from the window to the wizened nut of a woman behind the Laundromat counter. "Pardon?"

"Your clothes. I get them." The clerk shuffled to the sedately rotating rack of clothes in plastic bags and returned to the counter with the dress and coat. "The blood come out completely. There was no problem." Her words were rich with the language of her youth.

"Thank you." Eileen pulled out a bill and waited for change, her attention straying to the window once more. The distant sketch of a plane against the sky lifted slowly out of sight. She fancied it was Borgio's flight to Albany.

He'd called that morning from O'Hare to see how she was feeling and to say good-bye, suggesting they stay in touch "if you should have a moment."

"I have to ask," she'd dared between brushing her hair and putting on earrings. "Does anyone else know?" Her reflection had held its breath. What a surprise for Eileen to realize she'd done the same.

"Not now. It has been many lives since I told," Borgio had said over their tenuous connection. He'd sounded wistful, separated by more than miles. "I must be through the security now. Will you be well?"

Eileen hadn't known how to answer that morning. Now his business card was tucked in the back pocket of her wallet.

The clerk counted back Eileen's change, nudging the tip jar by the register as if by accident. "You have a good day, okay?"

"You too," Eileen managed with a socially convenient smile. She dropped the coins into the jar, slid the bills in her wallet, and stopped with her hand in her purse. She took a deep breath, thinking of now and then. "Excuse me?"

The clerk closed the register drawer. "Yes?"

Eileen handed her a half-empty pack of cigarettes and a blue Bic lighter. "Could you throw these away, please?"

Author's Note

I'm not good in crowds (trust me on this), and a convention is one big crowd the size and shape of the hotel. Because of this, and limited financial resources, I can manage one, maybe two, conventions a year and then only because I help man the table for my partner's game store. During a passing conversation at a Norwescon (mumbles) years ago, a friend mentioned how one of her RPG characters became immortal when his family died, filling him with their unused years. The idea never left me, and after much massaging it came into this world and was eventually picked up by Jim Baen's UNIVERSE, not their usual fare but Eric Flint liked the story and, besides, it would appear in the magazine's next to the last issue so what could it hurt. This story was my first professional sale and the first time my name appeared on the cover of a publication. The story illustration was exquisite, a close up of one of Borgio's eyes, the reflections of palms and ancient monuments deep within. Sadly, my copy of the illustration grew legs and wandered off years ago, but the memory still takes my breath away.

Black Widow

June, 2068
2 kilometers outside Kunming

"**Y**ou got it, Mattie! It's yours! Own it!"
Cheyko's laugh is lightning from the crew bay, my one-woman cheering squad as I slam dance the Seahawk-FK troop wing through the clouds.

I give local groundcom a tight beam to clear the way and drop to the hot zone from 43,000 feet before the window closes. Land without so much as a scratch in the paint, lucky for them. Scotson suits in a weasel the moment we set down and is gone the moment the Crank gives the all clear and the doors open. Scotson's our eyes and ears. Easier to neutralize a target when you can find it first.

"I thought there were ten in your squad, Sergeant Crank," the field ops says when nine of us report in. Aussie, a full bird with two drop stripes, graying, looks like she's seen her share of time. The ops tent is a disaster of insulated crates, fold out tables, and a solar coffeemaker nursing half a pot of tar.

"He's taking a dump," the Crank says, and passes her our order packet.

Got to love the Crank. Her husband Wesley served in the 101st War Dog Strikers with my Manuel. We both wear the War Dog insignia over our hearts, to the right of the red hourglass for the 81st Black Widows.

We pitch tent on the far side of the mess, then grab eats. The regular forces love us. Pity us. Black Widows, the wives and husbands of the fallen who have chosen to serve in their memory. We should be somber, reserved. In mourning.

Hell no. We fist slam and jaw through the line like there isn't a war on the other side of the perimeter. We make a show of being the show. We keep our propriety to ourselves and the dark places in the night.

Eat, then back to the tents, strip down our gear, and bring it back up again. You can trust a memory to always have your back, but you never trust gear you haven't specced yourself.

I upload my personal and suit debriefs, standard Black Widow procedure. Serve the past, preserve the present, honor the future. Weirded me out five years ago, thinking that PacCommand wanted eyes on everything we do and say, but the world is changing too quickly to let our sacrifices be forgotten. Someday my son Leo will unravel the meaning of my enlistment. I hope the uploads help him understand how much I loved his father.

How much we both loved our only child.

Fiedler, Williams, and I play deuces out for an hour until someone scratches at the flap and the field ops steps in. Doesn't wait for us to stand, but doesn't try to make friendly. Has her own coffee. Once upon a time, I would have served biscuits then excused myself. Now I look her in the eye and wait.

She perches on a confiscated packing crate table. "Your orders are clean. Looks like you're go any time now."

"Yessir." The Crank doesn't look up from her sketchpad. Word art for her grandchildren, she says, and she's not bad. She made one for Leo's eighth birthday last year. He loved it.

"PacCommand is taking heat from Delhi. We'll eventually push into China, and Tokyo wants everything cleared and ready."

"Yessir."

The field ops slurps her coffee. "Never had a Black Widow unit come through before. Is it true?"

"Is what true, sir?"

She runs a finger around the mug's rim. "What they say about Black Widows."

"What's that, sir?"

We've heard it all before. Black Widows are magic. Americo spies who sold our souls to the Devil. Ghouls who harbor the dead in our duffel bags. We were never married, or in love. Never prayed God would take us that instant when we opened the screen door and the survivor advocate said "Missus Matapang? May I come in?"

We are more, and less. We're honor and survivor benefits for our children so they'll have a leg up in this shithole, overcrowded world. We hope that the dead would be proud of our service. We hope to survive the tangled web we weave.

The field ops clears her throat. "My cousin just petitioned to enlist as a Widow in honor of his husband."

We don't say a word. The field ops is looking for a reason we can't give. Each enlistment is different. The Crank still doesn't look up from her sketchpad. From outside the tent comes the give and take of orders, the low rumble of tracked vehicles.

The field ops' shoulders slump. She shakes her head. "Your man still taking a dump?"

"Yessir," says the Crank.

The field ops finishes her coffee, crunches the cup, stands with shoulders back. "Tell him to lay off the curry next time."

"Will do, sir."

Then she's gone. No inspirationals, no huffings and puffings. Enough sense not to push for an answer she doesn't want to hear. I can respect that.

Not long after, I roll off for a sleep. Eyes closed, I lie with my Manuel in Laoag. The muggy night is fragrant against my skin. We've been assigned to teach at the refugee school two kilometers outside the city. Ocean levels continue to rise, and the fish are almost gone. Australia can't take any more refugees, so the Philippines are the first place many Pacific Islanders go on their way to anyplace else.

PacCommand is looking for insertion specialists. Manuel has talked about enlisting. The thought of him joining the Army unsettles me, but it would mean better rations for myself and Leo, a room to ourselves no matter how small.

My Manuel makes a joke, smiles, laughs. I can't hear what he says, but it doesn't matter. Nothing matters but the glory of his body against mine, his breath warm in my mouth when we kiss.

The Crank calls my name and my husband unravels. I hold on to his smile for as long as I can before I open my eyes and sit up. She tosses me my pack. "Scotson called in. We're go."

I tuck my Manuel in my heart for safe keeping. Six years, three months, two weeks, four days. I remember the advocate's sad smile, how he put his hat under his left arm. "Missus Matapang? May I come in?"

This is my world since enlisting to serve in my Manuel's honor. I suit up.

Badger suits are thicker than weasels, better armored, more bring it on but enough sneak that we leave the regulars blind. The insulated badger suits keep out the worst of the heat, but the dry filtered air burns my nose before we are four kilometers out.

Two weeks ago the Americo-Chinese fleet surrendered, and now PacCommand wants to break their overland lines into India. We're here to cut out the resistance cells in the hills outside Kunming without killing the sub-continent patient.

Why PacCommand doesn't just slash and burn the whole run isn't my business. Ngubi says that's what she'd do. She enlisted to honor her wife, one of the Dingo Cats out of Melbourne. The Crank says we don't get paid to think outside the mission. I agree, though some days I wish more people were paid to think instead of fight.

We uplink four times before we get a solid signal. Readings give us the headsup on a local militia unit to the southeast long before they know we are here. We curl north to keep out of their way. Command wants to keep the locals friendly, another reason for insertion teams instead of full assaults. No sense giving them someone new to hate when the old hates are gone.

The terrain is like the locals, beaten up but not down. Stone fists punch the sky; burned out cracks run deep and dirty as God's ass as my Manuel used to say. Bones crunch underfoot, sounding like metal on a bad tooth feels. Rocks, bones, and debris are what it's all about. I don't belong here—I'm a child of muggy green nights and steaming coastal days—but I respect the people with strength enough to call this place home.

Off road there is no straight line, not even for a joke. Up, down, around, watch your step and hope the map doesn't glitch into a doubleback. Mostly up, though. I fall in behind Cheyko. She is a short, squat brick wall of a woman, as wide as she is tall, and wears two patches next to her Black Widow hourglass, a Cutthroat 171st and a 52nd Lightning Cat. She once confided that she fought for the memory of both her husband and her only daughter. After the admission, Cheyko carried her bottle of sake into the storeroom and locked the door behind her. It took the Crank most of the next day to talk her out again.

We scope a burial on the far side of a ravine near a burned out village. According to uplink, the village has no name. According to my eyes, grief and death are its only residents. Three women and two men, the women all in black from head to toe, one man leaning on a crutch in place of his missing right leg. Three small bodies wrapped in tarps. Kids, maybe? Leo is about the same size. My heart dies a little at the sight.

The man with two legs drags one woman from the bodies, shaking and hugging her by turns. The group's wails cut sharp and mournful through my audio. Another woman sees us and reaches out with both hands to call us over or keep us away. Brick stops long enough to cross herself, but there is nothing else to it. Her husband served with the 4th Burning Lotus out of Bangkok.

I clap Brick on the shoulder. "Come on."

She nods, follows. Black Widows don't look back. We can't afford to.

Scotson calls in two hours out. "Sarge, I'm in and it's dirty." He sounds clear enough that I could turn around and give him a thumbs up; I ping him ten kilometers east by northeast.

"Go ahead," the Crank says. She signals a halt. I wish she'd done it someplace flat.

"Uploading now."

Seconds later the stream slides in on a secure worm channel designed to eat its tail. I accept the download and the feed fills my heads-up display. Two caves less than a quarter mile apart with a marker that they could be part of the same crawl. Shots of a camouflaged fuel depot, water tank. Four plank-and-stone shelters with weapon signatures outside the southernmost cave. Maybe eighty armed Americo-Chinese infantry, no serious brass or sign of Red Shocks. Glad of that. We'd faced Red Shocks outside Janakpur, and again in a running fight through what's left of Lalitpur. They're tough.

The cave crawls could get ugly but the rest looks neat. "What's the dirty?" the Crank says.

"Wait for the truck." Scotson comes back.

Not even a minute later, a truck rumbles in from the north and most everyone at the northernmost cave gathers to unload the cargo. I check the time mark: roughly five minutes ago. The recorded stream sways and bounces; Scotson has moved in for a closer look.

Three Americo-Chinese with long, dirty faces peel back the canvas at the rear and out come Indian kids, filthy, scrawny, barefoot, and frightened. A soldier in the truck hands the kids down one at a time. Their hands are secured in front of them with thin wire. They wear rusty steel cable collars attached to a thicker lead cable. Attached to the end of the lead cable is a black box the size of a small duffel bag. Heavy, judging by the heft; important, judging by the care used to pass it down.

"What the ... ?" Williams says low.

I catch a flash of red in the upper left hand corner of the feed: mSv; Gray; Potential Load.

"Sumbitch," says the Crank.

"There are five, repeat five, sets of kids, each with a nuke," Scotson says. "Low grade and dirty by the readings. I'm picking up an electrical charge around the kids but that could be slop from the nukes."

The rubble that was Cairo, the wasteland that is now North Africa. I drag myself away from the thoughts of another nuclear strike, Leo gone in a flash. "I'll spec your sensor suite when we rendezvous."

No one calls me on how my voice shakes.

The children are led into the cave. Most keep their heads down, all look to be out of tears. There isn't a fighter in the lot of them. Probably what's kept them alive.

All eyes are on the Crank. She rubs the War Dog insignia over her heart. "Set up a distraction."

Just in case. She doesn't say it, but we hear it. Always have a back-up, because it's too late when you're in heavy.

"Launching fakers." For a split second Scotson has eight signals, then back to one. "Fakers go."

"Call in when you have a rendezvous point," the Crank says. "Keep your head down."

"Copy that." And Scotson is gone, not even a ping on my system.

We keep moving, not much jawing before and none now. Dammit. Kids. Were they hostage insurance? Bargaining options? A way to keep the nukes safe? Did I become a Black Widow so I could honor my Manuel's memory by killing kids?

We have orders to hit fast and move on. Would my Manuel have considered the children acceptable losses?

Scotson eventually calls in coordinates. We rendezvous short of four clicks later in a clutch of boulders with an eye leading to the caves. I spec Scotson's suit while he debriefs.

"I mark the Americo-Chinese as a unit held back for guerilla strikes," he says. His face is haggard. He sucks water from his suit canteen. "They're in those caves tight."

"What else is new?" Butchman pops the clip in and out of his blunt nose TR40. Some pace, Butchman pops. He fights for his wife, one of the 63rd Jade Tigers. "PacCommand should have called for strikes weeks ago, but the Japs want all the glory."

"You're not PacCommand so what you think doesn't matter," the Crank says from her rock. "The situation is what it is."

Williams speaks up. "What about the kids, Sarge?"

Williams has two kids. She's the newest member of the unit. Her wife was a pilot for the 28th Pathfinders.

"Yeah." The Crank flexes her elbows, rubs her face. "Aarons?"

Aarons is the Black Widow psych. We need one, so when he talks we listen.

"There's always more mouths than there is food so far as the Americo-Chinese are concerned," Aarons says around the last mouthful of a ration bar, "but this is extreme even for them. They must be pretty desperate to shake us if they're willing to throw kids into the line of fire."

"We're not going to burn the kids too, right?" Gifu says. Her husband served in the 34th O'Reillyphants.

The Crank doesn't say anything for a long time. We don't say anything either. You don't rush the Crank unless there's a bullet headed her way. I continue my diagnostic of Scotson's weasel suit.

"Mattie?" the Crank says when she is ready.

I unplug my leads from the suit port at the small of Scotson's back. "Golden. A few millisievert on the dosimeter, but he's clean." I slap Scotson on the thigh. "I cleared two of your vents, and uploaded your personal and suit debriefs."

Scotson thumps me on the shoulder and specs the suit himself while I pack up. I like Scotson. He's good people. He wears his wife's 216th Wolverine insignia well.

The Crank rubs under her chin with the back of her left hand. "What's the extended dose?"

I shrug. "Depends on what you mean by extended. A hundred feet or so for an hour shouldn't be a problem. You want to dry hump a bomb, that's a different story."

"You think you can drive the truck?" says the Crank.

Cheyko grins, all teeth and chin. "Fuck, Sarge, this is Matapang. She could drive it even if it was chipped."

The Crank still looks at me.

"Easy," I say. For a chance to get those kids out of there, I would carry the truck on my back.

Williams smiles and Cheyko cracks a lightning laugh.

Scotson figures the best approach is from the south between the caves. They'll divide and we'll conquer. He'll keep far point going in, and circle around to come in over the caves when we introduce ourselves. Gifu sends a code burst to the field ops over a worm channel, a heads up of intent. Williams says Gifu should add an apology for making the perimeter watch look bad.

Scotson gives the word. I pull Leo out of my heart, hug him as hard as I can, and sub-vocalize into my pick-up, "Mama loves you."

The Crank, Williams, Butchman, Fiedler, and myself take the north cave; Cheyko, Brick, Aarons, and Gifu the south.

Two Americo-Chinese smoke and talk on a small boulder pocked with ammo tracks. The Crank gives the clear, I knife one, Fiedler the other, and we pull the bodies down without enough sound to notice. Butchman sets a charge on the fuel depot and we back behind the water tank.

4 ... 3 ... 2 ... 1 ...

Hellfire rains from the sky. Pools of eager fire spread over the rocky ground, lapping at dried brush and pant legs. I come in low behind the Crank, breaking arms and bashing heads.

While the enemy dies, I suck dry filtered air. In through the nose, out through the mouth. Kill them first, don't give them a chance to do the same to me. Don't allow them the dignity of humanity.

A torch falls against me. I catch it under the jaw with the butt of my TR40 and hear bone snap under the crackle of flames.

Fiedler goes down under fire. Butchman has her back, it's all good. Too late, I see an Americo-Chinese open up in my direction. The strafe runs up my right leg, does not penetrate, but throbs like I'm the nail between the hammer and the steel. I roll with the shots, come up behind two crates, return fire. He isn't armored.

Grenades go off behind me. The blasts knock me and the Crank flat; audio damps the sound to a low popping. The Crank gets back on her feet and makes for the cave. I howl and push after her. Cheyko comes back twice as loud over audio, my one-woman cheering squad again.

Brick: "Weapons huts secured."

Aarons: "Back door secured. Going in."

Nails on chalkboard static bursts over the channel, gone two seconds later. "Jammers blocked," Gifu says, crystal clear. "Engaging countermeasures."

Heart racing, muscles pumping. The hourglass fills me with venom, the War Dog howls in my veins. Don't think, just do. Go, Go, GO!

I ride the rush through bursts of weapons fire and into the cave. The rock cools the blazing heat signature of the outside. Voices call deeper in, Chinese: "Attack! Under attack!"

Two gurgling targets sprawl on splintered crates. I follow the Crank deeper in. Blind turns make for bad runs; we move slow as quick as we can.

"We're in," the Crank says.

Fiedler: "Coming behind you."

Williams: "Copy that."

Butchman: "Nest of them behind the water—shit!" Burst fire rattles high and sharp over the channel.

Scotson: "On it."

The mountain rumbles from above and dust blocks visuals for a few seconds.

Butchman: "Spot on."

We move farther in and come to a branch, the wider way going forward and a smaller one to the left. Both glow with heat, the one on the left more recent passage. Red flashes in the upper left corner of the heads-ups. I bring up my dosimeter read, still zero. Nukes to the left. More important, so are the children. The Crank looks back at me. We nod and head down.

It's a tight sideways squeeze in the badgers. Chinese voices come up from below. And kids whimpering, kids chained to dirty nukes, kids Leo's age. Fiedler: "I'm in."

Williams: "Same."

I try to ping them and get nothing through the rock.

Aarons: "We may have passage to the south door. Repeat, passage to the south door."

The Crank: "Copy that. Secure and scan. Williams and Fiedler, the main passage. Butchman, the cave."

Black Widows spin webs, trap prey.

Gunfire cracks stone ahead of us, bullets ricocheting like angry wasps. The Crank swears but doesn't return fire, pushing ahead. Blue chem-light sneaks through the dark beyond her. Three steps, four, and she clears the passage to show these murderous assholes that Black Widows bite hard.

Scotson: "Incoming long range chopper from the south! One Irondragon-5R, mark that two, repeat, two Irondragon-5Rs from the south! ETA seven minutes!"

Shit.

I hear movement behind us, twist my head for a look. An Americo-Chinese soldier, blackened, bleeding, crazed, looks back at me above the rocket launcher. He screams something, maybe not even words, and pulls the trigger. He goes down with the blast back, and then my world is on fire.

Pain, Christ God-awful make it stop falling burning shrieking pain eats me alive and shits me out in incendiary pieces. Rocks tumble jagged laughter, and I fall into Hell, where there are voices big and small, the Crank calling for Gifu, Mattie down! Mattie down! Why is she calling for a medic? And who is Mattie?

Hot stone bites my back. I can't see, can't think. A spike drives through my chest and I blink at the rush of adrenaline and nerve blocks. The world is the world again in sharp relief.

I roll my head to the right. I'm on my back, the Crank cutting open what's left of my badger. Blood glistens on her helmet. "You're bleeding, Sarge."

"Shut up." She lifts my head, takes off the back of my helmet—*where's the front?*—and curses. She goes, comes back, presses something to the left side of my mouth. I touch it with the tip of my tongue and hear/feel it against my head.

Leo. I hear Leo crying nearby. I tilt my head up—it doesn't move the way it should—and see Leos huddled against the far wall, black boxes at their feet. Aarons appears out of thin air. No, a tunnel. He stops, doesn't move at all, and that's when I know, without knowing how I know, that I'm Mattie and it's bad. He's badgered up, I can't see his face at all, but I know. "Hey, Aarons."

"Hey, Mattie," he says softly, or maybe I only hear softly. "Sarge?"

I grip the Crank's hand. Cold air, hot fear. It's all about the adrenaline now. How much longer? How much longer? I taste blood. "ETA?"

"Four minutes," she says.

"Leo."

The Crank leans in close. "What?"

"Cut Leo—the kids—free and give me—" I laugh, the sound comes without asking me first. "—grenades."

She stares at me.

"Sarge?"

Is that Aarons or me? Can't tell.

"And another hit of juice." That's me, I know. I forget how to breathe; it takes me a moment to remember.

"Cut them loose, Aarons."

Aarons starts in. He jabbers at the kids. Can't understand a word of it.

Someone else comes in, a squat wall on legs. Cheyko keeps her laugh to herself.

"Give me a hand," Aarons says.

"All troops to the north cave," the Crank says. I hear it with my ears, feel it with my head. Must still have the personal debrief node. "Time for a bus ride. Repeat, everyone to the north cave. Butchman, you're driving. Scotson, buy us some time."

Butchman: "Copy that."

Scotson: "Fakers hot for full simulation."

My Manuel is at my side. He bites his lip, frowns at me. Did I disappoint him? "Awoo ..." I don't have much of a howl.

The Crank detaches a strip of thumb grenades from her belt, sets it on the left side of my chest, presses a hypodermic into my left hand. "You have two juice hits left. I sealed what I could. You have a saline pack on your side."

I shiver, feeling sick. "Get Leo out."

The Crank puts a hand to my chest, says to the others: "The tunnel back there is no go. Let's clear out what we can of the rubble. Maybe we can squeeze through."

"The blast cracked a tight split to the main passage just inside the back door," Cheyko says, jerking her head back. "We can take that."

The Crank nods. "We'll strip the kids off the cable if we make it out."

Jabbering Aarons and mute Leos, I watch them float away leaving the boxes behind. "Against the ... wall," I say. Think I say.

My Manuel helps the Crank and Cheyko lift me enough to lean me against the back wall. I see less of my legs and look away. I know it should hurt, maybe it does, but it doesn't hurt me. My husband's frown hurts more. I twitch my left hand towards my chest. "Take."

The Crank motions Cheyko out, waits until we are alone, then strips off my hourglass and my War Dog. The Crank has my back. "I'll see to it these get to Leo." Her voice cracks. It's not the audio. She stuffs the patches into a belt pouch. "Light the strip off. That should be enough."

"Copy that."

And she's gone.

I breathe in the smell of burn and blood and cooked meat. The black boxes get me all dirty.

In, out, drift. Is that their all clear? Check the clock, juice myself.

If my wounds don't kill me, the radiation will. Hurry up, Amero-China boys. You murderous assholes. Trust a memory to have your back, Leo. We got nothing if we ain't got Mattie.

My Manuel kisses me. His breath is cold in my mouth.

Author's Note

The Clarion West writing workshop changed both my writing and my life, though not without a cost. During the second week of the program in 2010, I challenged myself to write something I've never tried, military science fiction. I talked to a couple of infantry friends, and asked their permission to include a few of their experiences in the story. They said sure. I even included the nickname of one of them because it was authentic. It was also the wrong thing to do.

I'd made a terrible mistake. I broke down as did many of my furious classmates. After that week, most refused to speak to me beyond the slightest courtesy of "Excuse me" or "Move, please" for the remaining four weeks of the program. Some have not spoken to me to this day, seven years after the fact.

This was a hard lesson in how what can be done in reality cannot always be done in fiction, or, as the friend in question said when I told him what had happened, "You can't fucking do that!" It was also the first step in realizing how sick I was in terms of my mental illness, and how hard I would have to fight if I wanted to survive. My mental illness was not to blame for my writing choices and ignorance, but the fallout fed the shadows snickering in the corners of my mind. I fought back by stripping the story down to its bare bones and building it up again, learning from my mistakes to create a powerful piece.

Representation matters. Representation done right matters even more.

Lost in Translation

On'cher extended its ocular stalks towards the black and white creature masticating fibrous grass. "What is it?"

The First Lhur'tan trembled pride. "It is a pan-dah. We grew it from the only viable genetic sequence remaining on the derelict human archive ship. The humans will be very happy that we give them the pan-dah as a welcome gift in eight rotations."

Recycling vents around the edges of the atmospheric barrier circulated the nitrogen-oxygen atmospheric mix and a curious array of chemical signatures from the unfamiliar flora. The enclosure and additional residential hall had been constructed at what some deemed a lavish expense in the name of another tedious first contact.

The pan-dah rolled on the ground until all four limbs waved in the air. On'cher settled on its pods. "What does a pan-dah do?"

The First Lhur'tan quivered knowledgeable. "Our translation of human writing is incomplete, but the instruction module indicates that the pan-dah eats, shoots, and leaves."

"Ah. A formidable creature." On'cher approached the pan-dah with pods extended, cilials at rest. "Greetings, pan-dah. I am On'cher, Second Lhur'tan in service to the Mur'wpsix Gelcenter. May your pods never tangle in anxious thought."

It repeated the greeting in Yugaelit, the vibratory thrumming of the T'z'tit, and as a puff of Hunwha passive communication spores.

The pan-dah extruded a thick green and brown mass from the end opposite its mastication. On'cher sucked in its ocular stalks and thickened its membrane. When the mass did not detonate, On'cher extended a singular stalk towards its superior.

The First Lhur'tan burbled acknowledgment. "Unfortunately, it is a lesser sentient."

On'cher extended the rest of its stalks. "And the substance?"

"That is the waste product of the pan-dah's consumption of bam-booz." The First Lhur'tan extended a glistening ocher pod towards the plot of tall grasses. "We formulated the bam-booz with information gathered from the human botanical archives."

On'cher had absorbed the humans quaint botanical files. "This bam-booz lacks awareness. Why am I here?"

"Human records indicate the panda is extinct on the human homeworld. They will reward our supreme gift with favorable trade conditions for their heavy metals. You will ensure a steady supply of bam-booz for the pan-dah."

On'cher undulated confusion. "I am the senior botanical liaison to the Hunwha embassy."

The First Lhur'tan extended two pods to the base of On'cher's ocular stalks. "Exactly."

"But, but this bam-booz does not even recognize the pan-dah's assaults."

"No matter."

On'cher's pods tangled. "I communicate with plants, not grow them."

"I trust in your expertise."

With that, the First Lhur'tan slithered through the atmospheric barrier.

The pan-dah rolled onto the mass of gooey waste and promptly entered a state of lessened metabolic activity.

On'cher coiled resignation. It retracted its ocular stalks and slithered after its superior.

On'cher knew forty-two ways to promote positive and mutually fulfilling relationships with an array of sentient species. It spent the first quarter of its defined corporeal existence developing an open and empathic consciousness with the Known. After two rotations, it had developed a notable dislike for the pan-dah.

The creature appeared to have no interests beyond consuming bam-booz, creating waste, and spending extended periods in a reduced metabolic state. It preferred On'cher's carefully tended hyper-grown bam-booz to the fibrous mature flora, and had a prodigious appetite.

The First Lhur'tan dismissed On'cher's concerns. "You will manage."

They slithered together through the flowstone formations of the meditation garden. On'cher preferred its time under a proper burnt umber sky; the yellow sun and blue sky of the pan-dah's enclosure had begun to feel strangely, uncomfortably alien. "The pan-dah metabolizes less than twenty percent of its intake of bam-booz. The bhan'tans say it is possible to make the pan-dah's digestion more efficient, there-by reducing its nutritive intake and allowing me more time for my usual duties."

The First Lhur'tan quivered knowledgeable. "Then it would be a Mur'wpsix pan-dah, not a human pan-dah."

"Then the bhan'tans can improve the nutritive value of the bam-booz itself."

"It must be human bam-booz, grown human ways."

On'cher twirled desperate hope. "But I am to curate an art exchange with the Hunwha embassy, and create a visual interface for the T'z'tit forerunner program. May I delegate the pan-dah to a Third or Forth Lhur'tan?"

The First Lhur'tan plopped denial. "A change of caretakers might anger the pan-dah. You will manage."

The Hunwha grove provided equally ineffectual support. The bushy Ambassador of Branches puffed soothing pollens in On'cher's direction. Think of all the amazing things On'cher would learn working with the pan-dah.

On'cher blorped, and stroked the purring black moss around it. "It has a calcified internal support system that has pierced its membrane. The bha'tans insist the structure is part of the pan-dah's genetic coding, which is patently ridiculous. I spend more time tending to the pan-dah's dietary needs than I do on my duties as Second Lhur'tan."

Another puff, this time with a hint of buoyant affection. The First Lhur'tan must have great investment in the worth of On'cher's chlorophyll to entrust such a duty to it.

On'cher flattened sarcasm. "Ha!"

After four rotations of planting, observing, quarbling, and replanting, On'cher felt decidedly un-lhur'tan.

The translation of the human tongue might well have been in error. The pan-dah no longer appeared as formidable as On'cher first thought, unless one counted the havoc it wreaked upon the fibrous grass. It still could not fathom what to do with the pan-dah's excessive waste material. Piles of it littered the enclosure. The waste emitted a pleasant chemical signature, yet pan-dah was as likely to roll in it as it was to ignore it completely. Maybe the pan-dah instinctively used the waste material as a form of camouflage to hide from natural predators. Maybe other creatures did not consume the pan-dah for fear of contracting its stupidity.

On'cher extended and retracted its ocular stalks thoughtful. If it could not change its lhur'tan duties, it would have to change the pan-dah. On'cher could, reluctantly, tolerate an environment rich in nitrogen and oxygen, but research indicated the pan-dah would not survive a proper methane-chlorine atmosphere. The humans apparently suffered under the same deficit. A most un-lhur'tan awareness. On'cher noted the lapse, one of several of late, and its need for corrective gelling.

What about protecting against the atmosphere? On'cher slithered out of the enclosure and returned a short time later with an emergency containment bubble. By then the pan-dah had lowered its metabolism. Typical. Another un-lhur'tan awareness.

On'cher draped the bubble over the pan-dah. The membrane settled over and around the creature's bulk like flowstone. It made certain the bubble had a suitable atmospheric sample for replication, then adjusted the controls to allow for non-gaseous interactions. It prodded the pan-dah with one pod. "Pan-dah, you must move."

The creature continued to make low noises indicative of its state.

On'cher poked at the pan-dah again, this time with two pods. In places not matted with waste product, the creature's fur felt like Hunwha moss. "Pan-dah, I respectfully request that you move."

The pan-dah shuddered and opened its ocular orbs. A pink orifice tentacle slid over its calcified protrusions. As it lumbered upright and began to manipulate one of its two swiveling audio organs with a front limb, the bubble completely enclosed the creature in a spherical amber membrane. The pan-dah did not appear concerned.

On'cher bounced authority. "Pan-dah, you are now properly contained to allow for mobility. The bubble will prevent all respiratory atmospheric exposure while still allowing you to interact with the environment."

The pan-dah rolled onto all four limbs and disappeared into the plot of bam-booz. The stalks passed in and out of the membrane without disturbing a leaf.

On'cher trembled pride. The pan-dah could cross the enclosure's atmospheric barrier and it follow on embassy rounds. The exposure to different races might even encourage an increase in the pan-dah's cognition. On'cher extended its pods, cilials at rest. "Pan-dah, I request that you follow me. I have a scheduled interface at the T'z'tit embassy."

The wet cracking of the creature's mastication rippled over On'cher's membrane. It coiled resignation and retracted its ocular stalks, wondering if the pan-dah had cognition to increase.

The answer was not cognition, but appetite.

On'cher removed the growth pads to its second gel residence and brought a supply of tender stalk segments to the enclosure each rotation. It presented stalks in order of need, shorter pieces to facilitate mobilization, longer pieces to placate the pan-dah when they reached a given destination. It did not take the pan-dah long to learn that if it wanted to eat it had to follow On'cher.

Trembling pride and elongating efficiency, On'cher spent two full rotations catching up on its duties as Second Lhur'tan. The T'z'tit interface blossomed to fruition, the Hunwha art exchange engaged sentients from nineteen separate systems, and through it all the pan-dah followed, masticated, and extruded.

The ambassadors seemed fascinated with the pan-dah. They collected in the common areas of the ambassadorial campus to watch On'cher lead the creature around. Bright leaves and feathers swayed enthusiasm, spores burst red vegetative queries, prisms reflected substratums of questioning light. "Will the hoo-mans also extrude?" "Adoration limbs limited range! Holographic reference, holographic reference!" "b@dmaae^" "Eat, yes?"

On'cher decided against leaving its charge unattended.

The First Lhur'tan curled pleasure at On'cher's resourcefulness. "I knew you would find a way to assimilate the pan-dah's care into your scheduled duties."

They pooled together in the meditation garden beneath a flowstone overhang while the panda masticated supine in its bubble. On'cher hoped the pan-dah appreciated the rightness of a sky with chards and rempults in full phase.

It tossed its charge another segment of bam-booz. The pan-dah's fur was clean and smooth, an unanticipated benefit of the current feeding program. "It has proven a most enlightening experience."

"The humans will be pleased that their new pan-dah has been so readily accepted by the other embassies."

On'cher trembled pride. "Gratitude to you, First Lhur'tan."

"The humans shall grant the Mur'wpsix preferred trade status, and I shall receive favorable notice from the Grand Gel."

On'cher extended all of its eyestalks. "Pardon?"

The First Lhur'tan curled pods around On'cher's ocular stalks. "And you as well."

The pan-dah rolled onto its waste to retrieve the next piece of bam-booz.

On Arrival Day, On'cher made a special point to chem-wash its charge's fur. Even with blended frustration of political excess, On'cher wanted to make a good impression.

After re-inflating the bubble and a minimal first feeding – an extrusion of waste at the presentation would no doubt prove disastrous, perhaps even fatal – On'cher slithered to its first gel residence with a stop to pick up a fresh supply of bam-booz. Where went the bam-booz, so went the pan-dah. On'cher dribbled mirth and hurried on its way.

The First Lhur'tan contacted On'cher repeatedly. Was the pan-dah prepared? Yes, of course. And the enclosure? On'cher contacted the enclosure's droins on a separate wavelength and set them to the task before assuring the First Lhur'tan that everything was complete. What about bam-booz? Did On'cher have extra bam-booz to keep its charge occupied? Already pouched. Did it think a sedative would be needed so the pan-dah would not startle and attack? On'cher peeled exasperation yet answered with a lhur'tan's calm assurance that no sedative would be needed. Not for the pan-dah, anyway.

On'cher slithered into the residence and darkened the entrance to indicate gel time. It had spent far too little time at the first gel residence and missed the meditations curled on the walls, the scent of ripe flurgg. Really, flurgg made a gel residence a home.

It slithered into the center pit and unwound calm thought. Time to prepare itself for the humans. Let the First Lhur'tan slurp selfish and tremble pride. On'cher served the Mur'wpsix Gelcenter, and trembled pride at its own accomplishments. Someday other Mur'wpsix would as well. The pit warmed to On'cher's stillness and began to corrective gel.

Feathered peace. On'cher received a contact. It continued to gel. Another contact, and it refused with a statement of gel time. Moments later, another contact came through on the First Lhur'tan's singular wavelength: "The human transport has entered the lower atmosphere. Why aren't you at the vestibule? Where is the pan-dah?"

On'cher blobbed surprise. It slithered out of the pit and lunged for the observation wall. No! It had over gelled. "I am decontaminating an elimination area, and will be there shortly."

"Elimination in your first gel residence?"

On'cher brought up viewer wavelengths for human embassy's enclosure. It could not find the pah-dah. It shifted to different viewers. Nothing. No signs of a disturbance or fight. A clean enclosure, but no pan-dah. On'cher puckered fear. "I had hoped to engage the pan-dah's interests with further cultural exchange. We will be there soon."

"Do not disappoint me, Second Lhur'tan On'cher, or you will lose more than your ranking."

No corrective gel could strip away On'cher's un-lhur'tan awareness.

It called for mobilization and met the automated unit along the glide path. Where was the pan-dah? Had On'cher been taken in by the creature's ruse of incompetence? Was it even now stalking the ambassadorial campus, or, worse, the pits of the Grand Gel? Was this all an elaborate human plot to allow their agent of destruction inside Mur'wpsix defenses? On'cher's pods tangled. Puckered fear, puckered fear.

At the human embassy, On'cher rushed into the pristine enclosure. "Pan-dah! Pan-dah, I have bam-booz! Pan-dah?"

No pan-dah, only alien vegetation swaying in the circulated air.

It hurried to the observation wall and brought up the viewer wavelengths. It scanned back time until it found the pan-dah in its containment bubble mobilizing through the enclosure's atmospheric boundary in reverse. The creature mobilized backwards to the edges of where the growth pads had been, then snuffled over to a few bits of bam-booz on the floor. On'cher had been undone by trembled pride. The pan-dah's appetite had led it to seek bam-booz outside the enclosure. On'cher had been in such a hurry to corrective gel, it mis-judged the creature's metabolism.

The First Lhur'tan made contact once more: "The humans have

landed. Where are you? What have you done with the pan-dah?"

Puckered fear. On'cher muted the inquiry and forward timed the outside viewers. The pan-dah mobilized away from the human embassy to the common grounds. A T'z'tit courier waved three tentacles in excited recognition before heading into its embassy. On'cher undulated confusion, twirled desperate hope. The T'z'tit couriers were particular about their duties and never varied their scheduled routes. Judging by the time marker, this courier had finished its route, so the pan-dah had to be close.

The Hunwha wavelength activated. An automated voice came through: "Second Lhur'tan? Are you available? Your pan-dah is eating one of our staff. Should we poison? Please advise."

On'cher knotted panic. It imagined it could identify the Hunwha spores of alarm. It slithered out of the enclosure as fast as it could. "Do nothing! I will be there momentarily!"

At the Hunwha embassy, a dozen different species coiled and withered at the entrance. From inside the vestibule came the sounds of squealing moss, rustling leaves, and determined mastication. The Ambassador of Branches puffed fear at On'cher. The pan-dah's reputation was no lie. On'cher had to stop the pan-dah before the victim needed grafting.

On'cher pulled out short lengths of bam-booz and slithered into the vestibule where the pan-dah sat stripping leaves from a tall grass Hunwha. The top of the staffer's stalks had been chewed away, leaving nothing but moist stubs. "Pan-dah, cease your consumption. I have fresh bam-booz."

The pan-dah made no response. On'cher struck it over the head with the bam-booz, and the pan-dah stopped eating long enough to look at On'cher. At the sight of the bamboo, it dropped the staffer and pulled On'cher's pod forward. On'cher released the bam-booz, and helped the Hunwha drag the wounded staffer away while the pan-dah was distracted.

The bushy ambassador released agitated pollen bursts. Now it understood why On'cher made offerings of the dead to the pan-dah. It was a beast, a monster! Should the Hunwha seal their embassy against another attack? Would the humans demand further sacrifice to satisfy the pan-dah's terrible hunger?

On'cher vibrated relief. "I don't think so, but it is best not to speak of this until I have had the opportunity to, to confer with the pan-dah."

Should the Ambassador of Branches file a formal report with the First Lhur'tan?

"No need for that. You have my word by soil and sun that the pan-dah shall not trouble the Hunwha again. Now, if I may ask your pardon ..."

On'cher backed out of the vestibule, laying segments of bam-booz as it went. The pan-dah followed, pausing to consume each one. On'cher contacted the First Lhur'tan who answered immediately: "Your insult to the human embassy shall not go unreported. We were forced to greet them without our intended gift of welcome, and for that –"

"Escort them to the enclosure. I will be there with the pan-dah."

"Your lack of planning and poor –"

On'cher continued to drop bam-booz in front of the pan-dah at widening intervals to encourage interest in mobilization. "My skills are not in question in this discussion. Your willingness to make a favorable presentation to the human embassy is. Escort them to the enclosure."

The First Lhur'tan was silent a moment. "Your estimations had better be correct."

The contact snapped closed, and On'cher slimed relief to the Known.

One stalk at a time, On'cher coaxed the pan-dah across the common areas and back into the enclosure. It instructed the droins to retrieve the bam-booz growth pads, spilled the remaining bam-booz onto the floor, and deflated the pan-dah's bubble. It then settled down to compose a request to build a physical enclosure for the formidable pan-dah for reasons of sentient safety.

It finished the request as the official mobilization arrived. The unit merged with the atmospheric barrier, the connection point resolved, and the First Lhurtan escorted the human embassy and a surrounding of Third and Fourth Lhur'tans into the enclosure.

At the sight of On'cher the First Lhur'tan striated outrage, yet kept all ocular stalks extended. It slithered to one side. "Cap-tayn Loo-iz, human embassy," it said, and strange metallic sounds came from a translator unit attached to one pod, "I present to you Second Lhur'tan On'cher, and our privileged gift of welcome to you."

On'cher extended its pods, cilials at rest. "Welcome, human embassy."

The pan-dah lay supine and masticated with single-minded intent.

The humans stood motionless. Twelve in all, they were covered in identical partial containments, all the same distasteful blue. The one with the darkest membrane opened its head orifice, closed it, lifted an upper limb toward the pan-dah. It made noises at the other humans, they made noises back, quick and high, alone and together. Some shaped their orifices up, some down. On'cher spun sympathy. The humans had calcified protrusions similar to the pan-dah's.

A smaller human shook its head, made a soft sound, and its ocular orbs began to leak. It brought its two upper limbs to its head orifice, then turned its back to On'cher. A threat? No, the human with the darkest membrane set its limb around the smallest one in what appeared to be a recognition of some sort. A tall human began to leak in a similar manner, and a round one.

On'cher undulated confusion. Had it offended?

The First Lhur'tan extended and retracted its ocular stalks thoughtful at On'cher, then made a deliberate gesture towards the middle section of the one who raised its limb. "Your translator, Captayn Loo-iz."

At the strange metallic sounds, the human fumbled at its middle section and produced a translator. The human made strange noises, and the translator said, "Greetings."

The First Lhur'tan considered On'cher with all ocular stalks, then signaled to a Fourth Lhur'tan. The underling slithered over to On'cher, presented a translator, and backed away.

On'cher hung the translator from an ocular stalk. "Greetings, Captayn Loo-iz."

The human brought a limb to its orifice and made a sharp noise. "Is that ... Is that a correct panda?"

The monotone translator voice had no emotion, but the human exhibited none of the ninety-eight recognized indications of hostility.

On'cher quivered knowledgeable. "It is a human pan-dah, yes."

The human focused both ocular orbs on the pan-dah. It made another sharp sound, wiped leakage from its ocular orbs. "We have not seen a human pan-dah in ... significant length of human measurement of time. Exclamation of surprise and wonderment."

On'cher trembled pride. "Do not tangle your pods in anxious thought. I will provide your nutritional specilists instruction on the care and harvest of bam-booz. The pan-dah eats shoots and leaves."

The pan-dah extruded waste and rolled on top of it.

Author's Note

"Where do you get your ideas?"

From conversations with my family.

My partner, oldest son, and I were running errands and the old saw about how a panda "eats, shoots, and leaves" came up. One-liners followed fast and furious, and I began to wonder out loud about what aliens might think when they encountered a panda for the first time if that is all anyone knew about it: "Ah, a formidable creature."

I don't often write science fiction, but sometimes a story hits that sweet spot and I laugh every time.

Truth Is A Stranger To Fiction

"More! More!" the Menagerie chants.

From his seat at the head of the table, Master Robinson nods for another tale.

The chimera comes up on its hind legs. I sidle behind its musty bulk to refill its mug with wine. The pitcher taps against the rim of the goblet, and a birdsong of silver and bone sounds high and sweet. Master Robinson smiles at me, and I love him.

The chimera smoothes its belly fur with a wide paw. "You were found under a giant cabbage leaf by a family of grigs," it says with three throats. "They took you to their acorn home and raised you as their only child, along with your seventy-eleven brothers and sisters. They plumped you up with henbane until you were thin as a damsel fly's wing, and a strong wind whisked you away."

The Menagerie hoots and howls with laughter, hooves and hands pounding the table, all save one slight form in midnight robes, wedged between the drake and the hippogryph. She has skin the color of sunset sands, and hair as splendid as a thundercloud. A gold and alabaster horn sprouts from the middle of her forehead, and tufts of down feather her chin and wrists. She only has eyes for Master Robinson, which I understand, yet her eyes are sad, which I do not.

Outside the pavilion, the night wind blows a lullaby to the dunes, a cold, lonely song. Inside, oil lamps and a full firebox warm the air, stories and wine the spirits. The thunderbird tells how Master Robinson's parents baked him inside a salt crust and then left him to cool on the windowsill, how they chased him into the sea and the crust washed away, forever making the water salty as tears. In a gravel voice, the catoblepas sings how Master Robinson was born in a bubble blown from a drunkard's pipe and floated away when the man passed out in his cups.

I reach the woman one pouring at a time. She has no cup. "Why are you so sad?"

She looks at me without turning her head. I marvel at her eyes, dark as her hair. "I'm not sad," she says so low I almost cannot hear her under the Menagerie's laughter.

"Your eyes are. Drinking will make you happy." I turn to fetch her a goblet.

She stops me with a hand on my arm. "I don't drink."

"Oh. I'm sorry."

Her eyes are happy and sad at the same time. "Don't be." She releases my arm, smiles. "What's your name?"

I smile back, proud of my name. "Sassy."

"Ah." She looks back to Master Robinson with sad eyes once more.

I pour wine and serve dishes of sweet treats and tiny, salted fish in oil, always to Master Robinson first and then the rest of the Menagerie. Master Robinson pats me on the head, calls me good girl, feeds me a treat and lets me drink from his cup. The kitsune, the raksasha, and the wyvern all tell tales in turn, and then the woman with sad eyes stands.

"You were born to a mother still a child herself," she says. Lamplight edges her lips and words with cinnamon. "She had been abandoned by your father, and tried to raise you on her own, but your mother's family was sick and the sickness had invaded her soul. By the time people came to take you from her, the girl was too sick to care, and when they told her she had to give up being your mother she didn't know any better than to say yes. So you were raised house to house, some good, some bad, but most indifferent, which is the worst kind of house because indifference hollows out a child's heart. And it took your mother many years and cures to finally find you, and tell you how sorry she is, and how much she loves you."

The Menagerie erupts in gay and glorious mirth.

"Fantastic," says the gargoyle, chuckling a landslide.

"The best one yet!" says the troll, holding its sides.

All save Master Robinson. Shadows hang around his face, hiding his eyes. He lifts his goblet with a shaking hand, spilling wine on his fine shirt. I hurry to refill his cup, but the pitcher is empty. He does not call me good girl or pat my head.

I scamper outside to refill the pitcher and find the woman standing by the barrel. As I move around her to reach the tap, she gives a soft squeak. "Oh, it's you."

I blink up at her, shivering in the night's lullaby. "Who else would I be?"

"No, I mean ... Never mind."

I position the pitcher under the spout, and the woman peels the down off her wrists and chin. She presses the sticky ends together until they form a puff too pale to have color in the dark. I watch with interest, still mindful of the pitcher so it does not overfill.

"Thank you, Sassy," she says, and pulls off the horn. She rubs the place where it sat with her fingers, flicking bits of something to the sand.

I close the tap. "For what?"

"For being there, here, for him."

"Master Robinson?"

She nods, put the horn and puff inside her robe. "Yeah. Master Robinson." She makes a sound almost like a laugh. "They laughed. I didn't know what to expect. I guess, I guess truth really is stranger than fiction."

I want to understand, but I have to get back inside to fill Master Robinson's goblet. "Okay."

"Take care of yourself, Sassy. Take care of ..." She must have run out of words because she stops talking and walks away, over the dunes and into the night.

I return to the pavilion and the Menagerie, where everyone laughs, Master Robinson hardest of all. Laughs until he cries.

Author's Note

Addiction runs in my family, and with it the attendant shadows stirring in the background, the abuses and co-dependencies, the fears of failure, the need to blame someone, anyone, else for the terrible things you have done. I caught stray memories of my childhood in a moonsilk net and sifted through them for the pain and heartache that colors this story. It wasn't easy to write, but I think I did okay.

Blue

With her eyelids sewn shut for so long, Elena worried she had forgotten blue. "It's the color of sky," she said while Nurse dressed Elena in her favorite shift, the one with soft lace at the throat and smooth round buttons at the wrists, "and Lydia's dress, the one she wore to the summer fair."

"No, blue is the color of leaves and young spring wheat," said Nurse. "You're thinking green."

Elena frowned. She wanted to shake her head, but knew better than to move without Nurse's guidance when dressing. Nurse had big hands. "Really? No, blue is the sky, isn't it? I thought—"

"The sky is green," said Nurse. "Lift your chin."

The Ministry needed to sew Elena's eyes shut. Something about infection, or infectious, or contagious, they said. Then they cauterized the wounds, and bound Elena's hands to her sides until everything healed. And Elena had an entire stage to herself at the harvest jamboree last autumn—well, to share with Nurse and members of the Ministry— so everyone could see her. Something about teaching, or a lesson, they said. Very educational, Elena supposed. Like the flutter of birds wings, thoughts did not stay long.

Her eyes still moved. They strained this way and that under her lids until her head ached and Nurse gave her medicinal broth. Would her eyes eventually wither to the size of dried peas and roll around in her sockets, rattle inside her skull? Sometimes, when she could no longer smell Nurse's antiseptic sweetness, Elena would crawl to the chair, drag it the seven brick bumps to the window, and carefully stand on the woven seat so she could press her face to the cool, smooth glass. Yellow light from outside painted red and black patterns on the inside of her lids. At least she remembered the sun being yellow. And the sky as blue as Lydia's dress.

She always made certain to wipe the oily spots off the window and push the chair back into place before Nurse returned. No, not always. Once she forgot. Nurse had rough hands.

"Last night I dreamt about a bird," Elena said between spoonfuls of porridge with plump, sweet raisins that popped between her teeth. "It flew through my window and landed at the foot of my bed, and had the most beautiful red plumage."

"Puppies are red, birds are brown," said Nurse.

"Yes, but in the dream the bird was—"

Nurse took the bowl of porridge and the spoon. "Puppies are red, birds are brown."

"Yes, brown. Birds are brown."

"And puppies?"

Elena folded her hands in her lap. "Are red. Puppies are red, birds are brown."

That afternoon a film crew set up a live feed in her room so people everywhere could watch her identify feathers by their textured shades of brown. A woman with cold hands and smoker's breath used a fine-haired brush to paint a thick, cool liquid over the puckered crescent scars of Elena's eyes. The cameras whirred, buzzed, and beeped. Two men, one with a voice of silk, the other gravel, complimented her. They asked if she was happy. Yes, very happy. Was she being treated well? Yes, very well. Was there anything she wanted her friends to know? Yes, they shouldn't worry, she was very happy and being treated very well. The Ministry approved. Inspired viewing, or required viewing, they said.

After the filming and dinner of lentil soup with bacon and onions, Nurse gave Elena three pieces of Turkish Delight that tickled the roof of her mouth and left her drowsy. Elena liked Turkish Delight; it made thinking sweet. Nurse turned on the helping music with the happy voices, and Elena played with her hair until she drifted off to sleep.

Lydia skipped down Vendors Lane at the summer fair, puckered flowers in her red and black hair. Lydia in a grass dress, under a young spring wheat sky, chattering on about how very happy she was, and how much she loved the Ministry. Loved, loved, very happy and very well, growing smaller and less substantial the more Elena chased her.

Elena woke with a fist stuffed in her mouth, holding back a scream she hadn't known was there. The helping music played on, happy, happy voices. She curled into a ball on her side and wanted to cry, but tears were gone, along with her sight, and something else, something important. Something about the sky.

Author's Note

I had a stroke in 2011. I got out of bed, stumbled into the bathroom (huh, that's strange), fell onto the toilet (weird), wiped and flushed with a trembling right hand (must have slept on it wrong). While brushing my teeth (my hand isn't doing what it should, what's up with that?), I watched the right side of my face droop in the mirror (dammit, Bell's Palsy again, another complex migraine). My partner rushed me to the the ER where the staff immediately wheeled me into a room. The first doctor thought I was faking (gee, thanks lady!), but brought in a neurologist who recommended I stay overnight and have a stroke work-up so they could have a baseline in case I ever did have a stroke (well, that's something, at least).

I was taken for an MRI, a carotid ultrasound, and an x-ray (finally, some progress). Surprise, surprise, it wasn't a complex migraine but a genuine stroke (wow!). The doctor went to the computer terminal on the other side of my room and brought up the films from the MRI (NEAT!). Much to the horror of the nurses, I got out of bed and tottered over to join him without a safety belt or any sort of support (so I'm wobbly, big deal). The doctor showed me the damaged areas, said the therapists would be in later to evaluate my needs, and promptly split (but I still have questions!). So did the nurses (wait!). I was alone ...

I remained in the hospital overnight for observation though there wasn't much to observe. There was no wound to tend, merely echoes of damage done. Caught in the stillness of my room, I pressed the tips of my fingers of both hands to my eyelids, pulling them tight against my face. I turned to the window, marveling at the red and black dance of sunlight through the thin skin. I rolled my eyes, so very much like peas rattling around my damaged head. I could no longer see the future, only red and black. I could not feel the future, only the strong hands of the nurses. I was not allowed out of bed without supervision.

That night, Elena curled around me and we whispered secrets, so many secrets, until she drifted off to sleep and I was left alone with the antiseptic sweetness of the night.

A Troll's Trade

Maybe I should have listened to me mudder, been a mason or a carpenter.

What do I do instead?

"A what?" she said, and turned the spit so fast the apple tumbled out of the goat's mouth and into the fire.

I picked me nose and spread it on a cracker with a bit of brie. "A florist."

"What would your Pa say?" She fished the apple out of the fire, and jammed it back in place. "He built our bridge with—"

"With the sweat off his nose before he got tricked by the Maiden of Merriwether and turned to cheese, yah, yah, I know. Chisels and mortar and nails aren't me thing, is all."

She sniffed. "Flowers are for wiping, not arranging."

I sighed. "Don't be like that. Sure they're soft, but you can do some—"

"My son the florist." Me mudder teared up. "Where are you going to live if'n you can't find a bridge?"

I was young, hornstrong, determined to make me own way. How was I to know there were more trolls than bridges? Who'd have thunk!

So, yeah, me mudder was right, and when she turned me out I wound up with no bridge to call me own.

I figured maybe I could live someplace else, become a trendsetter. It doesn't always got to be a bridge, right? I tried a vine trellis, even a vineyard row, but neither had that special hidey something that makes a place livable. Haylofts were awful high up, and root cellars offered no privacy. Chicken coops? No thank you; I have me pride.

So, I did the only thing I could. I went to live under a porch. It wasn't proper or even fancy, but it was a roof over me head. The folk family kept goats and chickens, had a garden with lovely sweet peas in the spring and winter squash blossoms in autumn. There was even a field a good skulk away with red and orange poppies, and rose mallow. I grabbed the kids' ankles at least twice a week to keep in shape. I could have wished the folk mum didn't always hold the most tender, but, well, florists can't be choosers.

Thing is, there isn't much room under a porch, not like there is under a proper bridge. Always dirty and spidery, no room for flowers or pots let alone a nice vase, and I could never stand up. Made for a nasty belly rash, that. Not even a place to set up a spit or me smallest cook pot.

I missed good food. Trolls were not meant to live on bark alone, so one night I cooked out in the open while the folk family slept, a baby goat with cowberry sauce like me mudder used to make. Grass burns faster and farther than I expected. Doesn't take long to grow back, though.

No, life under a porch was not for me. The local bridges were all taken, all except for the comfy stone bridge south of the city proper with the not so comfy ghosts. I heard tell of a gray beard who lived under a city bridge and was maybe looking for something less busier, so I went to see what we could work out. Well, he worked me out alrighty, right out from under his bridge with a roar and a tumble. Him and his silver coins woven into his back hair sos the trollops might find him fancy. Fah!

And it was such a nice bridge, a right full overpass. Worked stone arches, strong pylons, no ghosts.

Fuddleswort up north said I would be better off going over the Old Bones Range and find me a gulley bridge. Edfart said Fuddleswort was full of stinky soup, and I should get me a big pot, cook up a folk stew with peppers and baby fern, and make meself at folk home. Fuddleswort said baby fern didn't hold up, and to use kale.

"Baby fern."

"Kale."

"Baby fern!"

"Kale!"

They locked horns, and I left them to make out for themselves.

I almost crawled back home, but what with the rash and all I couldn't take the pain. There was nothing to it but to braid buttercup crowns and thunk trollish thoughts.

The answer? Money. And for money, I needed folks.

The folk pa seemed a decent sort as far as folk go. He did have the heaviest step, but he didn't tromp over me just because he could. A regular folk with no charms or trickery about him, which is good;

cheese is for eating, not being. As I understood it, he worked the market selling fresh eggs and his wife's bakings, more like burnings, actually, which was perfect for me.

I thunk me thoughts all the way through, and when he came down the two short steps early one morning to gather eggs I was ready for him.

I grabbed his ankle at the bottom step. The folk pa whooped and took a tumble, basket one way, hat another, and me holding on. He tried to jerk his foot away, and I jerked back. "I want to talk to you," I said. I glowied me eyes so he could see me. I must have glowied them too well because he fainted dead away. Folks.

A few seconds later he came to and tried to get his feet, but I still had one. "I just want to talk."

His eyes bugged and his face turned all sorts of colors before he settled down. There was enough of me hand and arm showing that he could follow it under the porch to me not so glowy eyes. "You're real," he said, rather, squeaked.

"Yah."

"The children. They said you—"

"I'm a troll. That's what I do."

He gulped. "Are you ... Are you going to eat me?"

Not without cooking him first. What does Edfart know. Grown folk are best braised. "No."

He managed a sit and then bent low for a closer look. "What are you doing under my porch?"

"It's me summer home. I need to use your fireplace."

He moved his leg. I didn't let go.

"My what?"

"Fireplace. Your fireplace."

"My fireplace?"

This wasn't going like I thunk it would. "That's what I said."

"All right. Why? And how did you get under there? I thought you trolls are, you know, big."

Like that, I pulled his leg all the way under the porch.

The folk pa squealed. "Okay, okay! You're a troll. Big troll, huge troll, massive, ginormous."

"Better." He smelled ripe with sweat, nothing a little oregano couldn't fix. I gave him his leg back.

To his credit, he didn't run. He got to his hands and knees, still peering under the porch. "So, if you don't mind my asking, why do you need my fireplace?"

"I want to cook."

His eyes bugged again. "Not the children, I hope."

Kid pie with potatoes and pearl onions. Me drool made the ground all muddy. "No."

The folk pa sold food so food it would be, though I'd a florist's wanting for flowers. I set out what I needed from market. He listened, nodding his head with all that floppy red hair. "I'll, um, I'll have to tell my wife. Midge. She's my wife."

"Yah."

He squinted his eyes for a better look. I glowied mine, and he decided he's seen enough.

"Right," he said, and mopped his brow with a muddy hand. "You'll do your cooking, and then you'll crawl back under the porch to eat. I hope."

"No, then you take it to market."

That's when he figured it was best to get on gathering eggs. I liked him more already.

That night, when the candles were guttered and the dark everywhere, I crept inside and found me fixings on the plank table. Houses give me the willies with their shuttered eyes and walls and doors; they're too housey. I put it out of me mind and set to work. True to our agreement, the grown folks stayed in their beds and left me good and alone. Good thing, too. I eat when I get nervous.

Before the first of them made a noise the next morning, a baker's make of cherry clafoutis wrapped in checked muslin waited on the table. I snuck out of the house just as the most tender set up a hungry squall. Lucky for him I'd made extra for me own hunger.

With the eggs gathered and whatever folk do in the mornings done, the folk pa set off to market with the eggs, me luscious clafoutis, and two of his wife's custard pies. "Have a good day," I said around me last mouthful.

He nodded, and stepped a little faster on his way.

As usual, he was home after sunset, baskets swinging from his arms and a frown on his face. He settled himself on the first step and sat without a word. I heard a muted tinkle, muffled metal on metal.

What was he waiting for? I cleared me throat and he nearly fell off the step.

"Oh, you are there," he said.

"Sit on the ground," I said.

He did. I couldn't see his face, but he worked the cap in his hands like a folk mum on washday. "You sold them all?"

"I did." He opened his cap, pulled out a few coins, held them low so I could see. "Five silver and three half-coppers. Your share."

"What about your wife's pies?"

His hands drooped, but he didn't let go of the coins. "Still have them both. Everyone wanted more of your tart things." He lifted the corner of the cloth over one basket. "I don't even think I can get the goats to eat these."

I wouldn't want to eat the goat that ate her pies. "Too bad."

He presented the coins a second time.

"Keep them for now," I said. "You'll be needing them for market tomorrow."

"All of them?"

He sounded somehow wistful, and that's when I was certain.

"We'll work something out," I said.

We started small, a few popovers here, a pile of raisin tarts there, on the folk holidays sugar buns stuffed with goat cheese and apricots. I added slugs and potash to me sugar buns, an acquired taste, I know. On the days he came home with empty baskets, I let him keep two silver coins and I buried the rest in a hole at the back of the porch. The kids soon had new shoes, and the oldest kid a red ribbon for her hair.

A baby goat went missing the night the folk pa counted out me hundredth piece of silver. No idea how that happened. Quite tasty with a toe jam glaze, though.

Like a good bridge, good business needed a strong foundation; the folk pa bought the fixings at market, and I did the cooking.

"We're bringing in enough that I put silver down on Ha'penny Jack's old stall today," he said one evening from his place at the front step. "I'm moving over tomorrow. It's big enough for a stool if I want, maybe even a second body if business keeps up. Midge thinks it's a good idea."

I wasn't in the mood to be happy for his larger stall. The rash was bad enough I had taken to staying on me back, and now the tip of me nose was sunburned from poking up through the porch slats. "Fine."

"You all right?"

"Just spiffy."

"No harm. Just asking."

I thunk about ways to rub me belly against the porch without catching me pelt in the cracks. What he thunk about, I hadn't a clue or care.

The sun was an orange memory when the folk pa said, "There is one thing, um ... Heh, I don't even know your name."

"Of course you don't," I said as testy as I pleased. "Trolls don't tell folks their names because folks with magic can do nasty things with them."

"Oh. I didn't know. What, um, what do I call you? 'Ginormous troll under the porch' is a bit awkward."

I huffed. "Call me Troll."

"Troll. Makes sense. I'm Sando Loggerson." He waited, shifted his feet, kicked up dust when I didn't want to sneeze. I let him wait.

"So, Troll. Midge and I were talking last night before you came in, and she wondered."

"Wondered what?"

"Well, if you could maybe share a few of your recipes."

There wasn't room to roll me eyes, either.

One late summer evening while I sat under the moon scratching and fretting on how me plans were taking longer than I thunk they should, Edfart and Fuddleswort surprised me with a visit. I don't get many visitors; don't really have a place for entertaining. Still, I set out some field greens with scabby bits and light vinaigrette. Only the best for friends, I say.

I couldn't make tails or nosehairs of me troubles, so I settled those two down and told the whole story.

Fuddleswort nodded, and picked his nose to garnish his salad. "Told you you should have looked for a gulley bridge."

"I don't want a gulley bridge," I said back.

"Says the troll with porch rash." He sniffed and went on eating. "Why not's just eats the folk and make a bridge of their house?"

Edfart said, picking scabby bits from between his teeth and sucking his finger clean.

Even the thought made me shiver. "Don't like houses, not at all."

"Don't got to keep it a house. Knock out the walls, leave the roof, and you gots yourself a bridge. Easy as mud pie."

Now, there was a thunk. I rolled it over between me horns. "No, still too housey. It's a bridge or nothin' for me."

Edfart gobbled up the rest of his greens. "Suit yourself." He stood and headed for the house.

Just like Edfart to not listen. "I said I wouldn't be knocking out the walls."

He waved at me over his shoulder. "I heard you. I'm still hungry is all."

Fuddleswort stood— "Now there's an idea." —and followed after.

"Hold on now." I came up and hurried right behind. "You can't be doin' that."

Edfart rubbed his belly. "The salad was nice, but no ways a meal for a growing troll."

Fuddleswort smacked his dead-fish lips. "Yeah. You said they gots an oven. We could whip up a crust and make pasties."

Human pasties with capers and fennel. Yeah. Almost as good as a braise.

Wait. No.

Quick like, I got ahead put out me arms. "There'll be no eatin' of the folks, understand?"

"No worries, there's plenty for us all." Edfart made to step around me, and I stepped with him. He frowned, and glowied his eyes. "Come on."

I stood up straight, head and horns above either of them. "They're my folks, and I says no eatin'."

"Like he said, there's plenty to go around." Fuddleswort wiped the drool off his chin. "Seeing's as you're the host, you get the first pick."

They made to go around on both sides. I grabbed a horn on each and shook them up good. "When I says no eatin', I mean NO E – " I couldn't give a proper roar or I'd wake the folk, so I choked it off quick. "—eatin'."

"Oi!" Edfart grabbed my wrist and tried to pull free. I held on troll tight. "Didn't your mother teach you no manners? It's rude not to share."

"Yeah." Fuddleswort waggled his head, but didn't do no better.

"What's all this?"

Yeah. What was all this? It wasn't like I didn't have a taste for the most tender, or even the older folk sometimes. So why wasn't I letting them have a sit down with me?

Maybe because I wanted the folk all to meself. Or could be I'd come to like having the folk around. Possibly. Sort of. A little.

I shook those two until their eyes rattled in their sockets. "They're my folk and I can do with them what I please, and what I please is no eatin'. Got that?"

I slammed their heads together like pig iron bells and dragged them back to the stream.

I dropped them down, and settled myself between them and the folk's house. Now and again Fuddleswort would look to the house, or Edfart would make to stand, and I'd glowy me eyes at them until they settled back down.

Finally, Edfart pulled up more greens and rubbed them around the inside of the salad bowl. He stuffed the whole scabby wad in his mouth and muttered around the stems.

I made like to reach for one of his horns. "What was that again?"

He swallowed the mouthful and hunched his head to his shoulders. "I said leave it to a florist to get all flowery soft."

"That's ri— " Me thinking came back and dropped the last piece into place light as a rose petal. Flowers? Flowers!

I grabbed Edfart by both horns and kissed the end of his warty nose. "Edfart, you're a genius!"

He wiped off the slobber. "Wait. What?"

"Flowers! Don't you sees? He just bought a bigger stall. I got so tangled up in thinking folks would pay for good food, I never thought they might pay for good flowers!"

Fuddleswort scratched the side of his head. "Do they pay before or after they wipe?" He covered his face with his hands. "Don't kiss me!"

Straight away I had Sando bring me flowers whenever he could. I used up the folks' pitchers and jars until he could bring home proper vases. While sweet and savory memories of me mudder filled the creepy house,

I used dried moss and earwax as a base for me arrangements. Balance, proportion, color, and earwax. Lots of earwax.

Sando took me creations to market, and most often they sold better than me bakings. Business was good, as much as nine silver my take some days. The grown folk talked of finding a house in the city for the family, and a proper bridge for me. I sent me mudder a scroll with the good news. She sent me back a phbtbtbtbtbt, I'll believe it when I see it.

Fuddleswort and Edfart were dumbfounded.

"What's all this about?" Fuddleswort said one mid-winter night as I handed him an arrangement of holly berry and ivy. The snow made his bridge look less rickety, more bridgety.

"I made it meself," I said, proud and a bit self-conscious. I was going places but still lived under the porch.

Edfart gave me a long sniff. "You smell like ... pansies!"

"Hothouse sweet peas, actually."

Fuddleswort held up the basket and looked it over. "What do I do with it?"

Edfart picked at a leaf. "I think it's a salad."

I slapped him upside the horns. "No, it's not a salad. You put it somewhere nice to look at it. Here." I took the arrangement from Fuddleswort and looked for a place where it wouldn't get stepped on or lost in the snow. No good. I looked at the soffits under the bridge, and then to Edfart. "Behind you! A dragon!"

Edfart whirled around. "Where?"

I yanked out one of his back hairs, and wrapped one end around the basket handle. I bent the other end into a hook, considered me options, and hung it as close to the middle of the stretch as I could. I stepped back. "There."

Edfart rubbed his back. "I still say salad."

Fuddleswort stared at the bit of color hanging in the middle of the snow and dark. "I dunno. Brightens the place up a bit, don'cha think?"

During spring and such, extra flowers and greenery were kept fresh in a bucket wedged between two rocks in the stream. At the end of every market six-day, I made an arrangement out of what was left for the plank table to make the folk house seem less housey. I didn't give the arrangements much thought after the fact until the night Sando and Midge came into the kitchen.

Mulberries are a favorite summer treat, me mudder's mulberry and frog kidney pie in particular. Fresh out of frog kidneys, I can't eat just one, I'd decided on mulberry pasties for market. In the middle of spooning out the next bit of filling, I heard a step and a low gasp behind me. I whirled around in a splatter of mulberry syrup.

Sando and Midge stood at the door to the loft stair, he shamefaced, she wide-eyed. "She said she would come down with or without me, so ..." Sando hitched a shoulder and smiled as best he could.

A hand on her elbow, he led her to the plank table where I worked.

The spoon dripped in time with their steps. I licked it, and stuck it behind me ear. "Mind the mess," I said.

Some part of me noticed that she didn't have the most tender with her, the rest of me was too surprised to care. Sando went to market, but he never did anything without her approval. She could end it all right here and I'd have to live under a porch foreverer. I'd be nothing but rash and stinky soup.

They stopped at the corner of the table. "Troll, this is my wife Midge," Sando said, gesturing to us both. "Midge, this is Troll."

Such a small woman; no wonder her step was so light.

Midge looked up, up, up at me. "You really are big, aren't you?"

I shook me head, the spoon knocking against a horn not as loud as me knocking knees. "Not so much. You're just short."

I smiled. She paled. I stopped smiling.

Sando put his arm around her. "What he means is— "

Midge shushed him with a look and a wave of her hand. She pushed the bowl of mulberries and trays of dough circles aside, and climbed onto the table. Her robe and shift bunched up around her twig legs, not that she seemed to notice but Sando did. As he pulled her clothes stuff back down, he flushed and gave me a sidelong look. Folks is the craziest people sometimes.

Midge brushed Sando's hands away, took two steps towards me, and looked me right in the throat. In fits and starts, she reached up and took me horns in her tiny folk hands. I let her pull me head down until we were eye-to-eye. Right to say that at that moment I'd have rather gone to live with the ghosts.

"Thank you for the lovely flowers," she said, and kissed me on the peeling tip of me nose. "Tomorrow I'll mix-up an oatmeal rub for that rash."

I'm a troll. I don't believe in happy endings, but comfortable ones aren't so bad.

The city council approved Sando's petition for a house, and he set to building. The family moved before the autumn rains. This new house has a room specifically for cooking. Another room; I'm not certain I like it.

Sando did something he calls hired to a kid, and now the kid minds the shop when Sando has other business. Sando's oldest kid seems quite taken with him. No idea what she sees in him, though; folks aren't much for looks. Midge helps me with bakings, and almost never burns things anymore. The younger kids love to take their friends across town to feed the ducks, particularly if they know I'm home.

Home. I'm a city troll now, and I have a city troll bridge. I'd paid another visit to the gray beard. He'd reached for me to show me what for, and I'd hit him over the head with me bag of silver. All them coins scattered out, and his eyes glowied right up. Said he wanted something smaller, less cluttered. I directed him to Sando's porch.

The overpass is more than enough for one troll, and comfortable for three. I call the main arch me own, and Fuddleswort has the east arch near the stables. Edfart likes his span bridge over Lockjaw Gorge too much to move. Me mudder is coming to visit this summer, and I wonder if she wouldn't fancy a place in the city, with rabbits and kids and squirrels fresh for the pot.

Yeah, maybe I should have listened to me mudder, but if I had I wouldn't have such splendid flowerboxes under a bridge I can call me own.

Author's Note

"A Troll's Trade" was my fourth week Clarion West story under the incredible, and sorely missed, Graham Joyce. I rarely write fantasy, but my brother suggested I write about a troll too poor to afford his own bridge so he went to live under a porch. The conversation left me to wonder why the troll didn't just build his own bridge, one thing led to another, and a florist troll was born.

If you haven't already, check out Wilson Fowley's narration of the story for Cast of Wonders, episode #182. He knocks it out of the park.

(My brother later ended up living under my back deck for months, but that's a trollish tale for another time.)

Afternote

I was there in the Clarion West classroom on the day Sandra describes in the afternote to "Black Widow." There was a lot of emotion in the classroom that day. A couple weeks later, I was there again when Sandra pissed off many of her classmates with yet another story. It worried me a little, because I was one of the people running the writing group that many local Clarion West graduates joined after the workshop. If she pissed off people in the workshop, what effect was she going to have on the group?

But I figured the group was robust enough to survive the injection of a new element and so, when a couple of people got fussy beforehand, I stood my ground and said, nope, we are open to anyone that comes through that workshop. And that was one of the smartest things I've done in this life.

Today I count Sandra one of my best friends. She can be off-putting, alarming, and say things in a restaurant that have every single person there turning to look at you. And she is gold, through and through. She has been through shit that most people would have crumpled like tinfoil under. She takes care of the creatures around her, to the point of adopting two kittens with special needs, despite all the other crap she has to deal with on a daily basis. She is one of the most amazing human beings I know, and better at being a human than I am.

And she is a fierce talent, with an equally fierce work ethic behind it. I poked her into putting together this collection and then poked her again until she coughed up two stories she hadn't planned on including, the aforementioned "Black Widows" and the devastating "Good Boy."

This collection shows her range, her depth, and her talent and I am very proud to have had a hand in bringing it before readers. I hope you've enjoyed it. If so, please spread the word by recommending it to a friend or reviewing it somewhere.

Cat Rambo

About the Author

Sandra lives in Washington state with her partner, sons, and an Albanian Mountain Moose disguised as a a dog. Her work has appeared in such venues as *Jim Baen's Universe*, *Daily Science Fiction*, *Crossed Genres*, *Galaxy's Edge*, and three of the four Escape Arists, Inc. podcasts. In addition to being a Clarion West 2010 graduate and an active member of the SFWA, she writes inflated autobiographical promotional bios.

You can find Sandra online at her blog www.writerodell.com, on Facebook, or you can follow her on Twitter @WriterOdell. Support her advocacy and writing on Patreon at http://patreon.com/writerodell.

CPSIA information can be obtained
at www.ICGtesting.com
Printed in the USA
LVHW02s1653290818
588518LV00006B/836/P